The Faithful
Side Chick

The Faithful Side Chick

Racquel Williams

www.urbanbooks.net

Urban Books, LLC
300 Farmingdale Road, N.Y.-Route 109
Farmingdale, NY 11735

The Faithful Side Chick

ISBN 13: 978-1-64556-478-2
EBOOK ISBN: 978-1-64556-479-9

First Trade Paperback Printing August 2023
Printed in the United States of America

10 9 8 7 6 5 4 3 2 1

Distributed by Kensington Publishing Corp.
Submit Orders to:
Customer Service
400 Hahn Road
Westminster, MD 21157-4627
Phone: 1-800-733-3000
Fax: 1-800-659-2436

Acknowledgments

First and foremost, I want to give all praises to Allah. Without his blessings, none of this would be possible.

To my support system, thank y'all for having my back and pushing me to be the best I can be. I love y'all.

To all my readers, the older readers and the newer ones, I love and appreciate y'all. Without all y'all's love and support, I would not be able to continue writing full time. I will forever be grateful.

Chapter One

Brooklyn

I'm sitting here thinking back on my life and can't help but laugh at how naive my ass was. See, all the signs were there, but I let my common sense and my Ivy League education all slip away just because this nigga fucked me good and sucked the life out of my pussy.

To understand how this drama unfolds, I have to go back to 2016. This was the year that brought out hoes and thots to Front Street and gave these side bitches a voice. I remember back in the day if a bitch was fucking your nigga, she used to do that shit on the low, hoping and praying the wife or girlfriend didn't find out. That shit is now a thing of the past. These new bitches are definitely on some *"Let's share this nigga"* kind of shit. A nigga can be married and have a family, and that still won't deter a bitch from jumping in the DM or hitting that nigga up on some *"Let's get together"* type of shit.

See, that's all motherfucking good . . . until they fuck around and bump into a bitch like me. Brooklyn was the name my dad, who was born and raised in Brooklyn, New York, gave me. My mom was from the island of Jamaica. She met my father as soon as she moved here. They started fucking around at a young age. She got pregnant at 14, and he was 16. My father was a well-known trap nigga that had a couple of trap houses all through the tristate. But on the other hand, my mother went to college and earned an accounting degree. In my opinion, I think she did that so she could learn how to clean my daddy's illegal money.

I was never exposed to that life. As a matter of fact, I went to live with my daddy's mother, who had moved to Richmond, Virginia. She was a schoolteacher and part-time librarian. Grandma was a dedicated Christian woman who made sure we were in church every Sunday morning, rain or shine. We were always there. I used to think Grandma was fucking the pastor because, in my young mind, I did not understand why Grandma was so damn loyal to this nigga. I ain't never seen them together, but only God could come down and tell me different. Anyway, I graduated high school, went on to college, and got me an associate degree in psychology, but I didn't stop until I got my master's in psychology. I wasn't surprised 'cause, from a young age, I used to try to get into the mind of these young niggas, often manipulating them to give me whatever it was that my heart desired, whether it was beating them out of the head or bleeding their pockets dry. I was a savage at the games I played.

I wasn't your average chick. I had brains, and I had a bossy mentality. Maybe this was one of the reasons why none of these niggas were in any rush to bag my ass. I saw how my father treated my mother like a queen, but everyone, including my mother, knew that Daddy was a whore. Rumors had it that he was slinging dick from the Bronx all the way to Brooklyn, and a few females done called his name as their baby daddy. See, Mama was no pushover, though. She stayed calm and handled all of Daddy's money. Then when he was gunned down in Harlem over ten years ago, Mama walked away a rich woman. I respect my mother, but shit, there was no way I would've dealt with his ass that long for the love of the money . . . or would I?

***

After getting my master's in psychology, I opened a counseling center with my portion of the money that Daddy left me. Before you knew it, I was raking in a good sum of money on my own. I cater to the juvenile system 'cause God knows some of these young motherfuckers were fucked up in the head and needed someone to help them figure their way out. That's where my staff and I came in.

The day after my thirtieth birthday, I was walking out of Planet Fitness. I had gained a few pounds over the winter and decided I needed to get them off me. I was never a skinny bitch, but I was always toned. Lately, I peeped a few cellulites creeping up on me. I quickly joined the gym, and I've been showing up faithfully ever since.

Anyway, I had just finished working out when I put my Kate Spade sunglasses on and exited the building. My phone vibrated, and I looked down to check it. It was a text from my homegirl. She's out here visiting a friend and spent a few days at my house with me. I promised her I would drop her off at the airport this evening.

"Excuse me," I heard a sexy, sultry voice say.

It was too late. I done walked dead into this man. I looked up, and we locked eyes. "I'm so sorry. I was paying attention to the phone," I tried explaining myself while feeling a little embarrassed.

"Nah, you straight, beautiful," he flashed an addictive smile at me.

"Have a good day," I said and started to walk off.

I heard someone running behind me, so I quickly turned around. Surprisingly, it was the nigga that I bumped into. I was confused. *I apologized, so what the fuck do he want now?* I thought.

"Excuse me, is something wrong?" I quizzed.

"Nothing is wrong. I just felt like I had to come strike up a conversation with you."

"Really, and why is that?" I was puzzled and annoyed. I had shit to do, and this nigga was holding me up.

"Where are my manners . . . My name is Jihad. What's your name, beautiful?"

"Nice to meet you, Jihad, but I ain't got time to be sitting here talking. I got some shit to do." I started walking off.

"Damn, ma, why the attitude? I just asked your name. You're behaving like I asked you for your account number." He came off a little too cocky for me.

"You know what? You're right. My name is Brooklyn. Now, can I go?" I asked sarcastically.

"Is that your name, or you just threw something out there 'cause I asked?"

"Jihad, I'm a grown-ass woman. Does it look like I'm into games?" I took off my glasses and stared down this nigga.

"Okay . . . Brooklyn, can I take you out sometime?"

"No disrespect, Jihad, but no. I'm not interested. Now, have you a blessed day."

Without waiting for a response, I put on my glasses and sped off toward my car. This nigga was really tripping. I accidentally bumped into him, and he took that as me trying to go out with him. These niggas must really think every female that they come across is either lonely as fuck or just desperate for the dick. I beg to differ 'cause my ass is far from lonely, and I got a few different size dildos that I use almost nightly or whenever my pussy starts fiening for some dick. Yes, I know, the dildo can never replace a man, but for now, it was doing the job. Sometimes, I fucked myself so damn good, pussy be sore for days. You should see me walking around with my legs close together because of the soreness from tearing my walls up with that plastic dick.

I got in my car and pulled off. I glanced in my mirror to see if he was still standing there, but he was nowhere in sight.

I really hate coming to Richmond International Airport. These damn cops out here be tripping, telling people to move along. Why the fuck would I move along if I'm trying to drop someone off? I pulled up.

"Brooklyn, my dear friend, I am going to miss you. Maybe you can come see us next time you get a vacation."

"You know I will. I been to Toronto quite a few times, and I love it there."

"Well, I'm in Pickering. Toronto is not that far, though. Just let me know, and we can get you."

"Okay, love. Have a safe flight."

"Okay, hon."

I watched as she dragged her bags into the building, waited a few seconds, then pulled off. This Richmond traffic was not easy this time of evening. I hope 95 South was not backed up. I was too tired this evening to be stuck in this heat.

Thursdays are usually my busiest days, so I wasn't surprised that the office was packed. By the time I realized that I hadn't taken a break or even drunk a glass of water, it was a little past four. Shit, I really was trying to make the gym today, especially since I couldn't go earlier. My first client was scheduled for 8:00 a.m., which my secretary mistakenly made 'cause my black ass don't usually work before 9:00 a.m.I thought about not hitting the gym, but I knew that was the devil playing with me. My entire life, I've kind of been on the chubby side. Finally, I got tired of looking at that belly roll in the mirror. So, one day I got up and decided to make a change. Shit, three months later, you should see my banging-ass body. I ain't where I want to be yet, but I was proud of myself. I also changed my eating habits. I cut down on red meat and started eating more fish and vegetables. For lunch, I often bring a bowl of fresh fruits that I picked up from the market.

Finally, I cut off my computer, grabbed my purse, locked my office, and headed out.

"You're leaving early?" my nosy-ass secretary, Nicolette, asked.

I wanted to say, "Yes, bitch. I *am* the boss, so I can leave whenever the fuck I want to," but instead, I smiled at her. "Yes, that was my last appointment. Plus, I didn't make the gym this morning."

"You really been on that exercising thing hard, huh? Let me find out you got a new man in yo' life," she giggled.

"Don't you think that's a little too personal?" I giggled.

"Umm, I'm sorry, boss lady. I didn't mean to imply anything."

"Please, set the alarm when you leave and deposit those checks first thing in the morning."

"Okay, will do."

I walked out, slamming the door behind me. See, I wasn't the kind to sit around and tell bitches my business. There were levels to this shit. I was the boss, and she was merely the help. Regardless of whether I was screwing a new man, I didn't see how it was any of her business.

I jumped into my car, pulled off, and cut on the music as I made my way to the house. After changing into my active wear, I made my way to the gym. I'm not going to lie. Going to the gym is a task, but whenever I'm finished working out, I always feel better mentally, even though physically, my ass be tired as a bitch.

I checked in and immediately got on the treadmill. Then I did my squats. I noticed someone watching me from the corner of my eye. I turned my head and went back to focusing on getting my workout on.

Finally, I grabbed my bag and was heading out the door when I heard someone clear their throat. I turned to look and noticed it was the same guy I bumped into the other day. I searched my brain. *Jihad. I think that's what he said his name was.*

"Hey, you. What you doing, stalking me?" I asked.

"Nah. Me stalk you? Never that," he laughed.

"So, what are you doing here? Are you a member of the gym?"

"Actually, I'm part owner of the gym. My brother, Jaseem, and I started this business years ago."

"Oh, nice. A brother that owns his own business." My whole tone changed toward him now that I realized he wasn't no bum chasing after me.

"Listen, Brooklyn, ever since I saw you the other day, I can't seem to get you off my mind. So, let me cut to the chase. I would love to take you out for lunch."

"Is that so? Hmm, lunchtime is way gone. I think it's almost supper," I said sarcastically.

"Yeah, I know. I was just throwing something out there, hoping you say yes. So, can I take you out on a dinner date?"

"I'll think about it. If you give me your number, and if I decide to take you up on your offer, I'll give you a call."

"Man, this sound like bullshit to me. I mean, if you not interested, just let me know straight up instead of stringing me on."

"Listen, I'm a grown-ass woman. If I wanted to tell you no, I would've. So, are you going to give me the number or not?"

"Damn, you a feisty one." He smiled, showing his teeth, which were pearly white. I did notice one of his teeth had a chip on it, though. That kind of makes him sexier when he smiles.

He gave me his number, and I walked away while he walked into the gym. I got into my ride and pulled off. I couldn't help but wonder what that was all about. Did he purposely bump into me just so he could ask me out? I was aware of the little games these niggas be playing.

As soon as I got into the house, I undressed. It was the best feeling to come up out of them clothes, letting this pussy air out and letting these breasts hang loose. I poured myself a glass of red wine while I set my bathwater. My body felt a little sorer than usual. I was hoping the hot water would do my body some justice.

I closed my eyes as I relaxed in the warm water with bubbles. Crazy enough, this nigga Jihad popped into my head. I ain't gon' front. I was curious to find out what the fuck he was about. I smiled to myself. It's been a minute since a dude piqued my interest, especially a Black brother. Don't get me wrong, I love my brothers, but I only dated one Black dude, and that was in my teenage years. All through college and my adult years, I only dated white dudes. The white dudes love my black, fluffy ass. And when I tell you they know how to eat pussy and ass, man, my freaky behind loved it. Often, I get a dirty look from the brothers or even the females, but shit, I love what I love.

The next day, my ass hurried to leave the office and head home. I wasted no time changing into my exercise clothes, grabbing my gym bag and water bottle, and heading out. In my mind, I tried to convince myself that I was eager to get to work out, but who the fuck was I fooling but my damn self? My fast ass wanted to see Jihad. I love the way his name rings out in my head . . . Hmmm. I wonder how it would sound rolling off my tongue when he was knee-deep in my guts?

Honk, honk!

Oh shit, I was tripping. My ass was so caught up in my thoughts I done swerved over in the right lane, causing the old bitch that's driving the beat-up-ass Buick to honk the horn at me while yelling, "Bitch, pay attention." I was in a good mood 'cause if I weren't, my ass would be on the 6:00 p.m. news for beating up somebody old-ass granny. So instead, I breathed hard and continued driving while keeping my eyes on the streets.

Five minutes later, I pulled into the gym parking lot. There were a lot of cars, which meant the gym was crowded. I really didn't give a damn 'bout who was there. My only concern was if Jihad's fine ass was there. I quickly parked and sashayed inside. I signed in and got into my routine. I wanted to turn around and peek the entire time I was there, but I tried not to. A bitch didn't want to come off as being desperate.

Thirty minutes later, I was finished. I grabbed my bag and walked out. I was hoping I would hear someone come running behind me, but I got to the car, and no one came running. I drove off feeling disappointed. Well, fuck it. I quickly dismissed him out of my mind. It was still early. I thought about going back to the office but quickly changed my mind. It was almost rush hour, and God knows my black ass didn't want to be stuck in traffic. I decided to head on home, but not before stopping at the Boston Market to grab dinner.

As soon as I got home, I took a quick shower. Ain't no better feeling than a fresh pussy. I put on a little housedress, poured me a glass of wine, and made a plate. I decided to sit in the living room while I relaxed, waiting for the evening news to come on. I took a few sips of the red wine and was definitely feeling lovely. Suddenly, my phone started ringing, so I grabbed it.

"Hellurrr," I tried to mimic Madea.

"Hey, you. Why is it that I haven't gotten a call from my best friend at all today?" My BFF, Jasmine, said with her loud ass.

"Girl, I was so damn busy today. First, I barely had time to breathe, and then I left early for the gym."

"Hmmm, is that so? Is this the same woman that complained about working out? I see that nigga got you doing crazy shit already. Let me find out you already got fucked."

"Bitch, you so crazy. No, I have not slept with Jihad, and if I did, I probably wouldn't be telling you."

"And you know that's a gotdamn lie. I know the minute you get that dick, you will be on my line either telling me he got some bomb-ass dick or his ass ain't got no damn use in the bed. Either way, I'll be hearing about it," she laughed.

"Well, you got me there." I joined in on the laughter.

We chatted for a few more minutes, then hung up. That crazy Jasmine was really my grandmother's adopted granddaughter. We grew up together and have been inseparable since. If she's rocking, then I'm definitely rolling, and vice versa. We done had our share of laughter, tears, and just going through life together, so she knows my ass all too well.

I put down the phone and took a few more sips of my wine. *Damn,* I held the glass up, and it was empty. So I got up to fix me another drink. Jasmine put me on to this Pinot Noir, and I've been addicted ever since. Ain't nothing like a glass of wine after a long day at the office. I heard my phone ringing again, so I walked into the living room. *Hmm, is that so?* I thought before I answered it.

"Hello," I tried to sound like I was asleep.

"I hope I didn't wake you up, beautiful." His deep accent rang through my ear.

"Hey, you. I was just resting my eyes a little," I lied.

"Well, get you some rest. I can hit you up tomorrow."

"No, I'm up now. What's going on with you?"

"I was calling to see if you want to join me for dinner?"

"I already ate. You should've invited me earlier."

"Well, in that case, what about a few drinks?"

He was not giving up, and what the hell? I do want to see him. "You can come by the house since I'm already settled in," I suggested.

"You sure you want to be alone with me in your crib?" he laughed.

"Shit, I'm a big girl. I can handle myself," I said, thinking about my 9 mm Glock in my bedroom drawer.

"Well, in this case, shoot me your address. I'ma close up in another twenty minutes, head home to shower, and then I'll be on my way."

While he was talking about taking a shower, my mind was thinking of all sorts of dirty things. So I hurried up and cleared my thoughts before my ass said the wrong thing.

"Okay."

"See you in a few, beautiful."

After I hung up, I sent him a text with my address. I know I took a shower when I came in, but shit, I needed to make sure my pussy was clean and well shaven. After showering, I rubbed my body with Victoria's Secret Oil Sleek, pulled out one of my sexy panty and bra sets, then put on a sexy minidress. Finally, I poured myself another glass of wine. By now, I was definitely feeling the buzz.

About an hour later, a text came in on my phone. It was Jihad letting me know he was on the way. I tried to calm my nerves, but I was excited to be around this young, attractive brother, and I could barely conceal it.

I opened the door and watched him walk up the driveway. "Hey, there, beautiful," he greeted me and gave me a quick hug and a kiss on the cheek.

I closed the door and walked into the living room. He took a seat on the sofa.

"I got some Grey Goose and a bottle of Pink Moscato for you."

"Hmm, a man with expensive taste. Thank you." I smiled at him as I took the bottles out of his hand.

We sat there drinking and talking mainly about our backgrounds and stuff. I tried not to give up too much information 'cause a bitch like me never kisses and tells. Plus, nowadays, you can't tell these niggas too much about you because they'll use that shit against you as soon as you get into an argument with their ass.

"So, tell me, Miss Brooklyn, how do you manage to stay child-free and no husband for so long? I hope I'm not asking too much."

"Well . . . let's see . . . Most of these dudes nowadays are intimidated by a woman like me. You know, one that got that boss mentality and knows how to run shit. And as far as kids, shit, I got to find the daddy first." I busted out laughing.

"I hear that," he said as his hand reached over and rubbed my leg.

I looked him in the eyes and instantly felt my body shiver. His hand continued up the dress I was wearing, traveling up to my breasts. I closed my eyes as he massaged my breast with his hand. My mind was telling me to stop acting like a ho, but my heart loved every bit of the feeling he was giving me. Then things started getting hot between us. Before you knew it, we were both going at it on the couch. My dress, bra, and panties were completely off.

"Let's go upstairs," I said.

He trailed behind me. I assumed he was watching my ass clap while I led him to the master bedroom. *Damn, I can't wait to feel this dick inside of me,* I thought as my clit throbbed. I stopped in front of him, wrapped my arms around his waist, then his body, and started kissing his neck. I unbuttoned his pants, allowing them to drop to his feet. I pulled his boxers down to his ankles, releasing his rock-hard dick. Then I ran my hand over it to get a feel of what he was working with. It wasn't no ten-inch dick. Maybe around eight and a half inches, but it was thick, just like I love it.

"Hmmmm, don't start nothing you can't finish," he whispered in my ear while he used his hands to cuff my tight, firm ass. Hmmmm, only if he knew I could finish whatever I started. I continued kissing his neck while massaging his dick, rubbing it against my clit.

"I want you really bad, beautiful," he whispered in my ear. My entire body trembled. I swear I felt like I was about to explode, and I hadn't even gotten the tip of the dick yet.

"So, what you waiting on?" I whispered back to him in a sexy tone.

I think that's all he needed to hear 'cause he picked me up and carried me to the bed, parting my legs and inserting his dick deep inside me. I'm glad I was wet, and his dick slid in without any major pain. Then he used his hand to grab my ass and pulled me up closer to him. I tried to move a little, but his firm hold on my ass made it impossible.

"This some good pussy," he whispered in my ear while he thrust deep inside of me.

I wanted to say something back to him, but shit, a bitch was under pressure. My ass really underestimated the width of the dick 'cause it seemed like it was stretching out my pussy.

"Aw, damn, it hurts," I moaned.

"But you loving it," his cocky ass responded, still not easing up.

I ain't gon' lie. He was kind of right. Even though I
was complaining, the fuck was sweet. I think I was only
complaining 'cause I'm used to throwing my ass all
around and handling a nigga. But this nigga's dick was
huge, which left no room for me to perform on the dick
like I would love to.

After about twenty minutes, multiple orgasms, and me
screaming and hollering, he finally pulled out and busted
all over my stomach. I lay there for a few minutes while
he was in the bathroom. I was out of breath and weak
from this dick lashing that I received from this nigga.

"You a'ight?" he asked as he walked out of the bathroom in his boxers.

"Yeah, I'm good," I lied. I really wanted to say, "Hell
nah, nigga. My pussy on fire," but I didn't. So instead,
I eased up off the bed and walked to the bathroom. I
tried not to let it seem so obvious that a fire was burning
between my legs.

My alarm startled me as I jumped up. I looked at the
time. It was 5:45 a.m., the time that I usually wake up.
That's when I realized this nigga was still lying in my
bed. Last night after sex, we both decided to rest for a few
minutes. Shit, that turned out to be this nigga spending
the night at my house. Hmmm. I sure hope he didn't
have no bitch at home 'cause if he did, his ass going to be
in a shitload of trouble.

I got out of bed and took a shower. Then I took out a
beige-colored pantsuit and placed it on the bed before
checking my email.

I noticed this nigga was still sprawled out in the bed,
sleeping like a newborn baby with a ton of cereal in the
formula. So after I got dressed, I made a pot of coffee and
glanced at my watch. It was almost 8:00 a.m.

"Wake up." I tapped him a few times.

"Hey, beautiful," he said as he sat up.

"Your ass was knocked out," I laughed.

"That's how you know you got some good pussy. Knock a nigga out." He grabbed his cell phone.

"Is that so? Hmm . . . Anyways, I got to be at the office by nine."

"Shit, you should've taken the day off."

"I wish, but I have a few patients that need to see me today."

"I know. I'm just kidding around. I'm glad you woke me up. My ass supposed to open the gym at six. Damn, that was two hours ago. Oh well, my brother should be there."

After he got dressed, I poured him a cup of coffee and made toast. Shit, that was the most he was going to get for breakfast. *My ass don't be doing no big cooking around here,* I thought.

"I really enjoyed myself last night, beautiful. I hope you don't have no intention to kick me to the side." Then he walked up to me, wrapped his hands around my waist, and whispered in my ear.

Cold chills ran down my spine as his dick pressed up on my skirt. I tried not to react, but deep inside, my inner freakiness was trying to pop out.

I turned around to face him and handed him a cup of coffee. "Well, I don't plan on it. I know we both have busy schedules, but I think we can make the time." I shot him a dirty, sneaky look.

"You're something else; you know that? But I'm loving it." He took a seat at the table while he sipped on his coffee.

We chatted for a few minutes, and then he left. After I closed the door, I smiled. Last night was a very good night. When I tell you that nigga has some good dick . . . trust me. I ain't lying. As a matter of fact, my shit still hurts. I pray no one notices the difference in my walking today at the office.

The entire day at the office I couldn't get Jihad off my mind. I was definitely feeling him. I know I was putting myself out there with a nigga that I barely knew, but what the fuck? I was a grown-ass woman who knew what she wanted. I mean, I was young with a booming career. So it wouldn't hurt to have a man that I can share my life with.

"Miss Evans?" My assistant walked in.

"Yes?"

"You were in your deep thoughts, huh? I've been yelling your name."

"What did you want?"

"Your 11:00 a.m. appointment called and said she's going to be twenty minutes late. I told her that's fine."

"Okay, yes, that's fine. That'll give me time to review her file before she gets here."

"Okay, and whatever it is you're thinking so heavily about must be some good stuff," she giggled as she closed my door.

I stared at the door as if that nosy bitch was still there. If it wasn't for her work ethic and the fact that she goes beyond and above when I need her, I would've let her ass go a long time ago. Unfortunately, she is one of those people who don't know her boundaries and keeps thinking we're friends. We're far from that. I'm the boss, and she's just a worker.

Chapter Two

Brooklyn

It didn't take long for Jihad and me to become insep-arable. We would meet after the gym, grab something to eat, and head home. We would shower together, eat, drink, and then make love. He was definitely a stallion. Sometimes I had to try my hardest to keep up with him, but that nigga was a beast in bed. I guess being five years older than him didn't help any. I've never dated a younger dude before, but being five years older than him wasn't all that bad.

My feelings for him went from just liking him to falling head over heels for him in no time. Part of me was warning me that I was moving too fast. But the way he makes me feel inside, I wasn't trying to hear that. I want him in my life, and it was time for me to make that known. Fucking and sucking every day was cool, but I wanted more. Scratch that. I *needed* more. We had a quiet candlelight dinner when I decided to bring up the conversation.

"Jihad, I need to talk to you about something," I said as I put down my fork.

"Don't tell me I'm about to become a daddy again?" He joked as he looked me in the eyes.

"Of course not," I blurted out without thinking.

"Damn, babes. You said that like it's such a bad thing."

"I didn't mean it like that. I just know we both have busy schedules, and having a baby will definitely require our full attention." I tried my best to clean it up.

"A'ight, I hear you. But what you need to holla at me about?" I could see he was a little bit annoyed.

"I mean, we've been dating for months now. You practically live here. So, I was thinking about us taking it to the next level. I mean, why don't you move in here? I know the going back and forth can become a bit hectic at times, especially when you got to get up early."

"I thought the same thing the other day, but I didn't want you to feel like I was moving too fast. Plus, you know I got my daughter. I mean, she can still live with mom dukes, but I would still have to go pick her up and drop her off at school."

"Well, I mean, you can always bring Briana with you. I have extra bedrooms, and we have excellent schools over here."

"Yeah, well, I'ma have to talk with her mom to see if she would be okay with that."

"I thought you had full custody of Briana?" I shot him a strange look.

"I have physical custody of her, but her mom and I share the weekends and holidays. You know Keisha kind of ratchet, so I'ma run it by her first. The last thing I need is some drama from her."

I agreed with him; he needs to handle that shit. I didn't have time for no loudmouthed baby mama and her antics.

"Okay, handle your business. It's up to you if you want to bring her over here. The offer still remains."

"You know you're a different kind of woman."

"Hmm, maybe you just need to stop making babies with ghetto, loudmouthed bitches."

"Ouch. That was a low blow."

"Sorry. You know I'ma call it like I see it."

"You know I love you and that no filter-ass attitude. I got to run, though. I'll be back around 9:00 p.m."

"Okay, love."

We kissed, and he left. Maybe I shouldn't have said that out loud, but I've never met his baby mama. From what I learned, she was a stripper when he met her, and they started dating. A few months later, she got pregnant. She wasn't ready to quit shaking her ass, so she gave her daughter to him and his mama. This was why I was confused about why he was so concerned about letting that ho know that he and his daughter were moving in. Why the fuck would he need approval from a bitch that left her child in the first place? This was definitely my cue to start paying attention to this nigga and his baby mama. I need to know if he was still fucking her on the low.

Alyssa

Bitches, bitches, bitches. Just because a motherfucking ring is on your finger and you and the nigga have the same last name, it doesn't mean you own the nigga. Yeah, I know I'ma ruffle a few feathers with this one, but I don't give a fuck. My mother was a side bitch for years, and I was the product of that relationship. See, I was too young to understand what was happening at the time. All I know is Daddy used to come to the house daily, but right around nine, ten o'clock, his ass would hug me and kiss me good night. I remember asking Mama why Daddy always had to leave. She would look at me and say, "Child, you too young to understand." Nah, what it was is this nigga had to make it home to his wife and his two other children.

It wasn't until my seventeenth birthday that I fully understood what the fuck was going on. My birthday party was happening, but Daddy had to go as usual. Yes, during my party, this nigga whispered to me he was leaving. I watched as Mama said something to him, threw a drink in his face, and dashed off. He followed right behind her. My nosy behind wanted to know what was going on and why my parents had just created a scene in front of all my little friends and a few grown-ups. I started to go into Mama's room, but the door was closed. I could hear loud talking, so I tiptoed closer to the door and placed my ear up against it.

"Jay, I'm tired of this shit. It's my baby's birthday. Scratch that. It's *our* baby's birthday, and you talkin' 'bout you gotta go home to this bitch."

"Gloria, you're being unfair. You know, if I could stay longer, I would. But Denise already texting me talking 'bout where I'm at."

"Fuck her, James. I don't give a fuck about that bitch or them kids you have wit' her ass. You promised me years ago you was gon' divorce that ho and marry me. Here we are seventeen years later, and you *still* ain't leave the bitch yet. How about I call up her ass and let her know her man, matter of fact, her *husband,* has been creeping around with me and fathered a beautiful daughter? How 'bout *that,* James?"

"Gloria, you know damn well you can't do that. I told you, Denise sick and that's the only reason why I'm still there with her. If you call her, you only gon' make her worse."

"You been saying that ho dying for years. Why the fuck she ain't dead yet?"

"You know what, Gloria? You a cold-ass bitch. I'm gone. I'll see you Friday when I get paid."

I heard him walking to the door, so I hurried off and walked away. I was back in the living room when he walked out and smiled at everyone. He came over to me, kissed my forehead, and walked out. A few minutes later, Mama walked out, pretending like nothing was going on. I could tell she was crying, and behind that smile, she was hurting.

"Mama, why did Daddy leave so soon?" I asked later that night while I helped her clean up the kitchen.

"Baby, he had some business to tend to," she smiled at me.

I didn't say anything else, but from that day, I never looked at him the same. To me, he was just another nigga. A few years later, he died, and Mama and I couldn't attend the funeral. I guess he told his wife about me on his deathbed, but the bitch didn't give a fuck. She sent word that Mama and I were not invited to his memorial service. Mama might've been crushed from it, but me, personally, I didn't give a fuck about that dead nigga or that bitch.

At age 18, I became a full-blown ho. I was fucking everything that was moving. I didn't discriminate. I was sucking dick and eating pussy on the regular.

It was late as fuck, and I was sneaking into the house. I thought Mama was sound asleep. I almost made it to the top of the stairs.

"Alyssa," Mama cut on the light and hollered.

I froze. *Damn, this bitch supposed to be asleep.*

"You listen to me, and you listen good. At this time of the morning, the only things open is McDonald's and legs. So you see, I can't tell you what to do wit' yo' pussy. But take it from an old whore, if you gon' fuck, make sure you getting paid. Ain't shit free in America and definitely not pussy."

I looked at her. This was strange 'cause I had never heard Mama talk like this before.

"Do you hear me? Don't be out here being no fool for these old broke-dick-ass niggas. You see, I did that, and look what the fuck happened to me. His wife living in a big old mansion while I'm in this small-ass, two-bedroom government housing. You think that bitch fucked him like I did? Hell nah. If she did, he wouldn't need me," she said as tears rolled down her face.

I walked back down the stairs. "Don't cry, Mama." I placed my arms around her and hugged her. Seeing my mama in so much damn turmoil hurt my entire soul. I mean, the nigga been dead, but she can't seem to get past it.

"Mama, come get in bed. It's late."

I know she was drunk 'cause the smell of that old cheap liquor she drinks was reeking through her pores. I led her to her room, and after sitting there for 'bout twenty minutes listening to her vent about this dead nigga, she finally passed out. I threw the cover on her, cut off the light, and tiptoed out of the room. I was tired and exhausted my damn self. I went to my room and climbed into bed without taking my clothes off. I needed sleep.

Chapter Three

Brooklyn

Jasmine and I were eating lunch at Applebee's. Ever since I started fucking Jihad, I'd been neglecting my BFF. So, when she popped up at the office and offered to take me out for lunch, I couldn't turn her down.

"Hmmm, so tell me, how is this family thing working out for you?"

"I mean, it's cool and everything."

"Well, you better than me 'cause I don't fuck niggas that already have kids. I mean, I just don't have the patience for the shit."

"Girl, trust me. I'm trying to adjust. I think the baby mama is more of a problem than Briana. I mean, this bitch has no respect. Can you believe this ho called his phone late one night while I was on top of him riding?"

"Bitch, you lying?" she laughed.

"I'm dead-ass serious."

"I was talking about you lying about riding that nigga. Your bougie ass was not riding no dick." She busted out laughing while looking at me over her glasses.

"Bitch, just because I don't brag about my fucking skills doesn't mean I don't know how to fuck a nigga good. I'm just quiet with the shit."

"Child, hush. But on a serious note, he needs to check that bitch and let her know she can't be calling his phone like that. I know her ass ain't calling about no damn child that time of night . . . Hmmm, she probably wanted to get fucked too."

"I thought about that, but I don't think he's cheating, and if he was, I doubt it was with her. He acts like he despises the ground she walks on."

"Listen, honey, niggas always talk shit about the bitches they fucking. That is only a ploy to throw you off. Honey, you better keep an eye on Mr. Jihad and his baby mama. You're my friend, and I would hate it if I got to drag a bitch behind you."

"You're so damn crazy, but Jihad and I are in a good place. You know I haven't felt this good in a long time. It's that type of gushy feeling. When I'm around him, my heart races. Like he's different from all these other niggas out here. You know what makes it even better? He got his own damn money."

"Well, that's *definitely* a great thing 'cause most of these niggas out here are broke and looking for a woman to pay their damn way."

"Bitch, I did say the dick was good, but good dick don't pay no damn bills. Shit, my pussy don't even get wet for no broke dick."

"Bitch, I'm trying to tell you."

The waitress brought over our food, and we got down to business. I happened to glance down at my phone and realized I had three missed calls from Jihad. *I'll call him back once I get to the office.*

After we ate, Jasmine paid, and we hugged and parted ways. I really miss my bitch. After that, we decided to do lunch at least once a week.

I returned to the office and tried calling Jihad's phone, but it went straight to voicemail. *He's probably on a call,*

I thought as I pulled into the parking lot. I parked and walked into the lobby of my office.

"Miss Evans," Nicolette tried saying something to me, but I waved her off and walked into my office.

"Hey, honey, what are you doing here?"

Jihad closed the door behind me.

"Where you been, Brooklyn?"

"Huh, what you mean? I was at lunch with Jasmine."

"Lunch with Jasmine, huh? Who is the nigga you fucking, Brooklyn?" He stepped toward me with a scary, cold look in his eyes.

"What the hell you talking about, Jihad? I was out with Jasmine."

"I called and called, but guess what? You were too busy fucking and sucking on another nigga's dick, so you couldn't pick up the phone," he yelled.

"You need to quit yelling and get the hell out of my office," I said through clenched teeth.

"You know what, Brooklyn? You wrong for this shit."

"Jihad, get the fuck out now."

"You putting me out? That nigga must've sucked on that pussy real good. Is he better than me, Brooklyn?"

"Something is seriously wrong with you. Get the fuck out before I get you thrown out."

I opened the door. He saw that I was dead-ass serious, so he shot me a dirty look and walked out.

"Is everything okay, Miss Evans?" Nicolette asked.

"Yes, everything is fine. Please hold my calls."

I closed the door and leaned against it. I couldn't believe what the hell just happened. I've never seen Jihad behave like this before. That look in his eyes sent chills down my spine.

I couldn't stay focused at work after what happened earlier. Around 3:00 p.m., I decided to leave the office. I didn't want to go home, so I went to the park and walked around for a little while. I needed to clear my head and try to make sense of this shit that happened.

Finally, I pulled up at the house a little past seven. Jihad's car wasn't in the driveway or the garage. I was glad he wasn't home 'cause I was tired and just needed to shower and lie down.

I walked into the kitchen to pour me a glass of wine.

"What's for dinner?" Briana walked in and said.

"Well, first, hello to you too. As for your question about dinner. There's some leftover rice and steak from yesterday. Heat up enough for you and your dad."

"I don't want no leftovers. Why can't you cook?"

I wanted to say, "*Li'l bitch, I'm* not *you damn mama*," but instead, I looked at her little disrespectful ass. "You can eat the leftovers or grab a cup of soup out of the cupboard and eat it. The choice is yours."

I grabbed my glass and walked out of the kitchen, leaving her ass behind. I swear, at first, I loved that little girl, but the longer I'm around her, I realize she's just a spoiled little brat that thinks the world revolves around her. See, she must not know I have zero tolerance for other people's disrespectful kids.

I took my shower and got into bed. That wine finally relaxed me a little. I checked my email and started responding to a few. Then I heard the garage door going up. That nigga was home. I was hoping his ass would've gone to his mama's house instead of coming here. But instead, he walked into the room with a bouquet in his hand. His eyes were bloodshot red.

"You need to go in the guest room tonight."

"Brooklyn, I'm sorry about today, baby. I don't know what got over me earlier. It's just that lately, I find myself falling deeper and deeper in love with you."

"Jihad, I don't want to hear this shit."

"Please, Brooklyn, baby, please, listen to me. I've fucked a lot of bitches in my lifetime, but I ain't never been in love before. I'm in love with you. All I can think about is you. I want to spend the rest of my life with you. Baby, I just don't know how to deal with these different emotions. I need you. I love you." He started crying.

I'd never seen a grown man break down in tears like this before, so I was shocked to see this muscular, well-toned, macho man on his knees crying to me. I didn't know what the fuck to say. I was really at a loss for words.

"Brooklyn, I promise no shit like that will ever happen again. I will go to counseling to make sure I keep my emotions in check. But please, baby, I can't live without you."

That statement right there should've been the warning for me to run far away from that nigga. But nah, instead, I felt sorry that he was going through this. I looked at him; he was broken. I took his hand, pulled him up to me, and hugged him.

"I love you, woman. I don't want to lose you," he whispered in my ear.

"I love you too," I said back to him.

Within minutes, he had my legs open wide and his head buried inside me. All my anger was gone. This nigga clenched on my pussy and sucked on my clit like a suction cup. Tears rolled down my face because of how good he was eating me out. My legs shivered, and my insides trembled as I exploded in his mouth, pussy juice all over his face like a milkshake.

He then entered me and started pounding down my walls. I wanted to say, "stop," but the fuck was so good I threw my legs on his back and held him tight. All the anger that I felt earlier was out the window. All I could think about was how good this dick was, and I hoped his ass didn't come quickly.

Chapter Four

Brooklyn

I'm always late. Shit, I'ma be late to my own gotdamn funeral, I thought as I pulled into the Red Lobster in Colonial Heights. Jihad called me at the office and told me to meet him here instead of going home. I swear I have no idea what this man has up his sleeve, but I can tell you, ever since that one incident at the office, his behind did a complete turnaround.

"Hey, are you here? I'm walking in now."

"Yes, come on in."

As soon as I walked in, I spotted Jihad standing at the front. I walked over to him, and he greeted me with a hug and kiss. "Hey, love. We're back here."

I followed him to the table that he had already secured. I noticed he had a bottle of my favorite wine on the table and a glass.

I took a seat, then looked at him. "Hmm, what's the special occasion?" I shot him a suspicious look.

"What you talking about, babes?"

"The impromptu dinner date . . . a bottle of expensive wine?"

"I was just at the gym and missing my woman. So, I told Jaseem I was out. You're a beautiful woman, and you deserve every bit of this. At times, I wish I could give you more. Nah, scratch that. I'm working hard at giving you more."

"I love the sound of that, Mr. Lewis."

He grabbed the bottle of wine, popped it open, and then poured me a glass. I love this treatment. I'm glad his ass notices that I'm royal and deserve to be treated as such.

I ordered an eight-ounce steak, well done, with a baked potato and rice on the side. While waiting for our meals, we sat there just talking about any and everything. This was one of the qualities that I liked about Jihad. He wasn't a boring person to be around. While we talked, I drank wine and dug into those biscuits. There was something 'bout these biscuits that were addictive. I know I was cutting bread and rice out of my diet, but shit, today was a cheating day.

After our food came, we ate in silence. I looked over at him while he ate. This man was sexy as fuck, and he wasn't no lazy-ass nigga either. I swear I felt blessed just to have him in my life. Over the past few weeks, our bond has definitely gotten stronger. *Maybe we are heading somewhere special . . .*

After we finished eating, he excused himself to go to the bathroom. It gave me a few minutes to check my emails. Suddenly, I felt someone tap me on the shoulder. I looked up. It was Jihad. Before I could question him 'bout what was going on, he was on his knees. I looked at him in confusion 'cause we were in the restaurant, and this nigga was acting crazy.

"Get up. What are you doing?"

He reached into his pocket and pulled out a box. I looked at him and looked back at the box. "Brooklyn, I know we had a rough patch, but that's behind us now. Will you marry me?"

My mouth flew wide open. I looked at this nigga to see if it was a cruel joke he was playing on me. But nah, that nigga was dead-ass serious.

"Close your mouth and answer me, woman."

"Damn, I'm sorry. Yes, yes, I will marry you."

He took the ring out of the box and slid it on my finger. He then followed up with a big, wet kiss. After that, we didn't give a damn who around us was looking. When we came up for air, we were surrounded by waiters and a few patrons clapping and cheering us on. I couldn't do anything but laugh. This nigga pulled a fast one on me.

When we left, he pulled off, and I followed him. I swear, while I drove, I couldn't stop glancing at the rock my man had just placed on my finger. The sun was out and bouncing off it. I had to take my eyes off it before I got blind.

I pulled up right behind him at the house. The evening was still young, so I planned on showing my appreciation.

"Hey, babes. Don't tell Briana about the engagement yet. I want to sit and talk with her first."

"All right."

So, what'd he think I was going to do? Take off my ring and wait until he pacifies that little grown-ass child. I think not. I will wear my shit, and if she asks, I will direct her to her daddy.

I quickly got all that negativity out of my mind. This was my special night, and I wasn't gon' let anyone fuck it up for me.

Chapter Five

Alyssa

I glanced in the mirror and didn't like what I saw. I wasn't big, but I could see my stomach pushing out a little. That was a no-no for me. I've always maintained a good weight, but lately, I've been eating late at night and drinking a little more. Blame it on my homegirl, Trina. Trina was a cool-ass chick that I met at my brother's birthday party over ten years ago. We hit it off well, and we've become inseparable ever since. I was shocked 'cause I usually don't click with bitches, but we're both Scorpios; our birthdays were days apart.

I need to get into somebody's gym to lose these extra pounds and shit. I pulled up Trina's number. That ho was probably sleeping.

"Hello," she whispered into the phone.

"Hell nah. Bitch, I know yo' ass ain't sleeping at no twelve o'clock. Bitch, you need to get that ass up. It's too damn nice for this shit."

"Bitchhhh. I was up all night fucking and sucking the nigga Raheem from 233rd."

"How you lying? That's the nigga that drive the Orange Challenger. The one that fuck wit' the loudmouthed Mellodie?"

"Yup, that's him. That nigga head was buried in my pussy all damn night. Shit, that bitch probably wondering what's that scent on her nigga's lips."

"Bitch, you is a whole fool. Fuck that ho. If she was on her job, her nigga would not be in another bitch's bed. Did that nigga throw some paper your way? That's the real question."

"Bitch, you know me better than that. Ain't nothing 'round here free and definitely *not* this bomb-ass pussy."

"That's my bitch. I know I taught you well. Anyway, bitch, now we need to find a gym."

"A gym? Bitch, you do enough fucking to let you lose weight. You must be lying there all lazy and shit. You got to get up and ride that dick like a bicycle."

"Ho, I don't do no lazy fuck. I'm serious, though. I'm too young to be getting a stomach. That's from all them damn meals we be eating."

"Uh-huh. Well, you need to find you a gym then, bishhh."

"I need a partner to go with me, and who better to ask than my bestie?"

"Bitch, I'm fine with being fluffy. Shit, I've been fluffy my entire life. That's why these skinny bitches' niggas be running to me. My grandma always told me, 'Don't fix it if it ain't broken.'"

"I ain't trying to hear that shit. I'm going to look up a gym, and we're going."

"Okay, Mother."

We both busted out laughing. This bitch was a real-life clown, but she was definitely my rider. I got her, and I know she got me. Shit, we even had several threesomes together. *That's* how close we were.

"A'ight, I'ma look up a gym that's not too expensive. I'ma meet up wit' you later."

"A'ight, bitch. I'ma go back to dreaming about this good-ass dick."

"Byeeee," I said playfully and hung up the phone.

I lit me up a blunt and started browsing the internet for a gym with a reasonable membership rate. I was determined to lose this damn stomach.

***

"Excuse me, ladies," a fine-ass brother with a beard said as he walked past Trina and me.

Trina grabbed my hand, trying to get my attention.

"Bitch, I know you see how fine that nigga is. And I also saw how he smiled at you."

"Bitch, you tripping. All the nigga said was, 'Excuse me.'"

"Yeah, right. He only said that to get your attention. Trust me. I've been around niggas my whole life. I know that trick."

"Uh-huh, whatever you said, bitch. You ready for this workout?"

"My fat ass gon' get on this treadmill."

"A'ight, cool. I'ma start on this bike. Say a prayer for me, bitch."

So, Mr. Handsome with the Beard was fine as fuck. I saw him pass by a few more times and glance at me. I know his ass was flirting with me, but he was doing it discreetly. I didn't want to come off thirsty, so I pretended to be busy exercising and not paying him any mind.

After an hour of working out, I was tired and ready to fall out. I walked over to the bench where Trina sat for twenty-five minutes. "Ho, you can have this shit. I'm not coming back. I almost died."

"It's only 'cause it's your first day. You'll be all right."

"Ladies, are y'all doing okay? I'm Jihad and one of the owners."

"Well, I'm Trina, and this is my bestie, the very single, no kids and no man-drama, Alyssa."

This bitch did not *just put my business out there like that.* I just want to punch her ass in the throat.

"Hello, Trina and Miss Alyssa. Welcome to my gym. I hope y'all had a good first day."

"My fat ass is tired, and I'm about to go to the car while Miss Alyssa tells you about her workout plans."

I stood there flabbergasted by this bitch. I wanted to run after her and snatch her weave off her head, but this old, fine-ass nigga was standing in my face. My head drifted to his well-toned body, and the speedo he had on wasn't doing much to hide his dick print. I quickly lifted my head, so he wouldn't notice I was checking him out—especially that dick.

"So, Alyssa, what are your plans, and what do you plan on accomplishing?"

"Huh, my plans?"

"Yes, your workout plans?"

"Well, I ain't really got no plans. I just want to lose this stomach and these extra pounds that I done put on."

"Oh, OK. Well, I can draw up a workout plan for you if you like. It will focus on the stomach and body toning."

"Well, I would definitely appreciate that, but I don't have no extra money to do all that. I'm a student, and I'm balling on a budget."

"Nah, nothing extra. Student? What are you studying?"

"Massage therapy."

"Hmmm, really? So, you're not only beautiful, but you're also smart."

"Is that an insult, Jihad?"

"Nah, I'm just blown away by your beauty, and finding out you're also smart is a plus. Anyway, here is my card. You can call me about anything. I'm here almost daily; if I'm not, you can hit my line." He handed me his business card.

"Okay, great. I got to go. I'll see you around, Jihad."

"I'll definitely be looking for you, Alyssa."

I sashayed off, twitching extra hard 'cause I knew his ass was still standing there. I got to my car, where this bitch was standing outside waiting on me.

"Damn, bitch, you could've unlocked the car."

"That's what yo' ass get for putting me out there like that."

"Bitch, I did yo' ass a favor. Did you get the number?"

"Nah, I ain't get the number. You know I'm chilling right now."

"Bitch, you trippin'. Let me see, is it because he not a dope boy? 'Cause the nigga looked paid. You see all those people in the gym? I know he got some damn money. Shit, this might be the come-up for you for real."

"Ho, is that all you think about? A come-up?"

"Bitch, yeah. And if yo' ass ain't thinking about it, I need to find me a new bitch that is trying to secure the bag."

I shook my head and laughed at this fool before I got into the car. "Bitch, I was just fooling around. I got his business card. He told me to call him whenever. You heard that *whenever*. I ain't see no ring on his finger, so Mr. Jihad might be single."

"Ring or not, that ain't never stopped you before."

"You're right, but a bitch is getting old. Maybe it's time for me to find a nigga for myself and have a few babies, you know?"

"Bitch, please. Just stop this foolery. You have your whole life ahead of you."

"Let's go 'cause yo' head ain't right."

"Nah, you seem to be the one that hit your head. I want my money-chasing, bag-securing bitch back now."

I pulled off laughing in my head at this bitch's craziness. I love her ass and wouldn't trade her for nothing.

I lay on my back, legs on Jihad's shoulders, while his head was buried deep inside my wet pussy. The desk was kind of hard, but the pleasure I received made up for that minor discomfort.

"Aweee, oweeiii, damn, aw, I love this," I whispered as my legs trembled and juices expelled from my body. Jihad hungrily licked my pussy clean until the last drop of come disappeared.

He then got up and pulled me closer to him. "Wait, do you have a condom?"

"Shit, nah. I want to feel you. Are you on birth control?"

"No, and I don't want to get pregnant," I whined.

"I got you. I'ma pull out."

Shit, I don't want to get pregnant by this nigga, but I was horny as fuck and wanted the dick. He didn't wait for me to give him an answer as he slid his dick inside. This nigga's dick wasn't only long; it was thick too. His ass looked like he was fucking with steroids. I ain't never had a dick this damn big. But I was determined to fuck the hell out of this nigga. So, I bossed up and slid all the way on the dick. My insides were screaming, "Bitch, you trippin'," but I wanted to leave an impression on this nigga, so I bore the pain and let him tear up my pussy.

"Oh my God, I can't believe I let you fuck me in the office. I wonder if anybody heard us?"

"The music is playing. You have to admit, though, we both wanted this. You can't deny the chemistry between us, and that's some good pussy you got there."

"Nigga, my pussy is on fire. It should be a damn crime to walk around with a dick this damn big." I shot him a serious look.

"You'll get used to it. You'd be surprised to know some women appreciate a brother with a good size."

"That's 'cause them hoes are crazy. I need my insides to stay fully intact."

Knock, knock. "Hold on."

He walked over to the door. "Who is it?"

"Yo, it's Jaseem."

"Hold on, bro. Gimme a second."

I was already dressed by the time he turned around. "I need to get up outta here."

"Chill, yo. That was only my brother. He cool, but I need to get back to work. I'll call you later when I finish here."

"Okay, cool." I grabbed my purse, straightened my clothes, and left.

I spotted a chick in workout clothes walking in just as I walked out. The bitch almost bumped me. I turned around to see who the fuck this attitude-ass bitch was, but she had already stepped into the office and slammed the door shut.

I was too damn tired to work out today. Shit, all that fucking I did should be considered working out. I decided to walk to my car, but I couldn't help but wonder who the hell that ho was.

Chapter Six

Jihad

Oh shit. That was a close call. As soon as Alyssa walked out of my office, I heard the door open. "Did you leave something?"

"Who? Leave what?"

I quickly turned around. I thought it was Alyssa who walked back in 'cause she left seconds ago.

"Hey, babes. I thought it was Jaseem coming back in."

"Who is that girl that just walked out?" She looked at me all suspicious.

"Huh, who?" I was buying time to get my shit straight.

"Jihad, that bitch that just walked out of yo' office seconds ago, who was that?"

"That's one of my clients. I had to go over her personal training plan with her."

"Oh, okay."

"Baby, you a'ight?"

"Yeah, I'm good. Had a rough day at work today, so I need to let off some steam. Plus, it's been awhile since I been here."

"Well, that's because you have yo' own personal trainer at home now." So I walked over to her and kissed her.

"You better stop playing, boy, before I get butt-ass naked in here."

"Shit, I'm horny anyway. Let me slide up in you really quick."

"In here?" She shot me a crazy look.

"Yeah, why not? This my office, and I can lock the door."

I walked over, locked the door, and pulled her close. Once I started kissing her and fondling her, she finally gave in. Before I knew it, her panties dropped to her ankles, and I was pounding her from the back. I grabbed her hips as she threw her ass back on me, almost knocking me to the ground.

"Oh shit. I'm about to bust, baby. Oh shit," I yelled out as I busted all up in her.

I leaned on the table for support 'cause my ass was worn the fuck out. It took me a few seconds to get a little strength together.

"Damn, somebody was backed up, huh?" She turned around and looked at me before walking off into the bathroom.

Shit. I hope this takes away any suspicions she had.

"You done wore out my ass," she said as she walked out of the bathroom.

"You know I love fucking you, babes."

"Uh-huh, now, I got to go out here limping."

"You'll be a'ight." I slapped her on the ass.

"I'm gone."

She grabbed her bags, unlocked the door, and left . . .

Fuck. That was a close one. *I gots to be more careful,* I thought as I slumped down in my chair. Shit, a nigga was beat. Busting back-to-back like that did a number on my body. I think I might close up early tonight.

Then I heard the door open again. I looked up, and it was my brother this time. "Yo, son, why you ain't hit me up when you saw Brooklyn walk in?"

"Man, I was in the back helping a lady. I was trying to come in here to grab something when you said hold on.

I spotted her when I walked back over to the entrance. I couldn't even do anything. I just stood there talking to her."

"Man, shit. As soon as Alyssa left, she walked in. I swear I would've been dead, my nigga."

"Yo, I don't even understand why you fucking around wit' that little hood bitch. Brooklyn is a boss bitch. You gon' fuck around and fuck up a good thing."

"Listen, big bro, I got this . . . Brooklyn is a boss bitch and all that good shit, but she older. Her pussy ain't that tight, but Alyssa got that young pussy. Every time I get up in there, I feel like I got to bust. My nigga, it's a different kind of feeling."

"I hear you, li'l bro. All I'm saying is, don't fuck up a good thing over pussy."

"I got you." Then I stood up and walked out.

I love my brother to death, but he's been married to the same old, churchgoing, boring bitch for the last ten years. See, I was more like my daddy. He had Mama home, but he was a beast in them streets. I had to say I done met over fifteen bitches that my daddy used to fuck by the time I reached 21. Daddy once told me, "As long as you taking care of home, it don't matter what you do in them streets." I've lived by that motto.

I done ran through so many of these bitches up in this bitch, it should be a crime. These hoes were lonely and yearned for a little attention. That's where I come in. I'm good for boosting confidence, and then the next thing you know, I'm in their drawers. It was mostly only the single bitches, but I done banged a few married bitches. Shit, their husband should be thanking me. I made their bitches healthy and much better in bed. In the end, we all win.

See, with Brooklyn, things were different. I watched her for days until I felt it was the right time to approach her. I immediately peeped that she was one of those bougie-ass bitches, which made me even more eager to get her. I know her type and the games they like to play, pretending like they don't want to fuck. It didn't take me long to get up in them drawers and have that bitch begging me to move in. At first, I was hesitant, but why not? I could still play the perfect nigga and still fuck these other hoes.

Everything was going great . . . until I called that bitch's phone, and she didn't pick up. See, that was *my* pussy, and there was *no way* I was gon' sit around and allow her to throw my pussy all over town. I almost snapped on her ass, but I had to chill out. I got things to do, and acting like this wasn't gon' get nothing accomplished like that. So, here I am, getting ready to get married in the name of love. Or is it something else?

I couldn't get enough of fucking Alyssa. After that close call, I started going over to her place. She didn't live on the best side of town, but as soon as I dive into the pussy, all my senses go out the window. Within two months, my ass was fucking her raw, busting in her. I done bought her a nice Honda Accord and gave her a grand a week. I hate to admit it, but this little bitch had me wide open.

I was trying my best to juggle these two bitches. Alyssa was really chill. As long as I fucked her and spent time with her, she was cool. But on the other hand, Brooklyn kept coming at me with the bullshit. I kept trying to lie, but I was running out of excuses. My ass needs to figure out this shit fast.

Chapter Seven

Brooklyn

"I don't know if I should go through with this wedding," I said to Jasmine as we had lunch at Friday's.

"What are you talkin' about, chick? We're just months away from your big day."

"I don't know. I feel like things are changing between Jihad and me."

"Bitch, you're just getting cold feet. You know if a nigga ain't no good for you, my ass gon' tell you. I must admit, I did not like him at first. But you seem to be happy with him. Ain't none of us got to live with him but you."

"I know. I know. Mama said the same exact thing. I love that man, and I just hope all this is real."

"I mean, if he was broke, then we would say he was after your money. But the nigga is paid. What else could he possibly want? You been through a lot, so your heart is being careful."

"You right, boo. See, that's why I need you to keep me on track."

"That's why we're best friends."

We busted out laughing and went back to eating and drinking wine. After lunch, we parted ways. I headed home 'cause I was finished with all my clients for the day. I just sat in the car for a few minutes when I pulled into the driveway. I tried to shake this feeling that I was having.

Then I saw the mailman pulling up to the mailbox.

"Hey, there, Miss Evans."

"How are you, Mr. Smith?"

He handed me my mail, and I walked up the driveway to the front door. It was nice outside, so I might come back out later when the sun goes down to wash my car. I walked into the house and decided to go upstairs and jump in the shower. As I made my way up the stairs, I heard sounds. Not just any sounds but sexual moans. I tiptoed toward Briana's room, pressed my ear on the door, and was shocked to hear what was going on. Immediately, I busted open the door.

"Oh my God! What are you doing in here?" Briana's fast ass jumped up butt-ass naked.

"No, the question is, what the hell are *you* doing in here?"

"Get out of my room. You ain't my damn mama. I can do what I want to do."

I could tell the boy was scared as hell.

"I'm so sorry. I'm about to go," he said.

"Yes, get the hell out of my house."

He grabbed his clothes and dashed past me.

"What you think you're doing bringing this nigga up in my house?"

"Lady, I'm 15 years old. My mama don't have no problem with me having a boyfriend, so why do you?"

"In case you didn't notice, this is *my* damn house, and you must abide by *my* rules. Yo' fast ass was supposed to be in school. Is this the shit you been doing behind our backs?"

"I'm about to call my mama and my daddy. I got nothing else to say to you. Now, get out of my room."

"Who the fuck you think you talkin' to, little girl? You can barely wash yo' ass, but you up in *my* damn house having sex. Yes, go ahead, call yo' damn parents before I strangle yo' little ass up in here," I snapped.

I had to walk off before I did something serious to this little grown-ass girl. Thank God for my degree in psychology 'cause it prepared me to deal with out-of-control teenagers. If she were my child, I would've torn up that ass. She wouldn't have any behind left to sit on.

I tried calling Jihad's phone, but it just kept going to voicemail. Where the fuck this nigga at when he needs to be over here getting a handle on his out-of-control-ass daughter?

After my shower, I made me a cup of soup. My head was pounding, so I took two Tylenol. When I checked my phone, and his ass still hadn't called back even though I left several messages and sent him a few texts. So I went through my phone and found his brother's number.

"Yo."

"Hey, Jaseem, is Jihad at the gym with you?"

"Oh, hey, Brooklyn. Nah, he left about thirty minutes ago."

"Did he say where he was going?"

"Nah, is something wrong?"

"No, I was worried 'cause I was calling his phone, but it kept going to voicemail."

"I'ma try calling him, but he might be on the way home."

"Okay, thanks."

I cut on the television. I was worn the hell out, physically and mentally. The closer it gets to this wedding, I can't help but wonder if I'm making the right decision by letting Jihad's daughter move in here. Her ass has been nothing but trouble since she got here.

Suddenly, I heard the doorbell ring. *Hmm, I wonder who the hell that is.* I got up and walked down the stairs.

"Who is it?"

"It's Keisha," a female yelled.

She didn't sound familiar, but I knew that name. That was Briana's mother's name. I opened the door. This ratchet-looking woman with a blue weave in her head and gold teeth in her mouth stood in front of me.

"May I help you?"

"Yes, bitch, you sure can. My daughter called me to tell me you done cussed her ass out 'cause her boyfriend was visiting. I mean, you ain't related to her. You just the bitch her daddy fucking right now."

"First off, I'm not *your* bitch. You look stupid as hell coming over here going off. I don't know how you run yo' little *hut*, but this *my* shit, and over here, little girls don't bring their nigga home to fuck."

I was about to read this ho her rights, but I saw Jihad suddenly pull up. He must've spotted what was going on 'cause his ass ran over to the door.

"What the hell's going on? What are you doing here, Keisha?"

"Nigga, I been calling you. What the fuck I told you about leaving our daughter alone with this bitch?"

"Yo, will you calm the fuck down? What the fuck happened?"

"I came home and caught yo' grown-ass daughter in her room having sex."

"What? Babe, are you sure?"

"Jihad, why don't you ask Briana? As a matter of fact, get this bitch out of my yard before I drag her ass."

"Drag who, bitch? Jihad, you better get yo' old-ass bitch before I lay hands on her."

"Man, shut the fuck up and go. I'll handle it."

"Yeah, make sure you let this ho know. She ain't no kin to Briana. If you don't, *I'll* be back over here."

"Man, go home."

I walked back into the house, mad as fuck. This bitch done brought her ass all the way to my steps to disrespect me, and all this nigga said was, "Go home." I dashed past his daughter and went up to my room, slamming the door.

"Babes, we need to talk," Jihad said as he walked into the room about twenty-five minutes later.

"Yeah, talk," I said with an attitude.

"First, let me apologize for how Keisha behaved. She was wrong. She has no business coming here. I spoke to Briana, and she said she and the boy was just studying when you came into the room. She said you got upset and started cussing her out."

"First off, I saw both of them butt-ass naked. Second, I didn't cuss at her ass. I wanted to drag her out of here, but out of respect for you, I didn't touch her ass. That little girl has been trouble from day one. She plays us against each other, and you keep falling for the bullshit. Keep it up, and her ass gon' be pregnant soon."

"Calm down, Brooklyn. I'm trying to get to the bottom of this. You're my soon-to-be-wife, and that's my baby girl. I feel like I'm being pulled in different directions."

"Jihad, believe what you want. I know what the hell I saw. I wonder how long she's been bringing boys up in here. Did you even know she's sexually active?"

"That kind of stuff her mother deals with."

"Really? Maybe *that's* the problem. Her ass is too damn stupid to be a mother."

"Baby, listen, just calm down. I'll get everything under control. Trust me." He reached over and kissed me on the forehead.

I wasn't trying to hear that shit, but I was too damn tired to go back and forth with him. That little grown-ass girl was his problem and definitely *not* mine.

Chapter Eight

Alyssa

I find myself thinking about Jihad all the time. It doesn't matter if we just left each other, I be wanting him more and more. I done had my share of niggas, but he was the first older nigga that I ever fucked with, and I have to admit, I was falling deeper and deeper in love with him. The way he made love to my body was like no other. Then after sex, we would lie up there talking about our future together.

"Hey, babes, you ever consider having a baby?"

"No. I mean, I have to find the right man first."

"So, you don't think I'm the right man?" He sat up and looked at me.

"I'm not saying that, boo. I just don't know how serious we are, you know, on your end."

"That's crazy. I thought we were in a committed relationship. I guess I was wrong."

"We're in a committed relationship. You know I'm falling in love with you."

"That's good 'cause I love you."

Wow. Just hearing those words come out of his mouth sent chills down my spine. I was a whore, and I've fucked many niggas. Jihad was different, though. He was attentive and cared about my feelings.

I called Jihad's phone. As soon as I picked up, I started crying.

"Yo, babes, what's wrong?" He sounded concerned.

"I can't go back to school." I cried harder.

"Why not? What are you talkin' about?"

"I don't have enough money to cover next semester, but I can't drop out. I've come too far." I bawled harder.

"Calm down, babes. How much money do you need?"

"Twenty-five thousand for the next semester. It's my last one."

"Shit, that's a lot of gotdamn money. How soon do you need it?"

"Jihad, I wasn't asking you for the money. I just needed someone to talk to. I'ma figure it out."

"Yo, you my woman, and if you hurting, then I'm hurting. When do you need it?"

"My counselor said by 5:00 p.m. Friday."

"A'ight, babes. Listen. I got you. Now, dry them tears. You know yo' man is solid."

"I know, baby. I was just so scared all my hard work would go down the drain."

"Aye, listen, I got to run, but I'll be over later to suck on that pussy."

"Okay, daddy, love you."

As soon as I hung up, I wiped away the fake tears.

"Bitch, what did that nigga say?" Trina asked.

"He said he got me."

"Bitch, you lying. You telling me this nigga just gon' put twenty-five grand in your hands, just like that?"

"This pussy got this nigga doing all kinds of shit. Bitch, we going shoppingggg. You hear me?" I jumped up and grabbed my bitch, hugging her tight.

"Bitch, I swear you a motherfucking savage. I don't know what the fuck you did to that nigga, but keep doing it, bitch, 'cause that nigga is willing to pay."

"Hmm, later, when he comes over, I got to think of new tricks to blow his mind. Bitch, are you down with this threesome?"

"Nah, bitch. That's a nigga that you have feelings for. You know we have rules against that."

"I don't give a fuck about no feelings. Bitch, let's fuck and suck this nigga into a coma tonight."

"Well, you know, as long as dollars are involved, my fat ass is down for whatever."

"Yup. Well, let's do it."

Later that night, when Jihad came over, I had dinner cooked, slow music playing, and the only lights on were from candles.

"Damn, babe, it's smelling good up in here. What's that . . . steak?" he inquired as he stepped into my apartment and kissed me on the lips while he grabbed my ass.

"Come on. I know you probably hungry." I took his hand and led him to my small area, where I squeezed a dining table into.

He sat there, and I served him his food. I then poured him a glass of Hennessy on the rocks. See, I've been paying attention to what he likes to eat and drink. The key to making your man happy is to pay close attention to him. Show him how important he really is.

I took a seat beside him and started eating. I must admit, I put my damn foot in this meat. It was so tender. It just dissolved in my mouth.

"Damn, babes. This is good."

"Thank you. I ain't no chef, but I know to do a little something," I smiled at him.

After dinner, we moved to the living room. The candles were lit, and slow music was playing.

"Relax and watch television while I clean up this kitchen. I got a surprise for you."

"For me? Oh shit." He looked at me suspiciously.

"Yea, for you, daddy." I smiled and winked at him.

I smiled to myself. This nigga had no idea what the fuck we had in store for him. All I know is we will blow his mind and fuck and suck the life out of him.

"Yo, who is this?" Jihad's eyes popped open as my bitch Trina entered the room. He was in the living room chilling, watching the sports channel, so he had no idea I had let her in.

"Oh, bae, remember I said I had a surprise for you? Well, this is my bestie, Trina. We got a little something for you."

I walked over to him and pulled him up off the couch.

"What's going on, babe?" He shot me a suspicious look.

"Come on, boo." I pulled him to the bedroom.

"Take yo' clothes off."

"Huh?"

"You heard the lady. Take yo' clothes off, love."

He looked at Trina, then looked back at me. By this time, I was already getting naked. Trina came over to me, and we started kissing. Shit, this wasn't new to us. We been fucking and sucking on each other since middle school.

"Oh shit, babe. This how you roll?"

I didn't respond. I started sucking on her breast while massaging her clit. The room temperature was rising, and my pussy was on fire. I pushed her back on the bed where Jihad was laid back, enjoying the show and massaging his dick. I parted her legs far apart. Then I crept up between her legs and started licking her clit. The pungent smell of her natural juice hit my nose. I used my tongue to dig deep into her love cave while she ground on my tongue. I sucked on her pussy like I was feasting on my last meal.

"Aaarg, oh yessss," she moaned.

I didn't ease up any. Her legs started to tremble, and her body tensed up. Juices started to flow out of her pussy. "Aweee, aweee," she screamed out.

"Come here. Come ride this dick." Jihad moved over and grabbed her arm.

She obliged and got on him. I watched as she slid down on Jihad's rock-hard dick.

"C'mon, baby. Ride that dick," I cheered her on.

That only excited her more 'cause she rode Jihad like a cowgirl competing for the first prize. So I lay there playing with my pussy, which only got wetter by the sight of Jihad fucking my bitch.

For the next forty-five minutes, we took turns fucking and sucking. I know Jihad was a beast, but I didn't realize how strong he was until he fucked my girl and me without showing a bit of fatigue. In the end, we all fell out on the bed. I winked at my girl before I dozed off.

Jihad

Being with Brooklyn has become more of a routine. We did the same shit every day. At times, I was fucking her, and all I could think about was Alyssa's young little pussy. If it were possible to put both bitches together, they would definitely make the perfect bitch. On the one hand, Brooklyn has money, a house, and she's all about her business, but the pussy ain't nothing to brag to your homeboy about. Alyssa, on the other hand, she got a lot of needs, always wants money, she's in school, and definitely looking for a nigga to take care of her. But that pussy stays wet, and the way it grips my dick does something to a nigga. Not to mention the multiple threesomes I have with her and her homegirl. Man, that little bitch is worth every single dollar that I spent on her.

"Yo, bro, we need to talk." My brother interrupted my deep thoughts when he walked into the office. Shit, I was happy I was sitting down 'cause this dick was rock hard; seems like it was busting out of my gym pants.

"Whaddup, yo? Shit, I'm tired as fuck. I was just dozing off," I lied.

"The business is in danger. We are behind on the loan, and the profit is dropping viciously. Plus, the money we put aside to keep the business running is missing several thousand dollars. We need to call it quits or develop a better marketing strategy that will get more clients in here. But we can't go on like this."

I sat there listening to him. I knew this conversation was coming soon. The truth is, when we first started, the gym was booming, clients were coming in every day, and the money was rolling in. My spending started getting out of control, but that wasn't what did it. I was fucking with this bitch, a white bitch. We were fucking a good six months. Everything was going good . . . until the bitch started to catch feelings. I told her it was over, and she cried and begged me not to break it off. I wasn't trying to hear that shit, so I threw her ass out. I thought that was the end of it . . . until I got a call that she was suing me and the gym for sexual harassment. I wanted to fight the charges, but my brother wanted it to go away. He was worried about the damage it would do to the gym's reputation. The lawyers got involved, and we ended up settling for a huge sum of money. The insurance company paid, but our premium shot up, and word got out about the lawsuit. We started losing a lot of the female clientele. We tried to lower the prices and brought in more equipment, but it never bounced back from that rumor. Now, here we are in desperate need of a blessing.

"Yo, we can try to get an advertising team in here to see if they can turn things around for the better."

"Bro, to be honest, unless we get some serious money, I can't go on like this. I'm not bringing in no income, and my wife's starting to breathe down my neck. So I'm thinking about going back to school. I warned you that this might happen."

"What the fuck you saying? This *my* fault?" I stood up.

"Bro, we had a good thing going. I warned you about fooling around with these bitches. Unfortunately, you didn't listen, and you let a white bitch bring us down."

"I told you that ho was lying. That ho gave me the pussy and then got mad after I dumped her ass. This ain't my fault a ho lied. Yo, fuck you if you feel like this. I put my money in this shit too."

"Yo, son, you heard what I said. I done put too much money in this shit. I ain't putting another dollar in it. You can keep this shit. My marriage is in jeopardy behind this shit 'cause I done took money out of our personal account. I can't do it anymore. What was once a vision is now a fucking nightmare."

Here we are about to go broke, and this nigga worried about this bitch breathing down his neck. "Yo, we gon' figure it out. Trust me. We done been down a rough road before, and we dug ourselves out. We got this, bro."

"A'ight, we only got a month to figure it out," he said before he walked out of the office.

Man, this nigga be on the bullshit. I know that bitch he's married to has something to do with him behaving like this. Fuck that. I just need to figure out something fast.

After sitting at my desk trying to come up with different ways to get some money, nothing seemed to pan out. I tried my bank a few months ago, but they denied me. Credit was fucked up because of the late payments on the loan for the building. Shit, the only other way I can get this money was to get a loan from . . . shit . . . Brooklyn got money in the bank. I wasn't sure how much money, but from how she spends and how her business is doing, I know her account is fat. The thing is, she has no idea I'm broke. As a matter of fact, that ring I bought her maxed out my American Express card and put me in a deeper financial bind. Shit, I can go directly to her ass and tell her the truth, but would she still marry me if she knows I'm broke and about to lose the business? Would she ride for her nigga?

I grabbed my keys and my bag and headed out the door. I walked past a few clients standing by the door. As usual, the bitches stay flirting with me. I shot them a smile and kept it pushing. This was one of the things that I loved about this place, the different pussy that I got to fuck. Not that I couldn't do it without the gym, but this made it easier.

I thought about calling Brooklyn, but I decided to surprise her. I stopped by the flower shop, grabbed her a bouquet, and then stopped by the liquor store and grabbed a bottle of wine. On my way to her office, I stopped and grabbed us lunch.

After I parked, I walked into her building.

"Hello, Nicolette."

"Mr. Evans, how are you? What a pleasant surprise."

"I'm doing good. Is the misses in?"

"Yes, I can call to let her know you're here."

"No, please don't. I'm trying to surprise her with lunch."

"Oh, very romantic. In that case, please, go on in."

"Thanks."

I made my way to Brooklyn's office. In my head, I was still trying to figure out how I was about to get her to see things my way. I knocked once before I pushed the door open.

"Oh, hey, honey. What are you doing here?" She looked shocked.

"I wanted to bring my woman lunch, unless she's already eaten."

"Oh my. You're just amazing. I was just sitting here saying to myself how hungry I am."

"Well, your man got your favorite from your favorite restaurant, and here, these are for you." I handed her the bouquet of roses.

"Wow, Mr. Evans, what is going on?" She shot me a strange look.

"Listen, woman, if I could do this every day, trust me, I would. You're the most beautiful and amazing woman that I've ever laid my eyes on. You deserve this and so much more."

"You know, Jihad, all my life, I longed for a man that is for me. I mean, I been with different niggas, but either they were after my money, or they were just full of shit. You, you don't want anything, and yet, you give me your unconditional love. You go the distance to show me you're for me. I can't wait to be your wife."

"Well, I'm glad you said that. How about we forget the big wedding? We go down by the courthouse and get married. I mean, I know I sound crazy, but, baby, I love you so much, and I really don't want to wait much longer. We can always have a big wedding later."

"You serious? I mean, I've always wanted a nice wedding. After all, I only plan on doing this one time."

"Baby, weddings are for other people to celebrate. What matters is giving you my last name, my heart, my soul, and making you mine."

She sat there looking at me. I hope this damn speech was getting to her somewhat 'cause I was fucking broke and had no money to contribute to this bullshit-ass wedding that she wants.

"What about the people that we already told about the wedding? I already gave the wedding planner a deposit?"

"Baby, I can give that back to you, or once we plan on doing a big one, we can use that deposit. We can get the marriage license and go right down to the courthouse."

"Okay, you're right. As long as we're married, I can plan something later."

"Thank you, baby. I swear, Brooklyn, I can't wait to be your husband. Now, let's eat, and look what I got." I put the bottle of wine on her desk.

"You know I'm at work. I can't drink."

"A small glass of wine isn't going to hurt you. Do you know all these professionals, even judges, have a glass of wine on their lunch break?"

"I swear, you are something else, Jihad," she smiled.

"You have no idea." I smiled back at her.

Chapter Nine

Brooklyn

What the hell is going on with this man, I thought as I sat in my office, eating lunch and drinking wine with Jihad. He shocked the hell out of me when he walked in here with lunch, but then he wanted to go to the courthouse to get married. I mean, I didn't want to have no big-ass wedding, but I at least wanted to have one that I could invite Mama and the rest of my family to.

I realized that he was serious about going down by the courthouse and getting hitched. I mean, some bitches wish a nigga would propose to them, and here, I have a man that is rushing to marry my ass, and I was tripping about a damn wedding. After Jihad pleading and me coming to my senses, I decided to do it. I love Jihad, and as long as we're married, that's all that matters. Seeing how happy he was when I told him I would confirmed to me that I was marrying my soul mate.

After we had lunch and Jihad left, I looked at the clock. I still had about thirty minutes before my next appointment, so I decided to wash up fast. The last thing I needed was for a client to smell alcohol on my breath.

I sat back at the desk, thinking I would be married in a few days. I pulled up Jasmine's number.

"Hey, you."

"Bitch, you would not believe what just happened."

"Spit it out. You know I hate secrets. What, you pregnant?"

"See, there you go, being funny. Nah, bitch, Jihad wants us to go the courthouse and get married."

"Say what? Bitch, you tripping."

"Nah, I'm not. He said we can do a big wedding later on down the road."

"And what's the rush? I mean, there's nothing wrong with a man rushing to be your husband, but did he give a reason?"

I could tell her mind was spinning over there.

"Girl, he brought lunch and flowers, and then he busted out with that. I was shocked too, but after he told me his reasoning, I agreed with him."

"Fuck his reasoning behind it. Is this what *you* want?"

"I mean, you know I've always dreamed of a wedding, but I can do that later. It ain't like I'm canceling it."

"Brooklyn, did you consider getting a prenup?"

"Huh?"

"Have you considered getting a prenup? I know he got his own money and all, but you have way more to lose."

"No, I haven't, but Jihad has his own money—"

"Stop thinking with your heart and start thinking like the boss bitch I know you are. All the niggas on TV that went after their wives' money had their own money. Look at Halle Berry, Jill Scott, and Mary J. All their husbands have money, but that don't stop their ass from trying to get alimony and some more shit. You're my best friend, and I need to make sure your money is straight. Can't be too in love where you become naive."

"I understand, boo."

"Fuck understanding me. I need you to *act* on it before you become this nigga's wife. I don't know, but something don't seem right. However . . . You my bitch, and if you riding, then I'm definitely rolling. That nigga better be playing it straight 'cause if he's not. I'm coming for that ass."

"Girl, if I didn't know you got a law license, I would mistake you for a thug."

"Fuck this degree. I'm a thug at heart. Nah, but I'm serious, bitch. Get that prenup."

"All right, girl. I'm going to talk to Jihad about it tonight."

"A'ight, chick. I got to run, but I'll call you tomorrow."

"All right, babes."

How do you come out and tell the man you love and are about to marry that you need a prenup? Wow, this conversation should be interesting this evening. Jasmine is right, though. I got money from my dad's estate, plus my business is worth a lot. So I really need to protect myself. Not that I think Jihad would do anything crazy, but Jasmine is right. Niggas nowadays been going after the money.

It was a long day at the office. My behind didn't get off until 7:00 p.m. I don't know why I push myself this hard when I really don't have to. It's more that I love what I do, helping families through difficult times.

I took a quick shower and made a salad. After today's lunch, I decided to stick with something light. When I heard the front door slam shut, I jumped off the bed to see what the hell was going on. Brianna ran up the stairs. I turned around and went to her room, knocked, and waited.

"What do you want, lady?"

"Why are you slamming the door like that?"

"It's just a freaking door. Dang, you let everything bother you. Can you stop breathing down my neck?"

"Breathing down your neck? Should I remind you this my gotdamn house? Not your daddy's and definitely *not* yo' mama's house."

"How can I forget this is your house? You remind me every chance you get. So if you have an issue with me, you should talk to my daddy. Oh, I get it. You too scared to say anything about me 'cause he might leave you. Hmmm. Not a bad idea."

The more this little bitch speaks, the more I realize how much I despise her. I work with disrespectful kids and their families, but this one tops them all. I opened the door, looked at her, and smiled.

"Is that what you hope for? So your father can go back to your mother? Is *this* what it's all about, Brianna?" I stood there analyzing her.

"Go back to her? My father never *left* my mother. Lady, I swear you got to be the dumbest if you think my dad ain't still with my mother. Anyway, I got homework to do. Can you close the door?"

I watched as she smiled at me and walked back to her bed. I wanted to rush in there and quiz her on what she just said, but I wouldn't give her the satisfaction. Instead, I slammed the door shut and walked to my room. What the fuck did she mean they're still together? That can't be true. She was just saying that to grab my attention, and honestly, she did. I picked up the phone to call Jihad but threw it back down. I need to be face-to-face with him when I talk to him about this.

Later that night, Jihad walked in around 11:00 p.m. He cut the light on and started taking his clothes off. "Hey, babes. Thought you were sleeping."

"Nah, we need to talk."

"A'ight, give me a second. I'm sweaty as hell and need to take a shower real quick."

"All right."

I patiently waited as he took his shower. I heard his phone ringing back-to-back to the point where it was getting annoying. I thought about getting up and checking it.

That thought was interrupted 'cause he walked out of the bathroom.

"Babes, what's bothering you?"

"Sit down. We really need to talk."

"I'm all ears." He took a seat on the edge of the bed.

"Brianna and I got into it earlier, and some words were exchanged. But out of everything she said, one thing stuck out to me. She told me that you and her mother are still together."

"Brianna said what?"

"You and her mother never left. So, my question is, are you still fucking her mama?"

"Hell nah. I told you I wouldn't fuck her if she were the last bitch on this earth. Baby, listen, you going to have to realize Brianna is an only child, and she wishes me and her mother were still together. She told me that numerous times. I explained to her that I didn't love her mother anymore."

"Listen, Jihad, I already told you I'm not for the games. Your daughter don't like me, and I'm cool with that. What I'm *not* cool with is being disrespected in my own damn house, and then this."

"Baby, baby. We about to get married. I don't want Keisha's trifling ass. Brianna only saying that to get under your skin. She's a child. You can't pay this any mind. If I wanted another woman, you think I would be rushing to make you my wife? Hell nah. I love you, woman, and that's the God honest truth."

"Yeah, I guess you're right. Jihad, what you think about a prenup?"

"A prenup? So, Brianna lied to you, and now you want a prenup? You think I'm after your money, Brooklyn?" He stood up and yelled in my face.

"First, you need to lower your fucking voice. This has nothing to do with Brianna. I was going to talk to you about it earlier."

"Yo, this is crazy. The woman I love and gave my heart to wants to sign a prenup. Let me guess. You scared I'm going to take your money and take it to my baby mother? You know what? This is sick. I ain't no leech, and I got my own gotdamn money. You don't see *me* asking for one."

"Jihad, you blowing this shit out of proportion. People sign prenups all the damn time."

"Yea, people that don't trust one another. You know what . . . I need to go. I need to get my head clear." He went into the closet to grab some clothes.

I got up off the bed and rushed over to him. "Jihad, baby, I didn't mean to upset you like this. It ain't about the money . . ."

"Get off me. I fucking love you. When I started fucking you, I didn't know shit about you. I didn't know if you had a dollar or not. I'ma stand-up nigga. I work for mine every goddamn day." He shoved me off him.

He got dressed in no time, grabbed his keys, and left the room. This nigga blew this shit to the extreme. I knew he would be a little upset, but to go off like this was a little too much.

All this damn drama was getting to be too much. My head was pounding, and I was tired as hell. I decided to call it an early night. *Maybe tomorrow will be better,* I thought.

Hours later, I rolled over and didn't feel Jihad on the other side of the bed. I instantly opened my eyes and looked. His spot was empty. I sat up and looked at the time. It was 5:00 a.m., and it seemed like he didn't make it home. To be sure, I got up and walked to the bathroom. It was empty. I walked downstairs to see if he was asleep on the couch since we had fought earlier. No, he wasn't there either. I returned upstairs, checked the guest room, and that too was empty. I went back into my room and grabbed my phone. I was checking to see if I missed any calls or got a text from him . . . but nothing. I called his number, but the phone went straight to voicemail. Where the hell could this man be? I thought about calling his brother, but it was too early to call a person's phone, especially looking for my man.

I lay back down, wondering where the fuck Jihad was. I wondered if he was laid up with another bitch, but I quickly dismissed that thought. I know you can't trust these niggas, but he has never given me any reason to believe he was fucking around on me. So I cut the television on, trying my best not to stress too much about where this man was.

By the time I left for work at 7:30 a.m., Jihad still had not made it home. I was starting to worry about him. I finally called his brother's phone and waited for him to respond.

"Hello."

"Good morning, Jaseem. Have you seen your brother?"

"No, I saw him yesterday when he left the gym. He's not home?"

"We had a minor argument yesterday evening, and he stormed out. I haven't seen him since, and his phone is turned off."

"That's strange, but you know how Jihad is. He might be at a hotel, trying to cool off. If I were you, I wouldn't be too worried. I'm sure he'll pop up today."

"I guess so. Thank you."

"No problem. Brooklyn, stop worrying. He'll pop up soon."

"Got you."

I hung up, not feeling any better. It was getting late, so I got into my car and pulled off. I really don't care where he was. I just want to make sure he was not dead or locked up.

I was finished with my first client and walked him to the door when I heard my cell phone going off. I quickly closed the door and rushed to pick it up.

"Hello."

"Brooklyn."

"Jihad, where the hell you been? I've been worried sick all damn night."

"Listen, I just needed to clear my head. So I got me a room in a hotel."

"A hotel, huh? So, it didn't cross your mind that I would be looking for you? So, what is *really* going on?"

"Brooklyn, nothing is going on. I hate that you feel like I'm after your money. So, after thinking all night, I decided that I would sign a prenup. And if that's not good enough for you, we can call off the wedding until you're 100 percent sure I'm in it for love, not money. To prove this, I will put you on my account. I don't have a lot, but enough to live off."

"Jihad, I want to marry you. Fuck the prenup. I love you, and I know you love me. I'm ready to do this."

"Are you sure, Brooklyn? I mean, we can wait."

"Yes, I'm sure. We can get the license this afternoon and marry in a few days."

"I love you, baby. I promise I won't let you down. I promise."

"I got to run, babes, but let's meet up around 12:30 p.m. We can go get the license then."

"I love you, woman."

"Love you too, bae."

After I hung up, I felt so much better. I wasn't sure I had made the right decision about the prenup, and I could hear Jasmine's voice in my head, screaming at me for being stupid. But I love Jihad, and to be honest, in my soul, I feel like he loves me too. I didn't want to let money come between what we had going on. Most women live their entire lives trying to find the right man. Jihad might not be perfect, but he was perfect for me, and I was ready to take the next step with him.

Alyssa

I looked over at Jihad, still asleep, and smiled. I could definitely get used to waking up every morning to this sexy-ass man. I reached over and rubbed his chest. He was tired from fucking all night. I swear this nigga was energetic and knows how to tear up the pussy.

"Good morning, beautiful," he whispered as he opened his eyes.

"Hey, you." I continued rubbing his chest.

"You see what you doing?" He grabbed his dick and pulled it out of his boxers.

"Oh my," I teased.

"Come sit on it real quick."

I didn't complain. I pulled off my panties and got on top of him, sliding down on his hard dick while he cuffed my breasts with his hands, massaging them. I tooted my ass in the air, allowing his dick to hit the bottom of my stomach.

"Fuck this dick, babes."

I love the way he talks dirty to me. That makes me ride the dick faster. Then he gripped my waist and pulled me down on him, holding me so I couldn't move anywhere.

"Shit, shit. I'm about to bust."

"Come all up in me, bae. Please, please," I pleaded.

"You sure?"

"Yessss," I said as I exploded all over his dick.

"Aarghh, aarghh. Shiiiit." He gripped my hips tighter and pulled me down hard.

His juices shot up in me as my body trembled. I didn't move. I just lay there on top of him while he held me.

"I love you," he whispered in my ear.

"I love you too."

That was a shock to me when he said he loved me. I was in love with him, but I was scared to tell him. Hearing him say it to me first was all the confirmation I needed.

His phone started to ring, which interrupted our bonding moment. He reached over and grabbed it off the nightstand. "Yo."

"Where you at, bro?"

"At Alyssa's house. Why? What's up?"

"You know Brooklyn is looking for you," I heard his brother say.

"A'ight, cool."

Without saying anything else, he hung up. I heard exactly what his brother said on the phone. This makes me wonder who the fuck Brooklyn is and why she would be looking for him.

"Aye, bae, who's Brooklyn?"

"Huh?"

"Your bother said Brooklyn is looking for you. Who's Brooklyn?"

"Oh, that. That's one of my clients. I forgot I had to meet with her this morning for a session."

"Oh, okay. You ain't fucking her, are you?" I got up off him and looked at him.

"Nah, she a client. You tripping," he chuckled.

"So was I," I said with attitude.

He sat up in the bed and took my face in his hand. "Listen, I love you, B. You have nothing to worry about."

"I love you too. Oh, before I forget, I need some money."

"How much money and how soon?"

"About three hundred. I got to pay the light bill."

"Okay, I got you."

"Thank you, daddy," I smiled at him.

"Well, I got to run. I'll see you later."

"Yea, I need to get up too. I have class in another hour."

He kissed me, got dressed, and left. I lay there tired from that fuck earlier. Finally, I cut off the room light, got under the cover, and decided to take a nap. I needed to enroll in school before Jihad found out I wasn't in school like I'd told him. Shit, that was the last thing I needed him to know.

I was lying on my bed chilling and thinking about how much my life has changed since I started fucking with Jihad. I went from fucking multiple niggas just to pay my bills to only fucking him. I ain't going to lie. I do miss the nigga Jahmiel that I be fucking. That nigga didn't have a ton of money. He was a local dope boy, but his head was off the chain. That nigga used to suck on my pussy for hours while I climaxed in his mouth. Shit, just thinking about him made my pussy moist. I reached for my phone and called his number.

"Aye, yo," his sexy Panamanian voice echoed through the phone.

"Hola, papi," I replied in my sexiest Spanish accent.

"What's good, B? I thought you ain't fuck wit' the kid no more."

"Boy, stop. I just been busy with school and trying to pay these bills."

"Shit, I feel that. So, what's good wit' you? Let me slide through and suck on that clit."

His words were a sweet melody to my ear. I smiled at the thought of his tongue on my clit.

"How fast can you get here?"

"I'm down on Jerome Avenue, so give me about half an hour, and I'll be there, baby girl."

"A'ight, daddy, I'll be waiting."

"A'ight. One."

Well, maybe this wasn't such a brilliant idea because Jihad expected me to be faithful to him. But shit, how do I know that Jihad ain't fucking one of them bitches at the gym? I remember that one bitch pushed past me that one day when I was leaving. Matter of fact, let me see where his ass is at right now. A bitch couldn't be too careful.

I called his number and waited for him to pick up. He didn't answer. I assumed he was busy at the gym, so I hung up. I just hope his ass don't bother to call when I was getting my pussy ate.

I jumped off the bed and walked to the shower. I hadn't shaved in a few days and needed to get my shit cleaned up before Jahmiel got here. I know he loves the pussy to be well kept. After I got out of the shower, I rubbed down with baby oil and put on sexy lingerie without any panties. There was no need for it because he would pull them off as soon as he arrived.

I looked at the phone, and Jihad still had not called back. Oh well, I'll hit his ass up later. Next, I heard the doorbell ringing, so I got up and strutted to the door. I looked through the peephole and saw Jahmiel, so I unlocked the door.

"Whaddup, yo?" he greeted me.

"Hey, you." I hugged him.

"Come on."

I walked off into my bedroom. I was kind of nervous, so I needed not to waste any time just in case Jihad started calling me.

"What you been up to, B?"

"Same shit, you know me," I said as I lifted the lingerie over my head, exposing my well shaved pussy.

"Damn, B. You ain't tryna waste no time, huh?"

"Ain't you the same nigga that always preach to me that time is money."

"Oh shit, I hear you, B."

He got my drift 'cause I got on my back and opened my legs far apart. He wasted no time. Within seconds, that nigga had me clutching his head and shoving it deeper into my pussy, suffocating him. I know most niggas knew how to suck pussy, but this nigga was blessed with a special kind of skill. He the kind that stretches out his tongue to snatch your soul through your pussy. I tried moving to ease the tension, but he had his hand cuffed under my ass and held me in place. There was no room for me to move, so I just lay there, trying not to explode.

My phone kept ringing, and as much as I wanted to reach over and pick it up, I dared not interrupt this art of making love to the pussy. My insides started shivering, and the veins in my head started standing up.

"Aweee, oh my God, I'm about to come. Godddd," I screamed as I used my strength to push out my juices.

He didn't move; he licked me from section to section until I was semidry. He then flipped me over and entered me. He grabbed my hips and pulled me closer to him while he thrust in and out of me. I was so into the dick . . . until that damn phone started ringing again. I buried my head under my pillow as I tried to tune out the phone's ringing and concentrate more on this dick sliding in and out of me.

Ring. Ring. Ring.

What the fuck is that? Is that the doorbell? I thought as I tried to think what that banging sound was. A few seconds went by, and I didn't hear anything. Jahmiel didn't miss a beat and didn't seem to hear what I heard. Maybe I was tripping.

I buried my head back under the pillow. This time, the banging on the door was louder and more consistent.

"Hold up." I tried to scoot away.

"Hold on, B. I'm about to bust." This nigga started pounding me harder.

My phone started ringing again, and the door kept banging. Now, I was beginning to panic. Before I could gather my thoughts, he pulled out and exploded on my ass.

"Damn, B. That pussy is gushing," he said before walking into the bathroom.

I would have loved the compliment any other time, but my mind was on the door. I grabbed my phone, only to notice around *fifteen* missed calls from Jihad. I opened the text.

Where you at? I'm at the door.

I blinked twice, then read the text again. That's when it registered in my head that Jihad was knocking at the door.

Oh fuck. This nigga is in my bathroom, and Jihad is outside, banging on my door. I quickly grabbed my lingerie and put it on. Then I grabbed my head. What the fuck am I going to do? God help me. I was going into panic mode.

"You good. Did you find out who's at the door?"

"Huh, no, I didn't."

"Oh, a'ight. Well, I got a run to make. Do you need anything?"

"No, I'm good."

"A'ight, B. Hit me if you need me."

"Jahmiel, hold on."

I dashed to the door and looked through the peephole, but I didn't see anyone. Maybe Jihad had left.

"Yo, you straight? You acting kind of weird. You sure you don't know who was at the door?"

"Nah, I'm good. It probably was the Chinese people delivering food and knocking on the wrong door."

I popped the lock. Jahmiel hugged me and was one foot out the door when I felt someone grab me.

"Bitch, who the fuck is this nigga?" Jihad stepped between Jahmiel and me and pushed into the door.

"Yo, nigga, get the fuck off her. Who the fuck is you?" Jahmiel asked.

"This my bitch. Who the fuck are *you,* and what you doing in *my* crib?"

"Yo, you got a nigga, B? Damn, that's foul. You just let me fuck you. My bad, my nigga. I ain't know this yo' ho," he said in the most disrespectful tone.

I felt low. I just finished fucking this nigga, and *this* was how he talked about me?"Yeah, nigga, you better get the fuck on before you get this beat down," Jihad released his grip on me and stepped closer to Jahmiel's face.

"Back the fuck up, pussy, before I lay you out in this hallway," Jahmiel said, pulling a gun and aiming it at Jihad's head.

"Oh my God! Stop, please; just go," I pleaded.

"Don't bitch up now, nigga. You want some of this smoke, nigga?" He released the safety.

This wasn't good. I could see in Jahmiel's eyes that he was about to do something stupid.

"You a young punk. If you ain't had that burner, I would beat yo' head to the white meat," Jihad chuckled.

"Nigga, this bitch saved you 'cause I like her, and if I kill you, I'ma have to body her ass too. I'm about to bounce, though, so you can taste my cum all up in yo' bitch's mouth."

"Get the fuck on, little young nigga."

He walked up to Jihad's face, smiled, and walked out the door while pointing the gun at Jihad before disappearing down the hallway.

I wanted to run, but Jihad had me pinned between him and the door. "Yo, you just fucked this nigga in the bed we fuck in?"

"Nah, I ain't fuck him. That's my homeboy, and he stopped by. I swear, baby, I ain't fuck him," I tried to lie.

"Bitch, you must think I'ma clown or something. I been calling yo' phone and banging on the motherfucking door. No fucking answer 'cause you in here with this nigga. How long you been fucking him?"

"I swear to you, Jihad, I wasn't fucking him."

Bap, bap!

"Bitch, shut the fuck up lying. I told yo' ass don't fucking play with me. Bitch, I'll kill you if I find out you giving away my pussy," he yelled as he shoved me down.

I thought more blows were coming, so I put my head down and covered my face.

"Bitch, I told you not to motherfucking play me. You fucking this little young nigga on me while I'm fucking paying yo' bills and yo' school shit. I do e'erything for you, bitch. I swear, bitch, I'm done. Lose my motherfucking number, ho."

He walked out the door and left. I was still too scared to move. After a few minutes, I got up and ran to the door, locking it. Then I ran to the couch and lay there, crying my heart out. Fuck, how did I allow this to happen? I always play niggas, but I never got caught like this. Not only that, but I also ain't never had no nigga put their motherfucking hands on me like this. I got up, ran to the bedroom, and called Trina. I needed somebody to talk to right now.

"Bitch, where you been? I been calling you."

"I need you to come over here," I tried to say in between sobs.

"Yo, what's wrong, Alyssa? You crying?"

"Just come over here, please."

I hung up before she could say anything else. Then I went to the bathroom to check on my face. It was burning. I stood in front of the mirror and ran my hand across my bruised cheek. Tears rolled down my face, stinging the raw skin. I grabbed a piece of cotton from the cabinet and opened the peroxide bottle. I needed to clean my face. I couldn't believe that Jihad did this to me. This nigga just told me a few days ago he loved me, and this is how he do me?

Suddenly, I heard the doorbell ringing. I threw the cotton into the trash and walked out of the bathroom. I looked through the peephole to make sure it was my bitch and not Jihad's bitch ass coming back. Finally, I opened the door.

"Are you okay, bitch? What happened?"

I busted out crying before I slammed the door and locked it.

"Look at my fucking face."

"Oh my God. What the fuck happened?" She reached out to touch it.

I eased back, preventing her from touching me. My face was on fire, and touching it would only make it worse.

"Bitch, answer me. Did Jihad do this to you? Don't tell me that motherfucker put his hands on you." She looked at me, waiting on a response.

"Bitch, I was in here with the nigga Jahmiel, and I heard a banging on the door. I didn't think it was Jihad. So, after we finished fucking around, dude decided to leave. To cut a long story short, soon as I opened the door, Jihad was waiting."

"Are you fucking serious, bitch? Why the fuck would you even invite that nigga over here? Bitch, that was a stupid move on yo' part. But that still didn't give that nigga no right to put his hands on you. Bitch, you need to call the motherfucking police on his ass now."

"Bitch, you know I don't fuck with twelve. I just can't believe that he would do this to me."

"I told yo' ass that nigga look like he ain't with the games. I swear I wish I was over here. We would've jumped his big ass. But you know, if you want, I can get my brothers and them to fuck up that nigga. Not kill him but show him what it's like to be beat the fuck up. He a weak-ass pussy to put his hands on you like that."

I sat there listening to her, but none of what she was saying was doing me any good. I swear I was in love with Jihad, even though he did this. I just can't believe he did this to me . . ."Listen, boo, you my bitch and everything, but you can't be playing around like this no more. These niggas out here are crazy, and they not scared to do some shit to a female. You could've used my fucking house or let that nigga get a hotel room."

"Bitch, I know I fucked up. I don't even give a fuck about Jahmiel. He's just a fuck to me. I love Jihad, and I might lose him forever."

"Bitch, that's *his* loss. He shouldn't have done that fuck shit. You a good-ass bitch, and you deserve way better than this shit." She moved closer to me and rubbed me on the back.

"Thanks, boo. I wish I had something to smoke or drink. You ain't got no Percocet?"

"Nah, I rushed out of the damn house. I knew something was up by the way you sounded. See, I'm still in my damn house shoes, and you know how I feel about bitches coming out of the house in these shits."

I looked down at her feet and busted out laughing. That bitch is correct. She despises bitches walking around outside in house shoes.

"Bitch, you laughing, but I'm dead-ass serious. I realized I still had them on when I was halfway here. I was like, fuck it, but I'm glad I could make you laugh. Now, you need to dry them damn tears. You a boss bitch, and this only a little hiccup. Fuck it. If Jihad don't want you, there's plenty of niggas out there that will pay to be with you. Shit, you been living way before this motherfucker came along. He don't deserve you anyway."

"I know, boo. I so appreciate you. I swear I feel better talking to you."

"That's what friends are for. You been there for me every time I go through my bullshit."

"Thanks, boo."

We hugged, and she left. I felt a little better after talking with her, but my heart was still hurting. I didn't have no weed, but I had a bottle of port wine. I got up and poured me a glass. The minute I started to drink, the deeper I sank into my feelings. Love's not supposed to hurt like this. *Jihad, why would you do me like this?* I was tempted to call him, but nah, fuck him. He beat up on me and don't even care enough to see how the fuck I was doing.

Jihad

Fuck you, bitch. I slammed my hand on the steering wheel. I can't believe this little bitch played me like this. I fuck this bitch good, eat her pussy, and spend all my damn money on her. Whatever the fuck she wants, she gets, and *this* is how she repaid me? By bringing this little bitch-ass nigga up in the crib and fucking him. Then to make matters worse, this little bitch-ass nigga pulled a motherfucking gun on me. I swear his ass lucky I left my gun in my office drawer. He would've been dead if this was another day. I made sure I saw his face clearly. On my daughter's life, if we ever crossed paths again, I'ma bury that bitch-ass nigga.

Back to this ho. The anger I felt inside, I wanted to rip this bitch's head off her body. She must not know who the fuck I am. I beat bitches the same way Ike beat Tina's trifling ass. That bitch lucky I left her alive. I was so fucking angry I couldn't go straight back to the gym. Instead, I headed to the park and pulled over. I needed a minute to get myself in order.

I opened the glove compartment and pulled out the small package of blow I had bought earlier. I've managed to keep my guilty pleasure from everybody, including Brooklyn. There were many times when she said I had disappeared, but in reality, I wasn't out fucking no other bitches. Instead, I be out getting high and be too fucked up to go home and face her. Other times, I blame it on being tired.

I opened the bag and poured some on a dollar bill. I looked around to make sure no one was walking by. No one was around, so I lowered my head and sniffed the line of coke that I had on the bill. I pulled up my nose as the coke hit my throat and entered my bloodstream. Then I closed the dollar bill and stuffed it in the armrest. I put the remaining bag of coke back into the glove compartment. Then I sat there enjoying the effect of the drugs. Minutes later, I felt a whole different mood overcome me. Suddenly, I was feeling like a brand-new man. I waited a few minutes before I started the car and pulled off.

"Whose pussy is this?" I asked Brooklyn as I thrust in and out of her doggie style.

"It's your pussy, daddy. It's your pussy, daddy," she yelled back as I applied pressure.

That's what I love to hear from my bitches. Before I got home, I did a few more lines of coke and drank me a glass of Grey Goose as soon as I got into the house. I got horny as fuck. But since my side bitch was cut off, I ain't had no choice but to bring my ass home to fuck Brooklyn.

"Take this dick, bitch, take this dick," I whispered in her ear as I fucked her.

"Awee, it hurts really bad, Jihad. Shit, my stomach's hurting bad."

"Chill, yo. Just enjoy the dick."

I was too fucking high to give a fuck about what she was saying right now. Matter of fact, I was about to bust. I tightened my grip on her hips and pulled her closer to me while I pushed my dick all the way up in her. It was coming, and I was ready to explode.

"Aaargh, shit. Shit. Fuck," I said before exploding all up in her.

I pulled my limp dick out and sat on the edge of the bed. A nigga was tired, and the coke was wearing off, so I was getting agitated and needed another hit.

"Are you okay? You were going a little hard tonight."

"My bad, yo. Yo' pussy so fucking good, I couldn't help it."

"Uh-huh. My shit's on fire."

I could tell she was irritated with me. She shot me a dirty look and walked off into the bathroom. Shit, that old ungrateful bitch should be happy that I'm still fucking that old, dry-ass pussy.

Finally, she returned to the room wearing her lingerie and got into bed. I got up and walked over to her. "Babes, I'm sorry. You know I never fucked you that hard before. I swear your pussy was just gripping my dick, and I allowed my dick to take control. I'm sorry. I won't ever fuck you that hard again." I massaged her shoulders.

"It's okay, but it was a little too hard. I had to run the cold water on my pussy to cool down the burning a little."

"My bad, yo. You want me to blow on it for you."

"You play too damn much. Blow on it? I don't know where you come up with this shit," she busted out laughing.

"I don't know my damn self. You said yo' pussy burning, so I figured if I blow on it, that should cool it down some."

We both busted out laughing at that. "I love you, woman, and that sex was the bomb. God gave you some good-ass pussy."

"Well, thank you."

"I'm about to leave for a little while."

"Go out? I thought you were in the house for the night?" She shot me a strange stare.

"Yeah, I was, but I remember I left my gun in the drawer at the gym. I don't feel comfortable leaving it there overnight. I know you're not aware, but a few years ago, somebody broke in there. Don't ask me how they got past the security cameras, but they did. So I'm just going to run up there. I'll be right back."

"All right." She gave me that look like she didn't believe what the fuck I was saying.

"C'mon, baby. You can throw something on and ride with me."

"No, go ahead. I'm tired. Plus, I have a big workload tomorrow."

"All right. In that case, get you some rest."

I grabbed my keys, kissed her on the cheek, and walked out of the room. Then I went to my daughter's room and knocked on the door.

"Who is it?"

"Girl, it's your daddy. Open the door."

"Hey, Daddy. I thought you were sleeping. Where you off to?" She gave me a big hug.

"About to make a quick run. Do you need something?"

"Yeah, can you grab me a four for four from Wendy's?"

"Brooklyn didn't get you any dinner?" I looked at her in shock.

"Nah. She came in and headed straight to her room. When you're not here, she don't care. But when you're here, she wants to be all nice to me. I told you that lady is not right."

"Baby, I need to tell you something." I took her hand.

"What's up, Daddy?"

"Brooklyn and I are about to get married."

"Daddy, you playing, right? You know that lady don't like me. You see the lies she made up about me. No, Daddy, you can't do this."

"Baby girl, listen to me. Do you trust your daddy?"

"Yes."

"Well, if you trust me, I need you to trust my decision. I will never let any harm come to you. Daddy will lay his life down for you, believe me." I looked into my daughter's eyes and meant everything I said to her.

"Did you tell Mom?"

"No, and I don't want you to either. I will talk with your mother later."

"You know Mom thought you were coming back to her."

"Baby girl, Mom thinks a lot of things that are not reality. But listen, I got to run. We'll talk some more later."

I kissed her and left. I could tell Briana was not too happy about me marrying Brooklyn. But baby girl was too young for me to explain things to her.

I rushed down the stairs just in case Brooklyn might have heard me and come out questioning me. I locked the door and walked to my car. I sat in the car for a few seconds before driving out.

My mind was all over the fucking place. I thought about all the shit that popped off today. I was kind of scared that Alyssa might have called the police. Shit, a sense of panic hit me suddenly. I played different possible scenarios in my head, and none of them were good. If I were to get locked up for beating on Alyssa, Brooklyn would be made aware of this. What the fuck would I tell her? What would be my reason for beating up on her? What if it goes to trial? Shit, Brooklyn would find out everything. *Oh God, I can't let this happen. Fuck, I need to do something fast.* I busted a U-turn and headed in the opposite direction.

On my way to Alyssa's house, I pulled out my stash of blow and did a few lines while trying to keep the steering wheel straight. Once there, I pulled up and jumped out of the car. On my way to her door, I called her number, but it just rang out. So I walked up and rang the doorbell. I know she was there because her car was parked outside.

"Open the door, Alyssa. I need to talk to you." I banged on the door.

"Go away. I have nothing to say to you," she finally said.

"Alyssa, please, baby. I'm so sorry. I swear, baby, I just need to talk to you," I pleaded.

"Jihad, go home. I have nothing to say to you."

"Alyssa, open this gotdamn door," I banged harder.

I know I wasn't doing a good job at convincing her that I was regretful for what I did, but this bitch was making me angry. I sounded like a fucking chump out here pleading with her, and she's playing her little games.

"Could you cut out all this damn yelling?" a little old grey-haired bitch opened her door and yelled.

"I'm sorry, ma'am. I'm just trying to get my girlfriend's attention. I'm worried about her," I lied.

"It's late, you prick. She's probably asleep. I'm warning you, keep it up, and I'll call the police," she said before slamming her door shut.

"Fuck you, you old fart," I yelled, but not loud enough for her to hear.

I banged a few more times, but Alyssa wasn't budging. I was coming down off my high, and my patience was wearing out. I kicked her door twice before I dashed off. This bitch really was tripping. Shit, I know I was wrong, but her ass was wrong as well. Now, she wants to play her childish-ass games by not opening the door.

Fuck her. I jumped into my car and pulled off, angry as fuck and sweating profusely.

Chapter Ten

Brooklyn

It was the night before I said, *"I do,"* and to say I wasn't nervous would be a lie. I didn't tell my family that I was going to the courthouse because, honestly, I didn't want to hear all the questions and concerns. They were happy for me when I told them I was getting married and looking forward to a big wedding. I know I would have to tell them as soon as I muster up the guts.

I looked over at Jihad as he lay there sleeping peacefully. I love this man with everything in me, and even though he had a few fuckups, I didn't see anything major. After all, we're all humans and make mistakes from time to time. I guess I should feel like the luckiest woman walking the planet right now 'cause he got good dick, has his own money, and is not cheating on me. I heard bitches say all the time that all men are dogs. Well, I beg to differ. It takes a bad chick like me to make a man appreciate what he has at home.

"Babes, you up?" He rolled over and reached over to me, rubbing my back.

"Yes, I'm up. I can barely sleep."

"You're not thinking about pulling out of this wedding, are you?"

"No, why would you think that?"

"Just been thinking . . . You're a beautiful woman, and you deserve nothing but the best. But sometimes, I feel like you have everything, so what do you want from a nigga like me?"

I sat up and looked at him. "I love you, Jihad. I have material things, but I need love. I need a partner who I can spend the rest of my life with. You walked into my life without warning and snatched up my soul. It's not about what you can do for me. It's more of our commitment to each other and our love. We have something that most people only dream of."

"See, you almost make a thug shed a tear. Brooklyn, you're a good woman. I asked God e'eryday, what did I do to deserve you?"

I swear I was tearing up inside as I listened to this man. I can spot bullshit from a mile away, but this nigga was being sincere. I even spotted a tear drop from his eye.

"Listen, Jihad, I can't promise every day gonna be sunny, but on the rainy days, I want you to know you have a woman who will love, honor, and ride with you through everything. Good or bad, right or wrong, I'll be there."

"Man, I fucking love you."

Before I could respond, he was on top of me. He pulled off my panties and slid up in me. I wrapped my legs around his back and threw this pussy on him. This wasn't one of those slow lovemaking moments. It was more like . . . I want this dick, and he wants this pussy kind of fuck.

I wore a lavender-colored skirt and a nice black shirt with a pair of nice heels and complimented it with a black clutch purse. My makeup girl came to the house and beat my face. I didn't want to be extra, just classy. My hair was pinned up in a nice, soft bun. The mister was sharp as hell also with his fine ass. When we both stepped into that courthouse, heads started turning. I smiled because this was the beginning of a lifetime of greatness.

I looked into his eyes as we exchanged our vows, and I was 100 percent sure I had made the right decision. Minutes later, we were pronounced husband and wife. We kissed, and everyone clapped. Well, almost everyone. From the corner of my eye, I saw Jasmine just standing there. Damn, this was my best friend, and she was supposed to be happy for me, especially at this moment—one of the biggest moments of my life.

I let go of Jihad and walked over to her. "What's that look for?" I quizzed.

"What look?" She played crazy.

"Bitch, quit playing. I see that displeased look written all across your face."

"Listen, you're my best friend, and I'm happy for you, okay?"

"All right."

I was slightly irritated, but I knew this wasn't the time or place for any kind of disagreement. Plus, this was *my* day, and I wasn't going to allow anyone or anything to fuck it up for us.

Later that evening, we boarded a Delta Flight to Montego Bay, Jamaica. We were staying at the Rayalton White Sands All-Inclusive Resort in Ocho Rios. My cousin had her honeymoon there a few years ago, and the place was gorgeous. I also checked them out and read the reviews. Jamaica was my mother's birth land, so I absolutely felt a connection.

The entire ride, Jihad seemed preoccupied. I mean, he just got married, but it was like he was distant. I brushed it off as him just feeling overwhelmed. After all, this was a big step for both of us. I closed my eyes, blocking out everything except how I would cut up when I reached Jamaica.

On our first day in Jamaica, we visited and learned about the culture. Then we closed the night out with a quiet dinner and wine.

"Hey, love, is everything okay?" I quizzed.

"E'erything good. Why?" Jihad responded as he took a sip of his Red Label Wine.

"Just curious. This is our honeymoon, and you've barely looked at me, much less touched me since we got here."

"Damn, Brooklyn, is that all you think about? I mean, I just fucked you the other day. You ever consider maybe I'm just tired?"

"Wow. Hold up a fucking minute. Why are you so aggressive? All I did was ask a fucking question," I snapped back, a little more forcefully than I intended.

"Listen, I'm going for a walk. I'm no longer hungry."

"What you mean? You're not going to eat your dinner that I paid for?"

"You know what, Brooklyn? I will pay for my own food."

He got up from the table and walked off. I thought of running behind him, but what the fuck? This nigga was putting on a show, and I refuse to be one of the clowns.

I waved to the waiter. The tall, dark-skinned man walked over to me.

"Yes, ma'am, how can I be of service to you?" he said in his best English accent.

"Let me get another glass of that wine."

"Do you mean the Red Label Wine?"

"Yes, that's it."

"Here you go, ma'am."

"Thank you, and please let me get the tab."

"Okay, ma'am." He smiled politely and walked off.

I didn't bother to sit there and sip. Instead, I took big gulps of the wine, finishing it off. Then I paid the bill and walked out of the restaurant. I was feeling tipsy, so

I clung to my purse and made my way up the stairs to my room. I fumbled in my purse until I found my key to the room, opened the door, and almost fell inside. Finally, I made it to the bed and lay across it. I knew I had too much to drink, so I planned on lying down a little to get some of the liquor out of my system.

It was a little past 9:00 a.m. when I finally woke up. The aroma of strong coffee filled the air. I got up, grabbed my robe, and walked to the small kitchen area.

"Hey, there, beautiful. I hope I didn't wake you up with the good smell of this coffee." Jihad was standing there dressed, making coffee.

I blinked twice to make sure this was the same nigga that snapped at me last night. Yes, it was him, but he was in a cheerful mood this time.

"Sit down. This coffee is called Blue Mountain, and it is grown right here in Jamaica. I promise you this is the best grain of coffee you will ever have in your entire life."

I took a seat. I loved the scent of the coffee, and my stomach was screaming for some. But my inner craziness also needed an explanation for that behavior last night, a night that we should have consummated our marriage.

"Here you go, my love." He placed a cup of hot coffee in front of me, along with two slices of toast. "Listen, before you say anything, I sincerely apologize for my behavior last night. I swear I don't know what got over me, but I felt like the world was caving in around me. I mean, I ain't no coward, but I think it finally hit me that I'm no longer single, and I have a family now that will depend on me. See, at first, I only had me and Briana to worry about, but now, I have you, your well-being, and your happiness. So I don't want to let you down, Brooklyn."

"Jihad, do you know stress kills? You are worried about things that are not even in the picture. When that judge pronounced us husband and wife, we became one. That means we figure things out together. This is new to me also, but I'm not gon' stress myself out. I'm just going to do what I need to do, so my husband can be happy."

"Babe, I'm sorry. Well, drink up. I got a day of activities all planned out for us while we enjoy the next few days of this tropical paradise."

"Hmmm, I love the sound of that." I smiled as I took a few sips of the coffee. He was correct. This coffee was smooth. I made a mental note to buy some to take it back to the States.

Four days later, and just like that, our honeymoon was over. However, it was everything. We spent the remaining time professing our love to each other and just getting to know each other more on a personal level. I even allowed him to eat my pussy and fuck me on the night beach. To say I was scared would be an understatement, but that didn't stop me. I mean, it was everything, but sadly, it had to end. I had patients waiting on me, and Jihad had a gym to run. Going back to our regular lives, I know there might be some obstacles along the way, but we were a unit, and there's nothing that our love couldn't conquer together.

Chapter Eleven

Jihad

What the fuck did you do that dumb shit for, Jihad?
A voice echoed in my head as I sat in the living room
drinking Patrón. It's been days since I returned from my
honeymoon, and I was in a fucked-ass mood more than
before. This bitch believes that because we were married,
she was supposed to have me in a grip. Bullshit. I ain't
never been no bitch's pet and wasn't about to start now.

I picked up my phone and dialed Alyssa's number. It's
been almost a week and a half, and this bitch was still
playing her little childish-ass games.

"Hello," she surprisingly answered the phone.

"Yo, what's good, babes? I need to talk to you."

"Jihad, after what you did to me, what do you want?"
she said in a high-pitched tone.

"Listen, baby, I'm so sorry. But please, let me come over
and explain it to you."

"Okay, but just for a few minutes."

"Thank you, babes. I promise you won't regret it."

"Hey, you," Brooklyn walked up on me, scaring the fuck
out of me.

"Hey, babes. I didn't hear you come in." I tried figuring
out how long she was standing there.

"Yeah, I just came in. Are you okay?"

"Yeah, I'm good. About to make a quick run. I have a potential new client trying to start coming to the gym."

"OK. Well, you seem pretty excited. I'm going to make a quick dinner, maybe something light."

"Sounds good, babes. I'll be back soon." I stood up, hugged her, gave her a quick kiss on the cheek, and dashed out of the living room.

It took me no time to shower, dress, and dash out the door. I was so eager to get Alyssa back into my arms. Most of all, I missed fucking her. I jumped into my car and peeled out of the driveway. I was in a good mood. I know the task ahead wasn't going to be easy. But being the nigga that I was, I know how to let bitches believe in every single word that I was saying.

I rang the doorbell and waited for her to answer.

"Who is it?" she hollered.

"It's me, babe. Open the door."

She opened the door and walked away. I couldn't help but notice she was in a sexy shirt and lace panties. My eyes followed her ass as she swung her hips into the living room.

I walked in right behind her. Her hair was in a ponytail, and her most beautiful features were visible. To say this bitch was sexy would do her no justice. She was a bad bitch in every sense. I walked over to her, dropped to my knees, and grabbed her hands.

"Alyssa, baby, there's no excuse for what I did. The only explanation I got is I'm in love with you, and when I saw that nigga in here, I snapped. I fucking love you, Alyssa. I want to marry you, and I want you to have my seed."

"Jihad, how can you say you love me and treat me like that? How could you?" She started crying.

I reached over and pulled her toward me, hugging her tightly. "Babes, I promise I will treat you right from this day on. Please, give me another chance. I mean, I ain't been able to eat, sleep, or even go to work since I fucked up. Look at me. It seems like I've been losing weight and everything." I stretched out my arm so she could take a look.

"Jihad, you have to promise me no matter what, you won't put your hands on me anymore. Promise me, please."

"Baby, I promise. I swear on my mama's life, that shit won't ever happen again."

"I love you, Jihad."

I smiled behind her back as we hugged. I knew then that I was back in for good.

I reached my hand under her shirt and started massaging her breast. Then my phone began to vibrate in my shorts pocket, but I ignored that shit. I was horny as fuck and was trying to get some good pussy.

Within minutes, we were butt-ass naked, fucking and sucking, mixing our juices together. My phone steadily kept ringing, and I kept on ignoring it. I was deep into her guts, tearing those walls down, and nothing was stopping it.

"You know I love you, right, babes?"

"I know, boo. I love you too."

I sat back on the couch, and she lay her head on my lap. I ran my hand through her hair as I thought about the love I was developing for her. I know it was wrong, but she was the one my heart desired. If only I could have made her my main bitch.

Alyssa finally fell asleep, and I decided to take a quick shower. I know Brooklyn must be wondering where the hell I am. Alyssa was lying there so peacefully, I tried my best not to wake her up.

I took a long shower and then got dressed. I thought about waking her, so she would know I was leaving but decided against it. Instead, I turned the lock on the door and headed on out.

Shit. I looked over at the time. It was going on damn near two o'clock in the morning. I started the car up, then checked how many times Brooklyn had called. Fuck, she called five times, back-to-back, and sent me three texts.

Her last text shortly after midnight read, I know you see me calling you, Jihad. Hmm, keep on playing games.

I shook my head and pulled off. I didn't plan on staying out this late. I just got caught up in all the sweetness that Alyssa had to offer.

I didn't even bother to go into the garage 'cause the sound of the door opening might wake her up. Instead, I parked the car out front and quietly opened the front door. I took off my shoes and placed them by the side. Then not cutting on any lights, I made my way up the stairs. The door was closed, so I gently grabbed the door-knob, turned it, and peeked my head in. I was in the clear. She was fast asleep, head buried under the cover. I tip-toed to my side and quickly took off my clothes. I waited a few seconds before getting into bed. I wasn't worried about her waking up now 'cause I would pretend like I woke up and had gone to use the bathroom.

I laid my head on my pillow, and all I could smell was the scent of Alyssa. Shit, I wish I could've lay beside her the entire night. Oh well, this will have to work for now.

Chapter Twelve

Alyssa

These niggas swear to God they had all the mother-fucking sense in the world. I was still upset with Jihad for putting his motherfucking hands on me, but the longer I held out from talking to him, the quicker I realized I was running out of money. I was deeply in love with Jihad, but losing him was not as crucial as losing that money.

"Baby, why you look like that? You feeling okay?" my mom quizzed as we sat in her living room eating and watching television. It's been weeks since I visited her, and I was really missing her. No matter what I was going through, Mama always knew how to comfort me.

"Yeah, Mama, I'm good." I tried my best to cover up what was going on with me.

"Who you fooling? Child, I can see through all that damn makeup you got on that something is going on with you. I noticed that shit the minute you walked through the door."

I looked at her. Even when I was younger, I ain't never been able to lie successfully to Mama. She's always managed to pull me on the bullshit. I wanted to talk to her, but I couldn't come out and tell her Jihad had put his hands on me. Mama's ass would snap if she knew it.

"Mama, it's nothing. I'm just a little tired, that's all," I tried harder at lying.

"Hmm, well, it's either you pregnant or you going through some bullshit with a man. Either way, baby girl, don't end up like yo' mama. I told you ever since you were young, these men are only good for busting a nut and taking care of you. So don't you go around loving on none of these no-good-ass niggas. Hmm, don't end up like me."

This was the reason why I didn't want to say anything. Every conversation always goes back to how Daddy dogged her. Fuck, it's been almost thirty damn years. I wish she would get some other dick and get over it already, but I couldn't dare say that to her, so I kept it simple.

"Mama, I told you I'm fine. I'm not knocked up, and I don't have no man to be having man problems."

"Uh-huh, keep on lying to yourself."

She must've seen the irritation plastered all over my face because she quickly dropped the subject. We went back to discussing other shit and other family members' business.

"All right, Mama, I got to go. I love you." I stood up and grabbed my purse and key.

"I love you too, baby girl."

She stood up, hugged me, and I left. I sat in my car in front of Mama's house, thinking. My bills were coming up, and I only had like $300 to my name. Even though I was holding on calling Jihad, my ass was running out of options. I had neglected the niggas that I used to fuck to get my bills paid so I could be with Jihad. Now, look at the fucked-up predicament I'm in. I shook my head as I pulled off. I could see Mama standing there in the window. I would hate it if I had to move back home with her. Fuck that. I will continue fucking and sucking on Jihad while he pays these damn bills.

I dialed his number, but it went straight to voicemail. So I decided not to leave a message. I was pretty sure his ass was desperate to get back with me . . .

***

No matter how much a dog strays, they always manage to find their way home. I was lying in bed watching *Snapped* on the ID channel when I heard my phone ringing. I reached over and grabbed it. I quickly noticed it was Jihad. I was ready to put on a show, so I sat up and mentally prepared. At first, I tried to play like I was still upset, but I knew I couldn't drag it out too much. After going back and forth with him, I finally gave in. It didn't take much 'cause his thirsty ass was back. I have to admit it, I really missed him, and by how he fucked me that night, I knew he was feeling the same way.

However, I was kind of irritated when I finally woke up and found Jihad was gone. At first, I thought he was in the bathroom or the kitchen. Then I got up and checked both places. That's when I realized that he was gone. Damn, what was so damn important that he had to sneak out? My mind started racing. There was only one way to find out the truth.

"Hello, beautiful."

"What time did you leave last night, and why the hell didn't you wake me up?" I snapped.

"Calm down, baby. My daughter called me around 1:00, and I had to go see about her."

"Daughter? You never mentioned that you had no damn daughter. You a fucking liar, Jihad." I was ready to hang up on his lying ass.

"Baby, I swear we have discussed Briana before. Matter of fact, I can't wait until you meet her. She's going to love you."

I didn't give a fuck about what he was saying. I would've remembered if my man had told me about a child. Now, I was curious about the reason behind his leaving. Did he *really* go check on his so-called child or fuck his so-called baby mama? Lord, these voices in my head were killing me.

"Listen, baby. I got to run, but I'll be over there soon as I get off work."

I didn't respond. I just hung up. Jihad was acting suspicious, and I wasn't feeling it. I had decided to give this nigga another chance, and he already fucking up. I swear this nigga will learn.

The weather outside was nice. There was no way in hell my ass would stay in the house, so I hit up my bitch. I was down to my last dollar, so going out to eat was definitely out of the plans unless that bitch decided to pay.

"Hola," her retarded ass said as she answered the phone.

"Bitch, what you doing?"

"Nada. Sitting my fat ass out on the steps. It's nice as hell out here too."

"I know. That's why I hit you up to see if you want to treat your bestie to lunch."

"Bitch, you know I don't get nothing but one check on the third of the month. I can buy you Chinese food, though."

"Oh shit, that'll work. Get ready. I'm on my way over there."

I slipped on a nice pair of booty shorts and a white wife beater, then slid my feet into my pink slides. I grabbed my purse, phone, and keys before I headed out the door. Not only was it hot, but it was also humid as hell. It seems like the devil was having a ball down there in hell. I see that I made the perfect choice of not wearing too many clothes. I got in my car and immediately cut on the AC. Then I cut on NBA YoungBoy *38 Baby* album. Lately, his music was all I played. I swear he was a little young nigga, but he could definitely get this pussy. I looked in my mirror before pulling off.

I pulled up and parked in the closest parking space. I had to grab the door when I got out of the car. I wasn't feeling too well. My head was dizzy, and my eyes were blurry.

"You a'ight, bitch?" Trina yelled out to me.

I could barely answer. I leaned against the car for support. She must've realized something wasn't right because she ran over to me. "What's wrong with you?"

"I don't know. I got out of the car and felt like I was about to faint."

"It's probably the heat or probably 'cause yo' ass hungry. Come on; come sit in the air real quick."

I closed the door and used her arm for support. We got into her apartment, and I lay down on the couch. After about ten minutes of lying there, I thought the feeling would go away, but instead, I felt worse. I was feeling light-headed and nauseated.

"You feeling any better, boo?"

"Girl, no. I'm trying to figure out why the hell I feel like this."

"Well, I'ma order this food. I'm pretty sure after you eat, you'll feel ten times better."

I just lay there. This feeling needed to go the fuck away. This was crazy 'cause I felt just fine when I left the house.

The Chinese people didn't waste any time bringing us our food. I had the usual, shrimp fried rice and chicken wings. But unfortunately, I heard too many damn stories about how the Chinese people were cooking all kinds of different animals and feeding them to us. I don't give a damn who likes it, but Alyssa's ass ain't eating that shit.

I lay back on the couch, trying my best to eat this food, but the smell was making my nausea worse.

"Bitch, you good? You look like you need to shit," Trina said jokingly.

She had no idea how bad I was feeling. I put the plate on the center table and rushed to her bathroom. I barely reached the toilet bowl before throwing up everything that had gone down a few minutes ago.

"Bitch, you good in there? Don't shit all over my toilet."

My head was buried in the toilet, tears rolling down my face. I've always hated vomiting since I was a little girl, and here I was, a grown woman, and the shit still was the most disgusting thing to me. After nothing was left to come up, I started dry heaving. Finally, I walked over to the sink and rinsed my mouth and face. I glanced in the mirror on my way out and noticed my eyes were weak. I have no idea what the fuck was going on with me.

"Bitch, is you good?"

"Man, nah. I just vomited everything I ate. I feel so damn weak, and my head is spinning."

"Hmm, you sound like you have food poisoning . . . Oh shit. Bitch, are you pregnant?"

"Pregnant? Why the fuck you and my mama keep trying to bring that shit down on me?"

"Fuck all that. When was the last time you seen your period?"

"That's my business, right? Trust me, I know I'm not pregnant."

"Bitch, you might be. First, you feeling dizzy and now vomiting. I been pregnant before, so I know the symptoms."

"Those might be *your* symptoms, but *not* mine. I'm *not* pregnant."

This bitch was tripping for real—or was she? My period usually came on the eighth of June. Now, it's July fifteenth, and my period is late. Shit, I didn't even realize that. I tried to get these fucked-up-ass thoughts out of my head. This can't be. My period has been late a few times before. So there was no need for me to be alarmed . . . right?

"Bitch, let's go buy a damn test. Family Dollar got them for a dollar."

"Bitch, for the last gotdamn time, I'm not pregnant. Now, pass me that blunt. Maybe it will help me to feel better."

She passed me the blunt, and I took a few pulls, but even the weed tasted different. I took a few more drags before giving it back to her. I just needed this feeling to go away. I lay my head back on the couch while she talked. I was so weak, so I stayed there, and before I knew it, I dozed off.

"Bitch, it's late. You spending the night over here?" I heard Trina say as she shook my arm.

I slowly opened my eyes. "What time is it?"

"Bitch, it's minutes to nine. Yo' ass was knocked out, snoring and shit. How you feeling? You know you can spend the night."

"No, I'ma go home. Shit, Jihad probably been calling me."

I reached down and grabbed my phone on the ground. It wasn't there. That was strange. That's where I put my phone at.

"What you looking for?"

"My phone. I had it right here beside me."

"No, boo boo, you put it on the table before you rushed to the bathroom. Here you go. It's right here." She handed it to me.

Oh fuck. I had over ten missed calls from Jihad and multiple text messages. As I read through the texts, this nigga was going off. I was feeling bad and don't need this kind of negative energy right now.

I sat up on the couch, trying to get myself together.

"Did your nigga call you?"

"Bitch, that nigga been blowing up my phone. Why you ain't wake me up and tell me?"

"I was in the room sleeping. I think I was knocked out too. Then my phone started ringing, and that's how I woke up."

"I got to go. This nigga really tripping in his texts and shit. I'm too sick to argue with his ass right now."

"Don't forget what happened last time. You sure you want to go home?"

"Bitch, trust me. Jihad knows that I ain't playing with him. He knows how serious I am and knows I will leave his ass if he ever tries that shit again. I ain't playing with his ass."

"I hear you, but if a nigga hits you once, trust me, he'll do it again."

"Bitch, trust me, he won't. Anyway, I got to go home."

"All right, bitch. Call me and let me know when you get there."

"A'ight."

This was terrible. It's been hours, and my ass wasn't feeling any better. I really hate the hospital, but I might need to go up in there if I don't feel any better. I cut the car on and was about to pull off when my phone started ringing.

"Hello," I answered.

"Yo, where the fuck you been?"

"Jihad, first off, can you quit yelling? Second, I was at my homegirl's house, and I fell asleep."

"Alyssa, you must think I'm a fucking clown. I been blowing up yo' phone for hours and no answer. Yo, I swear, if I find out yo' ass cheating on me, I'ma—"

"You gon' do *what,* Jihad? I already told yo' ass if you ever put yo' motherfucking hands on me again, it's a wrap. Ain't nobody cheating on yo' ass. I been sick all damn day, vomiting and shit."

"Where the fuck you at now?"

"I'm in my car about to head home."

"A'ight, yo, I'ma meet you there."

I couldn't get a word in because he hung up in my face. Old, rude-ass nigga. I swear I'm not in the mood for this shit tonight. I pulled off feeling disgusted at his behavior, yelling at me like I was his fucking child. Oh God, the nerve of this man.

Chapter Thirteen

Brooklyn

For the first two weeks of being Mrs. Lewis, things went great. Jihad and I were inseparable. Once he got off work, he would come straight home. From late-night dinners, laid up in the den watching movies, to sitting out in the sunroom just enjoying each other's company . . . This was definitely how I imagined living with my significant other.

I was off work early, so I threw a roast in the oven to cook slowly. I poured a glass of wine to get myself going. I was missing my husband and hoping he would hurry home. I try not to be too clingy, but I love spending time with him. When I said everything changed, I meant *everything*. The sex was turned up all the way. I never imagined I would ever enjoy a man licking my butt crack and blowing up my ass. The first time he did it, I felt a little uncomfortable. But as I loosened up, I realized it was a very stimulating feeling. I was open before the wedding, but now, I was gone. I loved *everything* about my husband. I really hope nothing changes between us.

I took a quick shower after making dinner and called Jihad's phone to see where he was and find out when he would be home. The phone didn't ring; it went straight to voicemail. Hmm, he's probably with a client and doesn't realize that his phone is off. I was hungry as hell, but I wanted to eat dinner with him. I waited another hour and called him again, but the same thing happened. This was strange as hell. Why would he have a dead phone walking around with him? Hmm, kind of got my mind wondering. All along, I kept telling myself it was nothing. Shit, he probably was on his way home this very minute.

Two more hours went by—and no Jihad. I was getting angry now. We have been eating dinner together, and if he felt he couldn't make it, he could've had the decency to call me and tell me something.

I was sick and fucking tired of waiting around, so I went downstairs, warmed up the food, and made me a plate. I was so damn hungry that I wasted no time eating up everything on my plate. I was drinking my wine and going over some emails while I sat at the dinner table when I heard the garage door going up.

Then he walked in. He walked straight into the kitchen. "Damn, bae, you startled me," he said.

"Hmm, where you coming from?"

"What you mean by that, babes? You know I was at the gym."

"So, your phone don't work?"

"Babes, it's been a rough-ass day. But, trust me, you don't know what I been through today."

He took a seat at the table across from me. I could tell something was bothering him, and as much as I would love to go off on his ass, I decided to play my wifely duties and find out what was going on with my husband.

"So, what's going on?"

"Babes, we about to lose the gym."

"What you mean by y'all about to lose the gym? I thought y'all was making money."

"I thought so too. I don't handle the books. I'm the dude that brings in the clients. It wasn't until today that my brother brought it to my attention. We owe a lot of money on the building, and the bank is going to take control of it."

"This is fucking crazy. How could y'all not know this? This is your life. This is how you make your money. I can't believe this." I shook my head in disbelief.

He didn't say anything. He just sat there and lay his head on the table. I've never seen him this broken before. I got up, poured him a glass of Grey Goose, and handed it to him.

"Can't you get the money out of your account?"

"My money is tied up. Invested in different projects. My account is almost empty."

I almost fell off the fucking stool that I was sitting on. Did this nigga say his account was *almost empty?* Don't get me wrong. I didn't marry the nigga for his money. But a bitch like me is independent. So why in God's name would I marry a broke nigga? The veins in my head started tightening up on me, and I immediately got a tension headache.

"Don't worry, babes. I see the look on your face. I got a $200,000 check coming from one of my investments. Earlier, my lawyer said it should be here no later than three weeks. It's just that this issue with the gym is going on now."

I wanted to jump up and hug him 'cause, baby, I was in panic mode a few seconds ago. I'm not a gold digger, but I was very much allergic to broke niggas. I've worked too hard to build a career and live the good life for me to take up anybody's son who can't hold his own. Hell, for all that, I could fuck myself for free.

"Well, that's positively great news. Maybe you can borrow the money from one of your business partners."

"I'm too embarrassed to do that. I still can't believe my brother would do this shit to us. Fuck that . . . to me. I bust my ass every day, and now this. I swear I can just put a bullet in my head right now." He put his head down on the table again.

I jumped off the stool and dashed over to him. "Don't you *ever* talk like that. This shit is not that serious. Listen, I'll write you a check for fifty grand. Use it and pay them people—"

"No, babes," he cut me off before I had a chance to finish my sentence, "I can't take your money. I'm your man. I'm supposed to give *you* money, *not* the other way around. I can't—"

"You need to shut up and listen. I didn't say I was *giving* you anything. I was about to say I will make you a *loan,* and you can pay me back when you get your check in three weeks. You're my husband, and your problem is also my problem."

"Are you sure, Brooklyn? Honey, I don't want to cause you no inconvenience. I know you got your business to run."

"I'm good. You can cash the check in the morning and handle your business, but you really need to talk with your brother. Let him know this can't happen again, or you will have to cut ties with him as far as doing business with him. This is your livelihood."

"Babes, you must've read my mind 'cause I was think-ing the same thing. I can't do this no more with him. I trusted him, and he fucked up like this. Man, I really want to beat his ass."

"That's your brother. Fighting him ain't gon' help noth-ing. But you need to be clear when you speak with him."

"Babes, I swear you are a blessing from God. I ain't never experienced a woman like you before. You have a heart of gold, and I just beg God to let me continue to be the husband you desire and for me to love you until I leave this earth."

"Are you going to eat?"

"Nah, I'ma run over here by my brother, and I'm going to tell him we got the money. As much as I'm angry with him, I know he was just as stressed out as I was. I'll eat when I come back in."

"All right 'cause I'm tired. I'm going to lie down."

"All right, babes." He kissed my hand.

I walked upstairs and got into my bed while Jihad showered. A minute ago, he was on the verge of crying, but I watched him as he got dressed. He was humming and seemed to be in an upbeat mood. I was glad I could step up to the plate and help my husband in his time of need.

Chapter Fourteen

Jihad

Not sure if it's the dick, the way I suck on her pussy, or if it was love, but Brooklyn shocked the hell out of me when she said she was going to write me a check for fifty grand. See, true enough, we owed the money on the gym, but that was something that I knew. My brother been down my neck lately, and I had to figure out something fast.

Right after we got married, I was in the office at the house. Brooklyn had mistakenly left her computer open, and there it was. See, I knew my bitch was caked up, but I had no idea how much. There were so many zeros in that account that I had to blink twice to make sure I wasn't being tricked. I realized then I had hit the jackpot when I married this bitch. My days of struggling were officially over.

I pulled up at Alyssa's crib. See, this bitch is playing with fire. I think she's fucking around on me. A few nights ago, her ass disappeared, then the bitch had the nerve to tell me she was over by her friend's house. Mind you, this was the same friend when I fucked both of them. So, why the fuck would I have faith that her ass wasn't over there fucking and sucking on that bitch? Just thinking about that shit made me angry all over again.

I parked my car and looked around to make sure no one was out in the parking lot. No one there, so I pulled out the dollar bill that had my blow in it. I lowered my head and took a few pulls. Then I sat there as the drug hit my brain. Within seconds, that anger disappeared, and I was floating on cloud nine. I folded the bill and put it back into my hiding spot, got out, and headed to her apartment.

I dialed her number as I walked up the stairs.

"Hello," she answered in her sexy voice.

"Open the door."

"A'ight."

The door was wide open when I walked up. Then there she was, standing with just a little shirt on. I wanted to cuss her ass out for standing there like that, but shit, those legs caught my attention, and my dick started rising in my pants.

"Hey, boo," she greeted me.

"What's up, love?" I grabbed her, pulled her toward me, and cuffed her ass cheeks.

I was ready to fuck, so I lifted her and took her to the kitchen table. Surprisingly, her ass didn't have on any underwear. I parted her legs, looked at her pretty, well shaved pussy, and licked my lips before I buried my head between her legs. I took a few seconds to inhale the sweet, flowery aroma. Then I wasted no more time. I licked her clit, using my tongue to dance around her love cave. After that, I latched on gently and sucked on her clit.

"Yes, daddy! Yes, aweee. I love you, Jihad," she whispered.

That only made me suck her pussy harder. I closed my eyes and just made love to her clit in a way that I knew would drive her crazy. She grabbed my head and pulled it in to her. I didn't ease up any, even though I couldn't breathe. Shit, this pussy was worth dying for.

After she busted all over my face, I grabbed her off the counter, took her to the couch, and entered her from the back. I rammed in and out of her while I gripped her hips, pulling her closer to the dick. She threw the ass back on me, matching my strokes. Our bodies were a unit and moved on one accord.

"Shit, I'm about to bust," I could barely manage to say before my juices shot up in her stomach. Then I pulled my limp dick out and walked to the bathroom. It seemed like we were fucking for close to an hour. But that's what coke do to you; sometimes, it will have you going and going.

"Let me find out you taking that viagra pill," she said as I walked into the living room.

"What the fuck kind of shit is that?" I shot her a look.

"Yo, you fucked me for a long-ass time. My pussy is sore from that beating you just gave it," she laughed, walking off to the bathroom.

I swear I love fucking her, and I hate to admit it, but I was in love with her. She was so full of life, and the fact that she let me fuck her friend was *definitely* a plus. I doubt Brooklyn's ass would ever have a threesome with me. Shit, I didn't plan on keeping fucking her, or if I do, it would be the minimum. Her dry-ass pussy be cutting up my dick. I told her ass one time to put some Vaseline on her pussy. Her ass got mad, accusing me of saying her pussy was dry. Shit, I was only trying to help her ass out.

"Babe, I need your help. I don't have no money to pay for school or to pay my bills this month. I think I might get put out."

"How much money you need?"

"I need like $3,000."

"A'ight, give me until Friday, and I got you."

"Thank you, daddy. I don't know how I'm ever going to repay you."

"All you got to do is keep this pussy clean, fuck me good, and I'll make sure you good."

"Hmmm, I can do that." She shot me a devilish grin.

"Oh, one more thing."

"What's that?" She looked at me.

"Don't you ever give my pussy away."

"I got you, daddy."

"You better. Anyway, I got to run. I'll be over here later tonight."

"Jihad, can I ask you a question?"

"Whaddup?"

"We *are* a couple, right? So why don't I ever get to come to *your* house?"

"Baby, I told you, my mother lives with me, and she's an older Christian woman. She don't like when I bring females over because she say we're living a life of sin. But don't worry, baby. Soon, we'll be married and have our own house."

"Are you serious, or you just playing?"

I walked over to her, took her hands, and stared into her eyes. "Listen to me, baby. From the moment I laid eyes on you, I knew you were the one. I can't wait for you to have my babies and wear my last name. I can't wait to show you off to the world." I then slowly kissed her, deeply and passionately. I had to make sure she knew how deep my love for her was.

"Boo, I'm just tired of sleeping alone every night. You know?"

"Be patient, babes. Your man got you. Anyway, I got to run. Love you, baby girl."

"Love you too," she said, pouting.

Walking down the stairs and back to my car, I heard my phone ringing. I took it out. I didn't recognize the number, so I didn't pick it up. Then I got into the car and pulled off.

Alyssa

I sat on the toilet in my apartment, looking at the test in my hand. Not just any test, but a fucking pregnancy test and those two red lines going across. I was spaced out for a few minutes as I tried to digest this crazy shit.

I finally found the strength to get my ass up off the toilet. I was confused or, more, shocked. I know I've been fucking without a condom, but shit, I *always* fuck without a condom, and I *never* got pregnant before. I could hear my mother's voice telling me I was knocked up. *Oh my fucking God, how did this happen?*

I sat on the edge of my bed in despair. Who the fuck was I pregnant by? I fucked Jihad and Jahmiel around the same time. I started backtracking the dates in my head. There's no way this is Jahmiel's baby. Shit, we've been fucking around for years, and that nigga been firing blanks. I know in my heart this is Jihad's baby. A smile came over my face. I can't wait to let him know I was pregnant. Now, we can finally be a family. No more of us living apart. I can finally have my man every night now.

My phone started to ring. I grabbed it and answered it.

"Hey, bitch," I answered.

"You sound better. Are you feeling better?" Trina asked.

"Bitch, I got something to tell you."

"What? You found out you pregnant?"

"Man, how the fuck would you know that?"

"Bitch, I told yo' ass. Your face got fatter, you been nauseated, vomiting, moody . . . all the signs of pregnancy.

I tried to tell you, but I'm glad you found out. Congrats, bitch. Now, I get to be a god mommy."

"Bitch, I don't know why you sound all happy and shit. I wasn't ready to be nobody's mama. I got shit I want to do, and having a baby wasn't part of the plan."

"Bitch, what you mean? You going to have Jihad's baby. You going to be paid forever, bitch. Now, you really ain't got to worry 'bout shit. That nigga will probably move yo' ass out of the hood."

"Bitch, you acting like a baby make everything right. Plus, bitch, I'm not sure it's Jihad's baby."

"Say what, ho?" she yelled in my ear.

"Bitch, remember, I told you I fucked Jahmiel the day Jihad caught him up in here."

"Oh shit, bitch. Your ass better be sure 'cause you know Jihad ain't the one to fuck with. You remember what his ass did to you last time."

"Damn, ho, you ain't got to keep reminding me. I've been fucking with the dates, and I'm leaning more toward Jihad. Plus, you know Jahmiel been busting blanks. I don't think he can make kids."

"Well, I'm just happy for you. It ain't like Jihad gon' know if it's not his baby. You already know I ain't saying shit. So, when you gon' tell him?"

"I was gon' wait 'til he comes over."

"Bitch, if I were you, I would make my way up to the gym and surprise his ass. That nigga will probably marry yo' ass right on the spot. I tell you, yo' ass done lucked up."

"Bitch, I done told you it's this good pussy that have the nigga gone. I don't be playing no games. I suck the color off that caramel dick, gargle on balls, and lick his asshole."

"Bitch, you nasty as fuck. I know you ain't licking that nigga's ass."

"Hmm, you better take notes. You might be able to bag one of these niggas that's paid. I told that nigga I need three grand, and that nigga didn't ask no questions. He just told me I'd get it on Friday. Bitch, I'm out here living my best gotdamn life."

"I hear you, bitch. I just can't imagine putting my tongue in my mouth up nobody's ass, but yeah, to each its own."

"Bitch, listen, I think I'ma get dressed and head up here by this gym. I can't wait to see his face when I tell him we're having a baby."

"A'ight, bitch. I wish you could record that shit."

"Bitch, he'd probably have a heart attack if I try to record him. You know how these niggas nowadays are. Secretive as fuck."

"Bitch, niggas are only secretive when they got something to hide. Jihad don't have no bitch, so he good. Like I said, you a lucky bitch."

"A'ight, yo. I got to bounce. I'll holla at you later."

"All right, bitch."

After I hung up the phone, I had to laugh to myself. I wish I could've seen the look on that ho's face when I told her I licked ass. Shit, a bitch can't be picky out here. It ain't like I'm doing it to every nigga. Hell nah, Jihad was my baby, and he deserves everything. It ain't like he ain't licking on every part of my body too.

I was dressed in no time. I grabbed the pregnancy test I kept so I could show him. These bitches out here play so many games, these niggas don't be believing them no more. One of the oldest games is to say you pregnant, so you can get the abortion money. Shit, I done did that shit to so many niggas, I lost count a long time ago. It's funny how niggas will come all up in a bitch, but bitch up the minute you tell them you're pregnant.

I headed out the door. My head was killing me, and I was nauseated as hell. Is this what pregnancy feels like? This was not a very good feeling. I was about a month pregnant, and my ass was already this sick. Shit, I don't know how bitches got all these damn kids out here, but I was excited to see Jihad. I knew he would come by after work, but as my bitch said, I decided to surprise him.

With the music blasting, all good thoughts of my Jihad floated around in my head. I claimed I was in love before, but this was my first real love. I was deeply in love with this man, and now that I have his baby growing inside of me, I can just imagine how much stronger our bond will be.

I smiled as I pulled up at the gym. Surprisingly, it wasn't as packed as it used to be. Hmm, these bitches probably tapped out like me. Shit, why should I still come to the gym when the trainer is in my bed every day? I chuckled to myself as I turned off the car and got out.

It's so damn hot out here, I thought as I stepped inside the gym. I looked around to see if I could spot him on the floor. Then I walked to the back, where he would be helping his clients. I didn't see him. I pulled my phone out to let him know I was here, but the phone just rang out. So I decided to go to his office. His ass probably ducked off in there, hiding from these old, annoying-ass bitches. He done told me stories of these groupie-ass bitches stalking him and shit. I know they asses are going to be jealous when they find out he has a whole bitch with a whole baby on the way.

I walked to the office. I lifted my hand to knock on the door, but the door flew open. I stepped in and . . . no. What is this I'm looking at? Jihad had a woman sitting on his lap. I know this bitch, but from where? My thoughts were moving too fast for me to really think.

He jumped up, almost pushing the bitch off him. "Hey, Cousin Alyssa. I didn't know you were coming by today."

I looked at him. I looked at the bitch. *Cousin?* Did this nigga just call me his fucking cousin? Who the fuck is this bitch?

"Who is this?" I asked.

"Oh, this is my beautiful wife, Brooklyn. I forgot you two haven't met before."

Wife . . . wife . . . wife . . . The word kept on playing around in my head.

"Oh, your cousin. Nice to meet you, Alyssa. It's good to finally meet one of Jihad's family members beside his brother."

I looked at this bitch standing in front of me. So this dumb ho believes I'm this nigga's cousin? Yo, what the fuck was really going on here?

"Nice to meet you finally. Jihad brags so much 'bout his woman, I knew it was only a matter of time before we bumped into each other."

"All right, baby. I'll see you later."

"Nice meeting you, Alyssa."

He ushered that bitch out the door so damn fast while I stood in the middle of the office. I was shaking inside, but I used my inner strength to stop myself from breaking down. Jihad . . . my Jihad. The nigga that tells me he loves me. The nigga that is my baby daddy is married . . .

"Baby, I know you about to cuss me out, but I can explain," this lying-ass, two-timing-ass nigga walked up behind me, put his arms around me, and said.

"G-e-t t-h-e f-u-c-k o-f-f m-e," I said in the coldest tone I could muster up.

"Baby, baby, listen to me. Please, let me explain. She's about to be my ex-wife. We're getting a divorce, baby. I couldn't tell her you my new woman because she and her lawyer will take everything from me in court. I won't have nothing—not this gym, no money, nothing, baby."

I turned around to look at this nigga. "Is this bitch the reason why you could never spend the night with me? When I call yo' phone after certain hours, you can't pick up? Oh my God . . . you're fucking married, and I'm preg—Oh my God."

"You're what, baby? You're what?"

I took the pregnancy test out of my bag and shoved it in his face. "I'm pregnant, Jihad. I'm carrying *your* baby, and you're married to another bitch. You think I'm mad about the ho. I'm mad because you could've told me. I didn't have to find out this way."

"Oh my God, baby. You're carrying my seed? Yessss, I love you, baby. I'm going to be the best father." This nigga danced around like everything was good.

"Jihad, I can't believe you did me like this. Everything you told me was a lie. About how you live with yo' mother, and *that's* why I couldn't come over? All along, you fucking me and this bitch at the same time."

This nigga dropped to his knees and grabbed my hands. "No, baby, you wrong. I don't fuck her. I only fuck you. I swear to you, baby. The bitch trying to bleed me dry, and that's the only reason why I try to be nice to her. I hate that bitch with e'erything in me. I can't wait for the papers to be signed so you, me, and our baby can move on. I can buy a big house somewhere, maybe in Connecticut. I can buy a building out there and start over fresh. Baby, you have to believe me. You're my life," he pleaded.

I didn't know what to believe. I was feeling so confused, and as crazy as it seemed, I was feeling hurt and broken, and every emotion you could think of was bottled up in me. I wanted to say fuck him, but I love him. I was carrying his baby. So what the fuck am I supposed to do?

"How could you do this to me?" I fell to my knees.

"Baby, I swear I didn't mean to. This bitch and I been over. Her pussy dry as fuck. Trust me. I don't even touch her, much less fuck her. Meeting you is the only thing that gives me any kind of happiness. I swear, since I met you, I feel whole again. I can't wait to make you my wife and give you my last name."

I was hearing him, but his words didn't make my pain any less. I loved this man. I wanted him in my life. But who the fuck this bitch think she is? A fucking *wife?* I hate bitches that think they own the nigga 'cause of a fucking ring. Memories of what my mother went through flooded my mind. I was the product of a married man. I recalled how badly this bitch treated my mother and me. I wasn't allowed to go to my daddy's funeral because of that bitter bitch.

You know what? Fuck this ho. If she was fucking and sucking on her man the right way, he wouldn't want this young pussy. You know what? I don't give a fuck if she was married to this nigga on paper. This is *my* man, and if she doesn't like it, she can come get this ass whooping. I quickly dried my tears and stood up.

"Baby, I swear I'm so sorry. I promise it will be over soon."

"Shut up, Jihad. You know what? I'm pissed that you didn't tell me you were married."

"I know, baby. Please, forgive me, babes."

"Shut up and fucking listen. I love you, and there's no way I will walk away because of this bitch. My baby deserves a chance to grow up with their mommy and daddy. But you need to get your shit in order 'cause I ain't waitin' around forever," I warned.

"Baby, thank you. I promise this bitch means nothing to me. I love *you.*"

He came closer and started kissing me. Right then, the office door flew open. I thought it was the bitch coming back, so I kissed him deeper.

"Yo, bro, I need to holla at you." It was his brother.

"Babe, I got to handle some business. I'll come by later."

"OK, boo."

I felt his brother didn't like me by how he looked at me. Oh well, fuck him. He better get used to it 'cause I was here to stay.

Jihad

"Yo, bro, what the fuck is you doing?"

"What the fuck you talking about, son?"

"Why the fuck you have this bitch up in here? Wasn't Brooklyn in here when she came in here?"

"Yo, chill out, bro. Yo, that shit was crazy. I had to make up some shit fast. I almost got busted," I laughed.

"Yo, you tripping. You got a good woman. A woman that bailed yo' ass out of some shit, and you stay running around with this little young-ass chick." He shook his head.

"Yo, nigga, who is you to judge me? Just 'cause you married a boring-ass bitch—"

Before I could finish my sentence, that nigga ran up on me and punched me in the eye. I grabbed him and slammed him on the ground. Next, we were on the ground, tussling.

"Fuck, nigga, you know you can't beat my ass," I said as I banged his head on the ground. Finally, I let go of his ass and stood up. Then I rushed to my desk and grabbed my gun out of my desk drawer.

"Nigga, run up, so I can blow yo' fucking brains out." I pointed my 9 mm at him. I didn't give a fuck if he was my kin or not. I was steaming with anger and couldn't think straight.

"You a bitch-ass nigga. What you gon' do? Shoot me over a bitch?"

"Run up, and you'll find out." I stared down that nigga.

He noticed how serious I was 'cause he grinned at me before leaving. I sat down in my chair. My eye was throbbing from that blow he gave me. I touched it and realized the skin was broken. I should go out there and put a bullet in his ass for this. Old, bitch-ass nigga. All he had to do was mind his motherfucking business.

I sat at the table across from Brooklyn, eating dinner. "What happened to yo' eye, babes?"

"Some bullshit happened with me and one of the customers today."

"A client did that, and you didn't call the police on him?"

"Babes, you know I'm from the streets. We don't call twelve. We handle shit on our own."

"I get that, but you're a business person. You can't be out here fighting. All it takes is for one spiteful client to report you, and then boom . . . a lawsuit follows. Babes, you need to start thinking corporate."

"You know what, Brooklyn? I already had a fucked-up day. The last thing I needed to hear is you preaching this corporate shit to me. I'm not you. I don't wear a fancy suit to work. I wear athletic wear. I don't have no big corporate account or fancy assistant out front. I handle my shit the way I can," I yelled.

"Excuse me, but you're doing all this 'cause I tried to educate you on some shit?"

"All I want is a fucking wife. One that stands behind me—not lectures me. I don't want a fucking mammy. I only want a fucking wife. Do you *know* how to do that?" I stood up and yelled.

I threw the fork on the table before I grabbed my keys and headed out the door. This bitch just pissed me the fuck off. It's bad enough that I didn't want to sit there eating this old dry-ass baked chicken. So I jumped into my car, pulled off, and dialed Alyssa's number.

"Hello."

"Yo, get dressed. We about to go out to eat."

"Okay, boo."

On my way to her place, my phone rang. It was Brooklyn. I pressed ignore. I really didn't give a fuck if that bitch knew that I sent her to voicemail. I was tired of her shit. Lately, I wished that bitch would encounter a heart attack and drop dead. That way, I could get every single dollar in her account without having to deal with her.

After paying the money we owed, I still had over thirty grand left. Enough money to put some in savings and also make sure Briana is good. Alyssa asked for three grand, so I'ma hit her off with that. I would put the rest of the money into my savings for a rainy day.

I pulled up to Alyssa's crib and honked the horn. I got a text from one of my cousins asking me what the fuck happened between my brother and me. Thinking back on what happened earlier made me angry again. I swear, this pussy nigga couldn't just leave the shit alone. Now, he got to run his mouth to the family. I swear I should've offed that nigga.

I looked up and noticed Alyssa walking to the car in a sexy, skintight dress. I gazed at her from her legs all the way up her thighs. Baby girl was sexy as fuck. I noticed she had gained a lot of weight but nothing major. So soon as she has the baby, I'll have her back in the gym. My bitch definitely has to be a reflection of me.

"Hey, boo," she said as she got into the car.

"Hey, babes, looking like a whole snack out here."

"Nah, nigga, fuck that. Fuck a snack. I'm a whole meal," she busted out laughing.

"My bad, babes. So, where do you want to eat?"

"Hmm, why don't you surprise me?"

"A woman that allows her man to choose? Shit, keep it up, and I'ma buy you a big old diamond ring."

"Uh-huh, you was gon' buy that anyway."

"Let me see . . . There's a little spot over there in Old Towne, The Croaker Spot. They have some of the best seafood in these streets."

"Seafood? Yes, Lord, I ain't had no real seafood in about a year."

"When I tell you this food is the truth, believe me."

I pulled up the address on the GPS and headed toward the restaurant. We laughed and talked like we'd known each other our entire lives on our way there. I swear Alyssa makes me so comfortable. I can just be myself around her. She should be my wife.

We ate, laughed, talked, and had a good time. I was so caught up in our conversation that I didn't see Jasmine, Brooklyn's best friend, walk up.

"I thought that was you, Jihad."

"Oh, yeah, Jasmine. How you doing?"

"I'm good. Where's Brooklyn?"

"Oh, she's at home."

"Oh, okay . . ." She stared at me with a stupid-ass look on her face.

"Oh, this is Alyssa, my cousin. Alyssa, this is Jasmine, my wife's best friend."

"Oh, hello, nice to meet you." Alyssa stretched out her hand to greet Jasmine.

"Hello," Jasmine said but didn't shake her hand.

She stared Alyssa down. I was starting to feel uncomfortable.

"Well, it was nice seeing you again. You should drop by the house more frequently."

"Jihad, I most definitely will do that. Anyway, I have a dinner date. Y'all please enjoy dinner." She walked off before I could respond.

After she left, Alyssa looked at me.

"Why you looking at me like that?"

"What's that bitch's problem? Did you see how she looked at me?"

"Baby, listen, I know it's an uncomfortable situation for you right now, but as I explained, I just need you to stay down while I get this shit under control."

"I don't know, Jihad. I mean, I ain't worried about the bitch or nothing, but I done heard niggas promise a bitch how they gon' leave their wives, then one year turns into two, and the nigga still married. I ain't trying to sit around and wait that long."

"Baby, there's no way I'm going to be with that bitch for that long. I've been thinking, though, and I have a plan. I just need to put it together."

"A plan? I like the sound of that. Hmm. I hope it involves money," she busted out laughing.

"You know yo' man too well. If it don't make dollars, it don't make sense." We busted out laughing together.

Even though I was laughing for the last few days, I've been plotting my next move.

After dinner, we went back to Alyssa's place, and we fucked. I noticed her pussy was wetter than usual and gripped my dick like glue. I lay on my back while she rode my dick. Being pregnant didn't slow her down. She stared me in the eyes and rode the dick. I gripped her hips and held her in position. She rotated her hips in a circular motion. I closed my eyes as my dick thrust in and out of her. Her pussy was so good, within minutes, I busted all up in her. I tried holding out, but that wetness wouldn't allow me to be great.

"Here you go." I handed her the three stacks that she asked for.

"Oh, thank you so much, daddy." She reached over and gave me a tongue kiss.

"Yo, when do you plan on going to the doctor?"

"Oh, the doctor? I need to go, but I don't have insurance."

"Find a good doctor, and don't worry 'bout no insurance. You having my seed, so I got you. I just need to make sure the baby is good."

"OK, boo, I'll get on that first thing Monday morning."

"All right, I got to go. I love you."

"Boo, I hate it now that I know you're going home to *her*." Alyssa started pouting.

I gently grabbed her face. "Listen to me. I'm not going home to anyone. That bitch is merely my roommate. Soon as this divorce is final, we'll be living our lives together."

"I know, boo. I just be missing you so much."

"I be missing you too, babes, but guess what? If we plan on having this paper, we have to do things the correct way. I helped this bitch, and there's no way I'ma walk away from this empty-handed. I'ma snatch everything I deserve and more."

"All right, boo."

We kissed, and I left. I glanced at the time. Shit, it was late as fuck. I started plotting my lie that I would run on Brooklyn when I got in the house. Either she accepts it, or she doesn't.

Chapter Fifteen

Brooklyn

I sat on the couch sipping red wine and thinking about all the possible reasons my new husband had not yet come home. It was damn near three in the morning, and this nigga ain't picking up his phone. That makes it worse. It's not that his bitch ass didn't see me calling him. The nigga had the audacity to press ignore. Hmm . . . I swear I hate to think Jihad was out there fucking around on me. But what other possible explanation is there? I asked his ass before if he was fucking Briana's mother. He acted like that was the craziest and most disrespectful shit I could ever say to him. I hate to sound like I'm not secure in my marriage, but with these sudden disappearances, a major red flag is going up in my head.

Finally, I heard the door open. I didn't wait. I jumped up off the couch and met him in the hallway. "Oh, hey, baby. I didn't know you were still up."

"Hey, baby. Where the fuck you been?"

"Where I been? I been out with the fellas shooting pool and drinking. You know how it is when you get around the guys. It ain't nothing, babes. I just lost track of time."

"Jihad, are you fucking around on me?"

"What? Baby, you *really* tripping."

"Pull yo' fucking pants down."

"Huh?" He shot me a dirty look.

"I said, pull yo' fucking pants down. I want to smell yo' dick."

"C'mon, Brooklyn. You tripping, baby."

"Am I, Jihad? See, I might be nice, but I ain't no got-damn fool. Yo' ass done disappeared a little too much for me. Now, is you gon' pull yo' pants down or what?"

"Brooklyn, what the fuck is yo' problem? You think every time I go through these doors, I'm fucking around on you, but you fucking wrong. You need to get yo' mind right. You very insecure, and you keep this up, you gon' lose a good man."

"I don't give a fuck about all this shit you talking about. Now, pull yo' fucking drawers down, so I can find out for myself if I'm wrong about my 'good man.'"

He looked at me with anger in his eyes and shook his head. "This here is some childish-ass-fuck shit. I don't know what kind of lame-ass niggas you're used to, but I'm not no bitch-ass nigga."

I didn't say a fucking word. I just stood there with my arms folded, waiting on this nigga to pull down his drawers.

"You fucking sick, yo. You want to smell my dick so fucking bad. Here you go, Brooklyn."

He pulled down his sweats and boxers, revealing his limp dick. I walked over to him, dropped to my knees, and smelled it. I then stood up.

"You satisfied now? Did you smell another bitch's pussy on it, or you smell sweat from me being out?"

"Uh-huh, I ain't catch you this time but know I *will* figure it out. Ain't no nigga keep disappearing until the wee hours of the morning. You know what's crazy? It started getting bad right after I wrote you that fucking check."

"How the fuck you gon' bring that up, B? See, this is the fucking reason why I didn't ask you for shit. You came out of your mouth telling me you were helping me. Now, I see you only did the shit so you could throw it back into my face. You know what, Brooklyn? I thought you were better, but you just like the rest of these other bitches."

Bap! Bap!

"Nigga, don't you *ever* come out your fucking mouth and call me no bitch. I ain't nothing like these two-dollar, old, synthetic, eyelash-falling-off bitches that you're used to. I'm the best motherfucking thing that will ever happen to you. But keep on, and I'll be gone before you know it."

He grabbed my arms and shoved me onto the couch. "Don't you ever put yo' fucking hands on me again. You hear me?" He shook me with force.

"Get the fuck off me. Nigga, you playing with the wrong one. I will get your ass locked up."

"Locked up? *You* the one that put your hands on me. Just admit you wrong. You thought I was out fucking around on you, and I proved you wrong."

"You know what, Jihad? Keep playing with me, and you gonna get burned. I hope whatever little bitch you fucking with is worth you losing everything." I got up and shot him a dirty look.

"Brooklyn, for the last gotdamn time, I didn't cheat on you, and I'm not cheating. You probably giving up the pussy to one of those doctor niggas you work with, so you trying to throw me off. Maybe I need to be sniffing yo' drawers. Who *you* fucking, Brooklyn?"

I looked at him and laughed. This old, silly-ass nigga don't even deserve a response. Instead, I walked upstairs. This nigga knows I'm a psychologist, so there's no way he can work reverse psychology on me. He's the only nigga that I was fucking and plan on fucking. I walked into my room and slammed the door. I don't care where the fuck he sleeps, but it won't be in my bed tonight.

Alyssa

Being pregnant was not what's up. I stayed nauseated, and everything I ate, I vomited right back up. It's been days since I've been out of this house. I heard the doorbell ringing nonstop. I wondered who the fuck this could be ringing my shit like this. It took me a few minutes to drag myself off the couch and walk toward the door.

"Who is it?" I yelled as I leaned on the door for support.

"It's yo' damn mama. Open the door."

Lord, what is this lady doing here? The last thing I needed to hear was her complaining.

"Hey, Ma," I said as I opened the door.

"'Hey, Ma,' my ass. I been calling you for days, and no response." She pushed past me.

I closed the door and walked back to the couch.

"Here, I brought you some homemade soup. It got carrots, potato, chicken, and dumplings in there."

"Ma, I ain't really hungry right now." I lay back on the couch.

"So, did you go to the doctor yet? Did you find out you pregnant?"

"Yes, Ma, I'm pregnant, but I didn't go to the doctor."

"Uh-huh. You think you can fool me. I knew yo' ass was pregnant. That big-ass nose on yo' face is spreading, and then you say you don't feel good. I know it. So, who's the daddy?"

"Ma, I don't want to talk 'bout it."

"Why? He married or something?" She looked at me.

"Yes, Ma, but he's getting a divorce."

"Ha-ha. A divorce, huh? You must've forgotten the hell *I* went through. Don't you sit back and leave it up to him. You too pretty to be sitting around waiting on no nigga. Now, you having a baby. You better let that nigga know he need to step up to the plate. You ain't gon' be nobody side bitch for long. You deserve to have a ring on your finger, and if that nigga can't leave that bitch he's married to, he need to move on."

"Ma, can you stop already? We already talked, and he knows what he needs to do."

"I hope he got some damn money 'cause this ain't no place to be raising no baby."

I wasn't going to keep responding to her. This was a touchy matter for Mama, and she will keep going on and on.

"Here, sit up and eat this food." She took the plastic bowl out of the bag and handed it to me. I took it from her. Even though I was nauseated, my stomach was touching my back.

"I was the same way when I was carrying you. Before I leave, I'ma run to the store to grab you a bottle of ginger ale and some saltine crackers. You also need to bring yo' ass to the doctor, so you can start taking your prenatal vitamins. All that vomiting can make you dehydrated."

"Thanks, Ma. What would I do without you?" I asked, being a smart-ass.

"Hmm, this gon' be my first grandbaby. I can't have you not taking care of yo' self. Don't be over here all sick and shit by yourself. That nigga, whoever the fuck he is, knocked you up, so he should be right here with you. Matter of fact, did he say he gon' move you up out of here? There's no space for no baby up in here."

"Ma, all you think about is money—"

"Shit, and if you have any kind of sense, you should be thinking the same thing too. Let me ask you a question.

You say this nigga married. So, nine times out of ten, him and the bitch living together, sleeping in the same bed, and fucking every night. With that being said, that bitch owns him on paper. If anything was to happen tomorrow, what the fuck you think going to happen? Wait, I know . . . That ho will get everything, and guess what? Yo' ass won't get shit—not a damn thing. Because all you were doing was fucking her man. The baby might get money from Social Security, but you get nothing but a fucking heartache. You think I'm old and don't have much sense, but, baby girl, smarten up. Open up an account and start putting money in there for the baby. Let this nigga move you up out of here, and wherever you go, make sure it's in your name. Not both of y'all, but *yours*. Stop thinking with your heart. Boss up and handle your shit. Shit, if I were you, I would get some insurance on this nigga. It's crazy out in these streets. That nigga can drop dead any day."

"Ma, can you stop? Trust me. I get everything you're saying."

"Hmm, yeah? Well, you can thank me later. I got to go to the store."

She walked out of the house, and the door closed behind her. I fixed the pillow under my back and sat up. Everything that Mama just said to me was on repeat in my mind. I swear this woman wasn't no fool. She was spitting some real-life shit to me. I felt everything she was saying in my soul. It takes someone else to say this shit to me to get me to think about it. I barely have a dollar to live off. If it weren't for Jihad, my ass probably would have to be out tricking all these other niggas out of their money. Shit has been good since I started fucking him, but what would I do if something *did* happen to him? This was something that I ain't really thought about.

I heard the doorbell again and figured it was Mama. Shit, her ass was gone long enough. I opened the door, and she walked in with her hands filled with bags.

"What's all this?" I pointed to the bags in her hands.

"I got you crackers, ginger ale, some milk, sandwich meat, tuna, eggs, cup of noodles, and water. I looked in this damn fridge, and it's empty. I threw away that food that you had in there for what seems like ages."

"Ma, you ain't had to do this. I was going to go to the store sometime this week."

"Well, now you don't have to go, but you need to put something on your stomach. You already looking like a crackhead. You need to eat, even if it's only soup. Also, you need to make that doctor's appointment."

"Yes, ma'am. Is there anything else you want me to do?" I asked sarcastically.

"Yes."

"What?"

"Get you some rest. Carrying a baby is not easy."

"Okay, Mother."

She walked into the kitchen, and I continued lying down.

"All right, baby girl, you all set. I'm going to run. I got some errands to do before it gets too late. Answer your damn phone when I call—having me all worried and shit . . . And let me know when your doctor's appointment is. If he can't go with you, I'll go."

"Okay, Ma, love you, and I will answer my phone."

I walked Mama to the door and locked it after she left. I was happy that she was gone. Now I could go back to lying down without interruptions. I was missing Jihad. Since I'm pregnant, I be wanting to lay up under him. I'm trying my hardest, but I want my man to myself, so I texted him.

Hey, boo, just thinking about you and missing you like crazy.

My phone started ringing. I smiled as I saw Jihad's number pop up there.

"Hey, there, beautiful." It doesn't matter how often I hear him say that same line. It still does something to me.

"Hey, baby daddy. Just missing you real bad."

"How about you show me how much you missing me by coming to the door butt-ass naked when I come by tonight?"

"Shit, that's easy, daddy. You know my pussy stay wet for you."

"Chill, Alyssa. You know I'm at work. I can't go help a client with my dick all hard and shit."

"Shit, why not? That bitch probably been wanting to fuck you on the low."

"Ha-ha, girl, you know you crazy, right?"

"Ain't that the reason why you love me?"

"You right. I love the fuck out of you, baby girl. But listen, I got to run. I'll be there to suck on that pussy for you later."

"Okay, daddy."

Damn, that man plays too much. Just talking to me nasty has my panties soaking wet. I lay on my back again, pulled off my panties, and right there, I started massaging my clit. Shit, I was horny as hell. I pushed my two fingers in and started grinding on them.

"Awee, shit, yessss," I moaned out.

I closed my eyes, pretending like I was riding Jihad's dick. My fingers were working magic 'cause within minutes of finger fucking myself, I exploded all over them. Then I put the fingers into my mouth, slowly licking all my sweet juices off them. I swear I felt much better. This will hold me off until Jihad makes his way over tonight.

Chapter Sixteen

Brooklyn

Jihad and I were barely on speaking terms after what happened last week. He insisted that I needed to apologize, but I was standing my ground. Yes, his dick might not have smelled like pussy, but I wasn't wrong for being suspicious. If it quacks like a duck, then it's a gotdamn duck. I don't have any proof that he's fucking around on me, but the fact remains, this nigga been moving suspiciously.

He moved back into our bedroom, but we barely exchanged any words. I watched him come home, bathe, and then leave. He would be gone for hours at a time, and then sneak in late many times. I wasn't sleeping. I just pretended like I was.

I noticed everything about him had changed since I cut him that check. I want to think I was tripping, but I see the changes. The story that he gave me also bothered me. I've met his brother, and he seems to be the kind of nigga that has his shit together, so how the fuck did he allow this to happen to the gym? Something didn't sit right with me. It was my lunch break, so I decided to grab a salad for lunch. Lately, I'm back to watching what I eat. I drove by the gym on my way back from grabbing the salad. After passing it, I decided to bust a U-turn and made my way into the parking lot.

I knew Jihad was off today because it was Briana's graduation day. I was waiting to see if I would get an invitation, but it never came. I was cool with it, though. I mean, I've tried numerous times to be in that girl's life, and each time, all I got was disrespect. I was at the point where I wanted to tell him to take her rude little ass to her mother's house and leave her over there.

I parked and got out. I was on my way into the gym when I heard someone call my name.

"Brooklyn."

I turned around, and it was Jihad's brother, Jaseem. Just the person I was looking for a quick visit.

"Hey, there, Jaseem. How you doing?"

"Shit, I could be better. Who you looking for, Jihad? He's not here."

"No, actually, I came down here to talk with you."

"Me, oh Lord, you heard about the fight. I swear, Brooklyn, I didn't start with that man."

"Fight? What fight? You and Jihad got to fighting?"

"Oh, you didn't know about it. Damn, it's nothing. So, why do you want to talk with me?" He shot me a strange look.

"Jaseem, listen, I know Jihad is your brother, but I don't know what's been happening with him lately. However, I'm more concerned about this gym. I had to loan him fifty grand, so y'all don't lose it. When I asked what happened, he said you were not staying up to date on the payments."

"That's what he said?" he laughed. "Just like my brother to blame me. You know what, Brooklyn? That is *your* husband, so you should talk with *him*. You're a smart woman. You can pick sense out of nonsense. I'm thinking about walking away from this anyway. There are other things I want to pursue."

"I hear that. Well, I see you not going to say too much about the situation here. I just hope Jihad is not lying to me about all this."

"Brooklyn, you married the man. Go home; talk with him. I don't have anything else to say."

"I hear you. Well, have a good day."

I didn't wait for a response and walked off. Something is going on between those two. I'm pretty sure he was the one Jihad got to fighting with and not a "client" as he claimed. Now, it all makes sense to me why he was so defensive when I told him he should've called the police. I hate that his brother wouldn't spill the beans on what was going on, but I do know it wasn't good.

I got back into my car and pulled off. The perfect man I married turned out to be not so perfect. It was like I was going around in a circle. I need to find out what the fuck Jihad was up to . . . What the fuck he's been hiding.

Jihad

Juggling two bitches at a time was getting more complicated than I thought. Brooklyn was breathing down my fucking neck every chance she got. Always accusing me of cheating or lying about some bullshit. Crazy thing is, this bitch was right. I *am* cheating, but she has no proof. I'm so careful with my shit; she'll never find out.

On the other hand, Alyssa has been nagging about me moving her out of the hood. Shit, I was trying to figure out how to still be at home and be with her. My fucking head was hurting trying to figure out this shit. I wish these bitches were the kind that would let us all live together.

"Ha-ha," I busted out laughing. That was a brilliant idea. I started pacing the gym, thinking. Shit, I was so excited.

I should be a freaking genius. The things that pop up in my head are nothing short of brillant. I grabbed my cell phone and dialed Alyssa's number.

"Hello," she answered. I could tell she was still asleep.

"Hey, sleepyhead, wake up."

"Hey, boo. I was up all night sick as fuck."

"Did you put something on your stomach?"

"I did, but I just vomited it right back up. I go to the doctor Thursday, so I hope the doctor can give me something to help with this vomiting 'cause I'm dying."

"I'm pretty sure they will. Aye, babes, how would you like to get a job?"

"A job? What do you mean? I just took off from school because I was sick, and now you want me to work?"

"Babes, relax. I have a plan for how we can be together immediately. We don't have to wait."

"Really? Hmm . . . And how did you come up with that?"

"Babes, I got the perfect plan. I just need to know you're on board with it."

"Sounds interesting, boo. What is it?"

"We'll talk about it as soon as I get over there later."

"OK, boo, I love you too."

"Okay, girl, get some rest."

After I got off the phone, I headed to my wife's office. I know we haven't talked lately, but it was time for this foolishness to end. Brooklyn was a lonely old bitch. All she needs is for me to suck that pussy, fuck her real good, and all is forgiven.

I looked around and noticed my bitch-ass brother was working, so I left. I had a plan in my head, hoping it would work out.

I stopped by the local flower shop and grabbed my wife a bouquet. I also stopped by Applebee's and grabbed a chicken salad for Brooklyn. I know she probably was working hard and didn't have a chance to go out and grab lunch.

Finally, I parked my car beside Brooklyn's, grabbed the salad and the flowers, and made my way toward the building. I rang the buzzer and waited.

"Yes, how may I help you?" Nicolette asked.

"It's Jihad. I'm here to surprise my wife."

"Okay, Mr. Evans."

I walked in and spotted Nicolette sitting at her desk as usual. I walked over to her.

"Hey there, beautiful."

"Good afternoon, Mr. Evans. Mrs. Evans is in her office. If you want to surprise her, now is the time to do it before her next client comes in."

"Nicolette, you can't tell me that you haven't considered what it would be like to be with a stud like me."

"*Excuse* me?"

"You heard me. Imagine me lifting you in the air and sucking on your pussy from the back."

"I-I-I think you need to go."

"Why? Because you scared of Brooklyn? This would be *our* little secret."

She got up from her desk and walked toward Brooklyn's office. I quickly grabbed her and started kissing her.

"Stop." She tried pulling away.

I slapped her. "Bitch, get off me. I'm here to see my wife. Are you fucking crazy?"

I pushed her down, dropping the salad and the flowers on the floor. Then I quickly ripped open my shirt and dashed for the office.

"Brooklyn, you need to get out here. Yo' fucking assistant just jumped on me," I yelled in a frantic state as I busted into her office.

"Huh? What are you talking about?" She jumped up from her desk.

"This bitch tried to kiss me and ripped my shirt when I refused."

Brooklyn looked at my ripped shirt and rushed out to the waiting area. That bitch was still on the ground. It seemed like she hit her head.

"Nicolette, what the hell is going on here? My husband said you came on to him!" Brooklyn yelled.

By now, she had managed to get up off the ground.

"You crazy bitch. I told you I didn't like you like that. Plus, my wife is your boss. What kind of crazy shit is that?"

"Mrs. Evans, he's lying. I was sitting here when he rang the buzzer, telling me he wanted to surprise you. I let him in—"

"This bitch is lying, Brooklyn. Ever since I've been coming to this office, she's been eying me differently. I'm going to call the fucking police. I want this bitch arrested."

"Mrs. Evans, are you buying this bull crap? I didn't touch his ass. This man attacked *me*." She started crying.

"Both of you shut the fuck up. I'm trying to make some sense of this. Jihad, she's been my assistant for years now—"

"And I'm your fucking *husband*. I'm telling you, this bitch just attacked me. If you don't call the police, *I* will."

"I swear to you—you know me. I've worked with you. I didn't touch this man. He's doing this for a reason. Mrs. Evans, please, believe me," she pleaded.

I pulled out my cell phone and dialed 911. Brooklyn realized I was dead-ass serious then. "Listen, Jihad, hang up the phone. The last thing I need is for the police to swarm up in here. Nicolette, please, gather your things and go quietly. I'll make sure you get severance pay along with your last paycheck."

"You're firing me behind some bogus-ass shit? Lady, you're stupider than I thought. I don't know what his motives are, but they're *not* good."

"Nicolette, I said get your stuff and get out. This is my husband, and I believe him."

Those were the only words that I needed to hear. For a minute there, I thought Brooklyn was siding with that bitch. I guess her ass got it together fast when I mentioned the police.

"This is *not* over. This man assaulted me, and you fired me on top of it. Y'all will hear from the police department *and* my lawyer real soon. This is not going down like this," she warned.

"Please, pack yo' stuff and leave. It's your word against my husband's. Why would he attack you while I'm in the office? This doesn't make any sense, but do know, if you come after me or make any kind of false claim against my husband, *I* will come after you my damn self," Brooklyn said in a fierce tone.

The bitch didn't respond. Instead, she threw her keys down on the desk, grabbed a small box, and walked out the glass door. Brooklyn followed closely behind her and locked the door.

"Are you okay? I'm so sorry this happened to you. This is crazy."

"Yes, I'm good. I've been around aggressive females before, but I have never run across one that was this bold. I was too shocked. It seemed like she was high or something."

"High? You mean on drugs? I've never known her to be on any kind of drugs. I need to get on here and change all my passwords now. This is crazy. I have clients coming in this evening. Oh my God, this is too much."

"Listen, babes, I'm so sorry. I was only trying to surprise you by bringing you flowers and a salad. I know the last week has been crazy for us. I was at the gym and was thinking about us. Finally, I decided I couldn't do this anymore. I miss you. I miss *us*."

"Aw, I miss us too, Jihad. I been feeling like you found someone else, so you didn't give a fuck about our marriage."

"You really tripping, babes. I admit I got some flaws that need working on, but I love you, woman. I keep telling you I'm not cheating on you. I have no reason to. Your pussy is too good. Why would I stray?" I looked her dead in the eyes.

"You right. Shit, my next appointment will be here in thirty minutes. This is crazy. What am I going to do?" She started panicking.

"Calm down, baby. I don't know nothing about your business, but I've been in a front office before. I'll work the desk for the remainder of the evening until you figure this out. I feel so bad because if I didn't come up here, none of this would have happened."

"Stop blaming yourself. You're the victim here. As you said, her ass probably was on some drugs."

I sat in the same chair that bitch was in half an hour ago. I could get used to this. Nah, this ain't my style, but I know someone who *could* fill this position.

Chapter Seventeen

Brooklyn

I sat in my chair, massaging my temples. I had a pounding headache that wouldn't go away. I tried my hardest to make sense of all this shit that went down between Jihad and my assistant. The more I thought about it, the more confused I was. It's crazy how you could work alongside someone and never really know them.

I called my attorney earlier and explained to him what went down. Before Nicolette left, she threatened me, and I wasn't taking that lightly at all.

"Babes, are you okay?" Jihad asked as he walked into my office at home and handed me a cup of coffee.

"Just what I needed," I smiled at him.

I took the cup out of his hand and sipped. "Damn, bae, did you empty the whole can of sugar in this?"

"Is it too sweet? I remembered you love your coffee on the sweet side. I can go make you another cup if you like."

"No, this will work. I just pray I don't get diabetes," I laughed.

I looked over at him as he sat on the couch. I smiled at him without him noticing. This past week has changed our relationship dynamics. Jihad was like a changed man. He'd also been at the office helping me out. I don't know how I could get this workload done if he weren't there. I certainly need to find someone to help soon. But I was skeptical of bringing someone new in after this shit that Nicolette pulled. It's hard for me to trust a stranger again.

He got up, walked over to me, and started massaging my shoulders. "Aye, babes, I'm going to have to return to the gym this coming week. I know I've been helping you out, but my clients been calling me. But guess what? I have someone that you can hire."

"Really? I don't know, Jihad, about bringing anyone else in right now. Look at the craziness that happened."

"No, babes, you remember my cousin that you met?"

"Yes, Alyssa. I think that's her name."

"Well, Cousin Alyssa just lost her job and called me yesterday asking if I knew anyone hiring. I told her I would have to look around, but now that we're talking, I think this would be good 'cause she's family, and you ain't got to worry about her trying to sleep with me."

"Yeah, you right, but does she have any experience? I deal with some very important clients. Confidentiality is my top priority. Also, she must be computer savvy. All the paperwork and appointments are logged in daily."

"Relax, baby. My cousin graduated at the top of her class in business management. Trust me. I would not recommend her, family or not, if I didn't think she could be an asset to your company."

"Okay, can you have her come in tomorrow? I'll interview her, and we can go from there."

"Got you, baby. I'll call her and let her know the good news. She'll be happy to hear that. I tell you, she's going through a rough divorce, so this will brighten her day. Now that this is out of the way, what's for dinner, love?"

"Dinner? Shit, my head is pounding. How about we order Chinese?"

"Sounds like a plan to me. I'll order it. You need to relax." He kissed me on the forehead and walked out of the office, closing the door behind him.

I sat in the Red Lobster, waiting on my bestie to join me. It's been weeks since we last talked. I didn't get a good vibe from her the day we got married, and I wanted to know what that was all about. I mean, we've been friends so damn long, I would think if something bothered her, she would come to me. With so much shit happening around me, she was the only solid person outside of my husband I knew I could trust.

"Hey, you," she said as she walked up to me and took a seat.

"Hey, girl, it's about time you got here," I joked.

"Don't forget you called me at the last minute to schedule lunch. So I had to cancel two appointments to make this lunch break."

"And that's one of the reasons why you're my best friend."

"How was your trip to Jamaica?"

"Wow, friend, it was beautiful. I think we should visit Jamaica the next time you and I go on vacation together. The food was the bomb, and the people were super friendly. We had a great time."

"That's good to know. So, how is married life treating you? You look good."

"Girl, it ain't nothing special. We started off kind of rocky, but things are looking up. I love the place that we're in right now."

"Hmm, how long have we been friends?"

"Bitch, I don't know . . . forever," I busted out laughing.

"You're right. Forever. So, I know when shit isn't right and when my best friend is trying to cover up something. So, spit it out. What's going on?"

"You know how you said I should get a prenup before we get married? Well, I didn't get one . . ."

"What you mean, you ain't get one?" She looked at me in shock.

"I know you kept telling me to get one, but I didn't believe I needed one because I was so in love, and I thought Jihad was doing good with his business and he had money. So for once, I felt like this was my partner. What's mine was his and so on."

"Okay . . . So why are we having this conversation? Obviously, you're going to do what you want."

"What changed is I think Jihad's business is in danger. I think he's broke."

"So, my educated friend with good credit and good pussy went and gave her heart away to a broke nigga. I don't know if I want to laugh at you or cry with you."

"How about just being a friend and listening?"

"Brooklyn, I am a friend, but a friend will let you know when you fucked up, and babyyyy, you fucked up. How did you find out?"

"The other day, he came home stressed out. I later found out they were getting ready to lose the gym. I felt bad because he sat there looking broken like he was ready to give up on life. I couldn't sit there and do nothing. I'm his wife. I took a vow that said, for better or worse."

"So, let me guess. You wrote him a check. How much money did you dish out to that nigga?"

"Fifty grand."

"Brooklyn, are you fucking *crazy?*"

"I know, but as I said, he's my husband, and I can't sit back and do nothing."

"Brooklyn, from the minute I met him, I smelled a rat on him. I don't buy all that Mr. Sweet Guy shit. That nigga knew he was broke, but he pretended he had money. If you ask me, that nigga did his homework. He knows you're not broke. Did he tell you I saw him?"

"Nah, where?"

"The Croaker Spot. I was meeting a client when I spotted him. I thought you guys were out eating. I walked over there . . . only to see him with another female."

"Another female?"

"Yes, he said she was his cousin. I spoke for a little, then walked off. There's something about him that rubs me wrong. At your wedding, I was only there because you asked me. I can see a snake-ass nigga from a mile away. But . . . You're my friend, and you fell for him and decided to marry him. I love you enough to respect your decisions, but I don't want to have anything to do with him."

"Damn, that's deep, and I love you too. Thank you for loving me. I hope he turns out to be the best man, and you'll see that he genuinely loves me."

"Do you *think* he genuinely loves you?" She stared me down.

"Yes, I do, but I wish he was real with me about his finances. Then it would have been my decision to make. Now, I'm wondering where the hell he got the money from to buy this ring?" I flashed my finger in the air.

"Hmmm, nice ring, but is it a *real* diamond?"

"Bitch, you really tripping. You know I'm very high maintenance, and I'm not running around with anything fake on my finger."

"I'm just checking, friend, since you done downgraded on the nigga. My friend I know would've made sure that nigga's bank account was flooded. But I get it. You doing it for the love of the dick. Boy, I tell you, that good dick can have a bitch out here acting all kinds of crazy," she busted out laughing.

The waitress walked over and smiled at us. "Hello, ladies. My name is Amanda. I'm your waitress and will be taking your orders. Can I get you ladies something to drink?"

"Hello, Amanda, can I get a Bahama Mama?"

"Yes, let me get one also," Jasmine said, barely able to control herself.

The waitress looked at both of us, smiled, and walked off. I looked at Jasmine, still over there, having the time of her life at my expense.

"You know you full of shit."

"You can't deny it. That shit was funny as hell. Admit you do need to lighten up."

"Yeah, you right." I side-eyed her.

We continued talking about careers and other business ventures. I love this chick 'cause we can go from
ratchet conversations to multimillion-dollar conversations within minutes.

We got our drinks and ordered our food, still laughing
and talking. By the time we finished, I was stuffed beyond understanding. It was a sin to feel like this. We paid,
hugged, and went our separate ways. I needed this honest conversation. Even though she can sometimes be a
little raw with it, I can do nothing but respect it.

Alyssa

"Baby, listen, my wife is hiring for a position at her job."

"And what does that have to do with me?" I looked at
Jihad as we sat eating steamed shrimp and crab legs.

"You remember I told you I had an idea? Well, how
about you get this job? That way, you can keep an eye on
her ass."

"You want me to get close to the other bitch you're
fucking? Kind of like babysitting her ass?"

"Alyssa, I thought you was a boss bitch. I want you to
get this fucking job. And you're my cousin, remember?
Soon, you will be coming to the house whenever you like.
You've been complaining about how I don't spend a lot
of time with you. Well, this would allow us to spend all
the time together, right under her fucking nose."

"Hmmm, sounds interesting. And how am I supposed
to get this job?"

"She runs a counseling business. You'll work at the
front desk, taking in new clients and setting appointments. You're computer savvy, and the rest is common
sense."

"I don't know, Jihad. What if this bitch come out of her
mouth wrong to me? You know my ass is going to go the

fuck off."

"Alyssa, think of the big picture here. Big-ass saving accounts . . . trips overseas . . . baby going to private school . . . This can all be us; all it takes is a little manipulation and hard work. Baby, that old bitch won't figure out shit, and if she does, by then, it will be too late. We a team, right?"

The sound of money, trips, and private schools had me sold. I didn't give a fuck about that bitch, and if Jihad had a plan for us, then I was down for it.

"I'm down, daddy. Don't I need a résumé to go in there?"

"Walla. I told you, your man got you." He reached over in his gym bag, pulled out a manila envelope, and handed it to me. I took it and opened it. It was a résumé well put together, with my name and places that I've worked.

"Go ahead, study that. Get familiar with the places and names. I doubt she'll ask for one, but just in case, you'll be covered. Just act normal because she's a psychologist. Her ass picks up on shit. Be on time tomorrow at 9:00 a.m."

"I got you, daddy. Anything for you," I joked.

"Oh, word? Come ride my face real quick."

"Ha-ha, how about we finish eating our food first? I don't want you to keep smelling shrimp and then think it's my pussy."

"Yeah, true."

We went back to fucking up our food. My mind was thinking all kinds of shit. Could this bitch be my big break to get out of the hood? Shit, I have no problem pretending to be "Cousin Alyssa" as long as I'm living the good life. And from the sound of it, that bitch is living the good life. Move over, bitch; a new Mrs. getting ready to take over.

I was dressed in a nice two-piece suit and a pair of pumps. It looked like a million-dollar suit, but the truth is, I grabbed it from Marshalls. The shoes I got on sale at Macy's. I felt like shit, but I was on a very important task today, so I threw a peppermint in my mouth and walked out the door. Then I put the address in my GPS and headed out.

This was definitely not my time of the morning. Plus, the traffic was horrible going to Chester at this time. What was supposed to be a twenty-minute drive took damn near forty minutes. I was uneasy and thought about turning back several times, but I kept hearing Jihad's voice in my head telling me this was going to be our big payday.

"You're here . . . Destination on the left," Waze instructed me.

I put on my blinker, turned left, then pulled into a space near the door, parked, and got out. I glanced at my phone. It was a few minutes before nine, so I was right on time. I made sure my hair was fixed and sashayed into the lobby, where I rang the bell.

"Who is it?"

"It's Alyssa. I'm here for an interview."

"Oh yes, come on in."

The door buzzed, so I opened it and walked in.

"Hello there, Alyssa. Nice to see you again," she greeted me.

"Nice seeing you again, Mrs. Evans." I almost choked, saying those damn words.

"Please, take a seat. Let me grab my notes."

I looked around as that bitch disappeared behind a big double door. This shit was big and looked expensive. So, this is what the good life feels like, huh?

"How was the traffic coming down here? I hope it wasn't too bad."

"Nah, not too bad."

"Okay, so you know my husband, y'all are cousins, so that makes us family. However, this is my business. It's a private counseling service. Have you ever worked around families or kids with behavioral problems?"

"Umm, not really . . ."

"That's fine if you haven't. I only brought that up to let you know we need to bend and be patient, and sometimes, this business can get overwhelming. You'll be working as my assistant, so you'll often be present at meetings with insurance companies. You will be the voice on the phone, taking calls and answering questions. You have to be on top of sending over prescriptions to pharmacies. The bottom line is you must be on top of everything when dealing with these clients. They and their families depend on us. Any questions?"

"How much is the pay?"

"It's $80,950 per year."

"Wow, that's good."

"Well, I'm glad you think so. You'll get paid vacations. We don't work weekends or holidays. When are you available to start?"

"I was thinking in the morning, if that's okay with you?"

"Yes, that's perfect. You have to dress in slacks. No jeans or sneakers allowed in the front office. You must look and speak professionally at all times."

"That's easy. I do that now."

"Oh great. I do need your identification and Social Security card. I will also run a background check on you. You'll be working with clients' personal information, so the law requires background checks."

"Oh, that's no problem."

I reached into my purse, took out the items, and handed them to her.

"Thanks, let me make copies."

This was the funniest shit to me. This bitch seems like she got all her shit together . . . educated bitch, big old office, lots of money, expensive shoes, and shit. But here I was in my little cheap suit, no damn money, and little education . . . And I'm the bitch that her husband was leaving her for. I was seconds away from laughing out loud. She reminds me of the bitch my daddy was with.

Anger swept over me. I disliked these high-and-mighty bitches that feel like 'cause they got their shit together, the nigga going to be faithful. Wrong, bitch. That nigga is loving on this little broke bitch—the one you think you doing a favor for. I wonder how this ho will feel when she discovers the help wasn't really the help but the bitch that's going to replace her.

"Here you go, love. I'll see you at nine tomorrow morning, and to avoid traffic in the mornings, you might want to leave a bit earlier."

"Gotcha. Well, thank you for bringing me on board. You won't be disappointed," I smiled at her.

"I have an idea I won't be. Have a great day. Here's my card. Call me if you have any more questions."

"I definitely will."

I took the card, stuffed it into my purse, and walked out. I was happy to be outside in the air. Being around that bitch was suffocating. Her voice was killing me with all that proper talk. I see why Jihad said that bitch was boring. She seems like the kind that can't suck or ride dick good. Oh well, bitch, I will handle all that and make sure your husband is *well* taken care of.

I was about to open the car when my phone started to ring. I looked at the screen and saw it was Jihad. "Let me find out you were timing me?"

I hurriedly got into the car and cut the AC on. It was too damn hot for this shit.

"Brooklyn just called, bragging about how pleasant you are. She said you got the job."

"Uh-huh. Do you know how hard it was for me to sit in front of that ho and pretend?"

"Baby, baby, I thought we had this under control."

"We do. I'm just telling you this wasn't easy, but I got it. Whatever you doing, you need to hurry up because I don't plan on playing the help forever."

"I got you, baby girl. The plan already in motion. Just trust your man."

"I trust you, baby, but I need some money too. I ain't got shit. No food, nothing."

"A'ight, I got you when I get off work. You need to get out of this heat."

"All right, love you."

"Love you more."

After we hung up, I dialed my bitch's number to share my good news with her.

"Yes, bitch, what's up?"

"Damn, who the fuck pissed you off?" I inquired.

"Girl, this fucking landlord. The AC been out since yesterday, and I've been calling this ho, leaving her messages, and still no response. If I got to go all the way to their main office downtown, I'm going to be one angry bitch. They don't want to hear my mouth today."

"Damn, that is fucked up. It's hot out here for that. You know you more than welcome to come over. Bitch, I called you to tell you my good news."

"What the fuck is that? You find out who yo' baby daddy is?"

"Bitchhhh, you is stupiiiid," I hollered into the phone.

"I'm just saying, bitch. But nah, boo, what's the good news?"

"I got me a J-O-B." I spelled it out for her.

"Bitch, I know yo' ass lying. You ain't getting no job unless it's lying on yo' back. So, who hired you to sell pussy?"

"Bitch, my days of selling pussy are over. I'm with Jihad now. I ain't got to do shit but fuck and suck him good. But I got a job working in an office with Jihad's wife."

"Wife? Bitch, what the fuck you talking about? You told me that nigga was single, so what the fuck going on?"

"It's a long story, bitch, but I found out he was married. I was in my feelings at first, but after he begged and begged me not to leave him, I decided to stay. I mean, him and the bitch getting a divorce, and he supposed to walk away with some big money."

"Bitch, you lying. I keep telling you, you a lucky bitch. Shit, fuck her. But how the fuck you got hired at her business?"

"Bitch, because I met the ho, and he introduced me as his cousin. Jihad's ass wants me to be around more, so he got me a job there."

"Man, that's why I told you these niggas ain't shit. This nigga has his wife *and* his side bitch working alongside each other. This is some reality-show drama brewing."

"Ho, I ain't nobody side bitch. Jihad is my man. That ho is the side ho. Before long, she won't be anything but a memory. I'm here to stay in Jihad's life. Me and my baby ain't going nowhere."

"You a bad bitch, but just be careful. This bitch might not be as stupid as y'all think she is."

"You know me . . . I don't trust these niggas or bitches. I'ma play right along, though. I love that man, and that bitch don't deserve to have him."

"That's right, bitch. So, when you start?"

"Tomorrow morning at nine. Anyway, bitch, let me know if you coming over. I'm tired and need to eat something."

"Cool, I'll let you know."

After I hung up, I made my way home. I was tired and nauseated. This peppermint wasn't making it any better. Lord, I don't know how I'm going to do this job thing while feeling like this.

Chapter Eighteen

Brooklyn

It's been a whole week that I haven't been feeling too well. First, I shook it off, thinking it was because I was tired. I've been putting in extra work since my assistant left, but it's been days since I hired Jihad's cousin, and my work load has gotten lighter. So, I have no understanding of why I was feeling like this.

"Hey, babes, are you okay? It's past twelve, and you're still in bed. Here, I brought you your favorite, coffee mixed with caramel." Jihad placed the cup on the nightstand.

"No, I don't feel too good. I think something is wrong with me," I barely whispered.

"Hmm, maybe it's exhaustion. You been on your grind hard lately. It's the weekend, so why don't you relax and let your man take care of you?"

"Hmm, sounds really good. I just wish I didn't feel like this."

"I know, babes, but you know your body has a way of telling you when you overdoing it. You can't always be a superwoman. You need to chill sometimes and let your man handle everything."

"I know, babes, I know."

"Well, drink up before it gets cold. Then I'll make some soup with carrots, yams, and chicken. My grandma used to give that to me when I was growing up. Oh, by the way, I told Alyssa you weren't feeling too well. She wants to stop and check on you."

"That's okay. I need to get up and take a shower."

"How 'bout I fix you a nice bath, and you can sit in there and relax. I'll even come wash your back for you . . ."

"Wow, maybe I need to get sick more often, so you can take care of me," I joked.

"No, I'm a brand-new man. I'll take care of you as long as I'm breathing. Aye, babes, you ever thought about us taking out life insurance? I mean, I want to make sure you'll be well taken care of if anything happens to me."

"You know what? Lately, I've been thinking about it. I have one policy, but my mother is on it. I need to do another one so you can be on it."

"Babes, I know this is a touchy subject, but shit happens in life. I know you got your own, but as your man and husband, I would hate for anything to happen to me, and you have to bear the burden of burying me and covering all my debts. So I say we get two policies that cover us."

"Okay, I'll get on them Monday." I sat up in bed while I drank my coffee. Jihad's ass was heavy-handed with the sugar lately. Shit was sweet as hell.

"All right, let me go set your bathwater and get you in there."

After he left the room, I couldn't help but smile. Each day with him is turning out to be better than the last one. I love this man.

"You ready, babes?"

I tried to get up off the bed, but my feet buckled underneath me. Jihad had to rush over and grab me.

"Damn, babes, you all right?"

"No, I'm dizzy. I can't stand up."

"Shit, just lie back down."

"No, I need to take a bath."

"Okay, let's go."

He picked me up and carried me to the tub. I was trying to figure out why the fuck I felt like this. I was dizzy and feeling weak, and my thoughts were confused. Something was happening to me, and I didn't know what it was. I was scared.

After Jihad washed me, I asked him to take me back to bed. I was tired and needed to lie down. He brought me the soup, and I drank it. Shit, even the soup had a slight sweet taste to it. Maybe I was hallucinating. No one puts sugar in soup.

"Hey, babes, you didn't put sugar in the soup, right?"

"Ha-ha, no, I didn't . . . Are you okay? You seem a little confused. I'm starting to worry about you."

"No, I'm okay. If I don't feel better by tomorrow, I'll see the doctor."

"Good, 'cause I got to make sure my baby is all right."

"What would I do without you, my king?" I smiled as he rubbed my head.

"Okay, I'm going to see about Briana. I'll be back in a few to check on you."

After Jihad left the room, I pulled the cover up to my chin. I was trembling uncontrollably. My only explanation was that I was coming down with the flu.

Knock, knock. I must've dozed off because a loud knock at the door woke me up. I pulled my head from under the cover.

"Come in."

"Hey, Brooklyn, it's me, Alyssa. Jihad told me you weren't feeling too well, so I stopped by to see you. Here. I brought you flowers and a balloon. How are you feeling?"

"I'm not feeling too good, but I'm sure it's nothing serious. Maybe the flu."

"Yes, I thought that when he told me. I know quite a few people who are battling the flu right now. Did you take anything for it?"

"I took some Pepto Bismol when I thought it was only an upset stomach. But that didn't work."

"Hmm, well, Jihad needs to get you some Tylenol Multisymptom. That'll probably help. Drink lots of water and get plenty of rest."

"Well, thank you."

"No problem, boss. I need you to feel better before it's time to go back to work."

"I will, babes."

"Okay, you get some rest. Going to check on my cousin before leaving."

"Thank you."

She walked out and closed the door. She was such a sweet girl. I'm kind of happy that Jihad brought her to the company. If she keeps up that attitude, she can be a real asset to the business.

My head was pounding badly now, and my eyes were blurry. This wasn't how I planned to spend my weekend, but I had no other choice. I needed to rest. Within seconds, I dozed off.

I opened my eyes and looked around. It was dark, and my television had gone off. I hate that damn timer on the TV. As soon as I get a little strength, I'll take off that shit. I cut the light on and grabbed my phone. I woke up in a sweat and was so thirsty. I needed something to drink. I dialed Jihad's number, but it went straight to voicemail. I glanced at the time. It was 11:15 p.m. I can't believe I slept all evening. You can tell my ass was sick.

I mustered up all the strength in me, dragged myself out of bed, and then opened my door. Damn, the entire house seemed dark. Jihad probably went out for a few or something. I wasn't strong enough, but I leaned on the wall for support as I walked through the hallway. Finally,

I reached the stairway by the guest bedroom. I was halfway past it when I noticed a light on in there. That was strange because no one used that room. I dragged myself to the door. I heard sounds . . . a woman moaning and yelling, "Yes, daddy." It must be the television. I pushed open the door to cut it off . . . and saw a woman's shadow bouncing up and down. I dragged myself closer. There was enough light from the television for me to see what was in front of me . . . Wait . . . Alyssa and Jihad? Wait, this can't be.

"Jihad, what are you doing?" I mumbled before I started shaking. I fell to the ground, still shaking uncontrollably, foam coming out of my mouth . . . I tried to make sense of what was happening but was confused. The room began spinning, and everything turned dark around me . . . *What the fuck is happening to me?* I thought.

Chapter Nineteen

Brooklyn

"Can you hear me?" I heard an unfamiliar voice ask.

I struggled to open my eyes. A whiff of brightness hit my pupils as they opened. Then I quickly closed them.

"Mrs. Lewis, how are you feeling?"

I forced my eyes open again to see who was speaking to me. A moment later, I noticed it was a short, stocky Filipino doctor. I glanced at my surroundings and realized I was in a hospital. Why the fuck was I in a hospital? I quickly searched my memory, but I was coming up empty.

"Doctor, why am I here? How did I get here?"

"I believe your husband brought you in. He found you unresponsive on the floor. You might've fallen."

"Unresponsive? What is wrong with me?" I shot the doctor a dirty look.

"Well, from what I came up with, you are dehydrated, and I think he mentioned a little nausea. I ran some tests on you, and your tests all seem normal. Your husband told me you were quite stressed for a few days, and he believes your body just shut down on you."

I don't recall none of this shit that he was talking about, so I just listened to him.

"So, how long do I have to be here?"

"Well, I have you on IV drip, antibiotics, and nausea medicine. You're good to go in the morning if all is well."

"Hey, sweetheart, you're awake. I was afraid you might still be asleep," Jihad said as he popped into the room with flowers and balloons.

He rushed over to me and kissed me on the forehead.

"Doc, how is she doing?"

"Mr. Lewis, I was just talking with your wife. Everything is looking good so far. Nothing is showing up in her blood that would have me alarmed. I would love to keep her overnight, and if all is well, you can take her home in the morning. But she still needs to rest for a few more days and take the antibiotic I'm going to prescribe."

"Doc, no worries. I'll take good care of her." Jihad rubbed my shoulder while he smiled.

"OK, guys, talk to y'all later." Then the doctor disappeared out the door.

"Hey, babes, how are you feeling?" Jihad said as he sat on the edge of the bed.

I had more questions than I had answers. What the fuck happened to me? I started to search my mind, but I couldn't remember shit. I remember feeling ill and Jihad bathing me, but this shit was strange. And I drank the soup he brought me. He stopped by to visit, but everything else was a blur after that. Even if I fainted because of dehydration, why the hell is my memory gone?

"Babes, this is strange." I turned to look at him.

"Huh? What's strange, love?" He turned his attention away from his phone and looked at me.

"Me passing out like that, and the doctor can't tell me what's going on with me. I mean, I've been feeling ill, but not like I was fucking dying. Did I say anything before I passed out?"

"Nah, love, you ain't said anything. I was downstairs watching the game when I heard a thump. I rushed upstairs, only to find you passed out outside the room. I think you were trying to come downstairs or something. But I told you to stay in bed, and I would take care of you. You're so hardheaded, babes. You could've hurt yourself."

I didn't say anything. What could I say? I couldn't remember shit.

Jihad

"Hey, babes," Alyssa greeted me as I entered the house.

"Hey, you. It's smelling good in here. What are you cooking?" I glanced at her ass as I followed her into Brooklyn's and my kitchen.

Yes, my side bitch was in our kitchen trying to cook something. Not sure how it tasted, but the house smelled damn good. Alyssa has been staying here since Brooklyn fell out.

"Well, take a seat, love. I made you some lasagna."

"*That's* what I'm talking about."

"Shit, you could be getting this treatment every day if you had just offed that bitch. But nah, the bitch is still alive, and I will have to go home to that little dingy-ass apartment while you and that ho live it up in this big old house. How long do you think I'ma sit around and wait for you to continue playing house with this bitch?"

"Yo, chill out talking like that. I'm yo' man, right?"

She looked at me with an attitude. "Yeah, but what that got to do with anything?"

"I'm your man, so trust me. I got this. Sooner or later, that bitch will be out of the picture, and it will be just us."

I got up and walked over to her. "Come here. All I need you to have is a little faith in me. Just a little, okay, babes?"

I pulled her closer to me and started kissing her passionately while I cuffed her ass. She kissed me back. My dick head was throbbing, and I wasted no time pulling off her pants. I picked her up, put her on the counter, spread her legs, and buried my head between her thighs.

"Awee, shit, daddy, stoooop," she moaned out.

I paid her no mind. Instead, I sucked harder on her clit. She grabbed my shoulders and pierced her fingers deep into me.

"Arghhh, oh shit. Damn, babes, this pussy is dripping wet," I mumbled as I lifted my head, trying to get a little air.

"Awee, oh, woieee," she moaned, and she exploded in my mouth within seconds.

Now, my dick was as hard as a rock. I stood up, ready to enter her wet pussy.

"What are y'all doin'?" Briana yelled.

I turned to see her standing in the kitchen. My eyes popped open as I looked down at Alyssa lying on the counter, butt-ass naked. How long was she standing there, and how much did she see and hear?

"Briana, get out of here," I yelled.

She looked at me with tears in her eyes and ran off. I heard her slam her room door.

"I'm sorry, boo. I didn't hear her come in."

"It's not your fault. Get dressed. I'ma go talk to her."

My dick was still throbbing, but now was not the time for me to be worried about that. I needed to get to Briana before she called her crazy-ass mama, Keisha. God knows the last thing I need is that crazy bitch to find out some shit like this.

I turned the knob, but the door was locked. "Briana, open this door."

"Go away, Daddy. I don't want to talk," she yelled back.

"Baby, c'mon, let me in. I need to apologize to you, baby. Please," I pleaded.

I was getting angry. This little bitch was as stubborn as her damn mama. As a matter of fact, she needed to get her shit together 'cause when this new baby comes along, her little ass will be shoved to the corner. I did my part in raising her. Now, her damn mama needs to step up instead of chasing different dicks around town.

"Bri, please, open the door. Don't do this to Daddy," I lowered my voice, pretending to sob.

There was complete silence, then the door finally opened. Her eyes were red, and the look plastered on her face let me know that she was hurt.

I walked into the room and closed the door. "C'mere, baby. I swear I didn't know you were home. Honestly, I thought you were still gone with your friend down the street."

"If that's our cousin, why are you messing around in the kitchen with her?" She shot me a strange look.

"Baby, come here. Sit down. We need to talk."

I placed my arm around her shoulder and took her hand. "Listen, baby; there are some things that grown people do that might confuse you."

"Like you fooling around with Cousin Alyssa?" She popped her eyes wide open.

"Briana, listen. Alyssa is not my real cousin. I just said that so Brooklyn wouldn't suspect anything."

"So, basically, Alyssa is your side chick you're hiding from Brooklyn. Daddy, I think you have a lot of drama going on."

"Yes, something kinda like that. But you got to promise me you won't say anything about this, not even to your mother."

"Hmm . . . How much you gon' pay me to keep yo' little secret?"

I turned to look at her and realized she was dead-ass serious.

"My own daughter is going to blackmail me like this? Oh man, what do you want?"

"Hmm, this one is kind of hard. Let's see . . . How about the new iPhone X?"

"New iPhone? I just bought the one you got a few months ago."

"Yes, but I want the X."

"A'ight, man, I got you next week, and, Briana, don't you ever say a word to a soul, and I mean a soul," I warned.

"Don't worry, Daddy. I got you. My lips are sealed."

"A'ight, I got to go."

I hurried up and walked out of the room. I can't believe I allowed her little ass to manipulate me into getting her a damn phone. Her ass is just like her damn mama—a con artist. I shook my head in disgust as I walked down the stairs, where I spotted Alyssa sitting in the living room on her phone, texting. "Hey, everything okay with you?"

"Yeah, everything's good. I just needed to talk with Briana real quick."

"Oh, okay. Did you tell her she's having a brother or a sister?"

"Nah, this wasn't the right time to tell her no shit like that. She just saw her daddy's head buried between her supposed cousin's thighs. I think this was a little bit too much for her, don't you think?"

"Yeah, I guess so. I just don't want you to think you gon' be hiding my baby and shit. I might be a motherfucking secret, but my damn child ain't going to be one," she said in an aggressive tone.

"Alyssa, why don't you lose the fucking attitude? I fucking love you. You and my seed ain't no motherfucking secret. You need to chill out and lemme handle my shit. In no time, we're going to have this big-ass house and more money than we could ever imagine. But I need you to stay focused and stick to the script. When you're around Brooklyn, you need to be cautious 'cause that bitch ain't no slouch, and the last thing I need is for her ass to find out some shit."

"Yeah, I hear you." She continued pouting.

I swear to God, I wasn't feeling this bitch's attitude. Here I was, trying my fucking best to provide a better life for her and my seed, and the only fucking thing I was getting is a fucking attitude. See, this is why I be dogging bitches. The minute you try to put feelings into their asses, this is how they act.

"Listen, babes, it's been a long-ass day, and I got to be at the gym early in the morning. I'ma take a shower. You can join me or continue giving me an attitude."

I got up off the couch and walked away. I was fucking frustrated. I needed to figure out what the fuck my next step was going to be.

The water was beating down on my body. It helped loosen my tense muscles. My mind was racing. So much shit was going on at the same time. Dealing with issues at the gym was also wearing me down. I was leaning toward letting the gym go and being done with my brother and his fucked-up ways.

Suddenly, I felt someone tap me. I opened my eyes, only to see Alyssa butt-ass naked standing in front of me. She stepped into the shower without speaking, and we started kissing aggressively. First, I grabbed her up against the shower wall and turned her around. Then wasting no time, I slid into her ass with force.

"Aargh, awee," she moaned out in ecstasy.

My head was in a fucked-up place, and I was punishing this pussy. I grabbed her hips and pulled her closer to my dick. I thrust in and out of her slippery, young pussy. Her moans and groans only excited me. I slipped in and out until my veins got larger, and within seconds, I exploded into her pregnant pussy.

Alyssa

"Bitch, I ain't seen your ass in how motherfucking long?" Trina asked.

"Girl, that's because my ass is so caught up with this nigga and his drama. Trust me. My ass is getting tired of him and his foolery already. Girl, and then his spoiled-ass daughter caught us in the kitchen. That nigga was down on his knees eating my pussy when her ass stood in the hallway."

"Bitch, you lying. What did she say when she saw y'all?" Trina said, sounding excited.

"Girl, I was too busy trying to get a nut. I didn't move a muscle when that little bitch stormed off. Shit, I was kind of upset that she interrupted us. I was about to get fucked good."

"OMG! Bitch, you are scandaloussss," she busted out laughing.

"No, ho, I'm not. That nigga should've made sure his brat wasn't around before he decided to turn me into the main course."

"Yeah, I hear that. So, how is the pregnancy coming along? I am so ready to find out if it's a boy or girl, so I can start boosting some fly-ass clothes."

"Bishhh, I'm ready too. I'm only four months—five long-ass months to go. I'm about sick of this shit already. I swear, sometimes, I'm tempted to have an abortion. What's worse is I don't know whose baby it is."

"Bitch, you still ain't figured out which one of them niggas is yo' baby daddy? Lawd, I would say give the little motherfucker to both them niggas . . . but there's one problem. One nigga has dark skin, and the next nigga yellow as hell. Oh boy, this is going to be a hard one."

"Bitch, I ain't tripping. I told Jihad he's the damn daddy, and *that* is who the daddy is. If my baby comes out a different color, he just gon' have to deal with it 'cause I got all kinds of color people in my family. By then, my ass should be straight, though. I'm planning to stack all my money, so if and when some shit pops off, me and my baby will be straight."

"Bitch, you talking like you don't love Jihad no more."

"I fucks with Jihad hard. I mean, I used to be in love with the nigga, but after that nigga put his hands on me, I stopped loving his ass. Then to top that off, his ass married."

"Yeah, that was foul as fuck how he put his hands on you like that. I wanted to off that nigga for you. I thought you would leave him alone, but you decided to stay. I don't like that shit, but you my bitch, so I respect your decision."

"Yeah, well, fuck him. I thought about leaving his ass alone right then and there, but I'm not no stupid bitch. This nigga about to be paid, and I ain't gon' let another bitch step in the picture and snatch up what is rightfully mines. Bitch, I might not be the smartest bitch out there, but I ain't no damn fool. That nigga owes me one way or the other. Anyway, bitch, it's late, and Mr. Lewis is waiting for me in bed."

"Oh shit, let me hang up. Hit me up tomorrow."

"A'ight, bitch."

I hung up and opened the door that led into the house. This was my first time seeing such a big-ass sunroom. I rubbed my hand on the wall as I made my way up the stairs. I stopped when I got to the top of the stairs and looked down, smiling. One day, this will all be mine.

Patience, Alyssa. I then walked to the room. He was asleep, snoring and all. I went into the drawer where this bitch had her nightgowns. I took out a few until I spotted the perfect one. I changed my clothes into one of the sexy Victoria's Secret nightgowns. I glanced at myself in the mirror. My stomach was poking out to the point where I could no longer hide it. I rubbed my hand across my body. I bet you I look better in this nightgown than that old-ass bitch . . . Hm . . . shit. I could probably keep this one since I already have it on. I smiled at myself in the mirror, then got in bed. I was tired and feeling nauseated.

"Babes, wake up," Jihad yelled.

I opened my eyes and looked at him like he had lost his fucking mind. "What's up?" I asked in a groggy voice.

"I got to open up the gym."

"Okay . . ."

"You need to get up. Brooklyn comes from the hospital today. Make sure you get everything out of here. I told you we need to be careful."

I sat up in bed with an attitude. So, this nigga woke me up to tell me his bitch was coming home? This some bullshit, I thought. But now wasn't the time to snap on this nigga, so I pulled myself together and got out of bed. In no time, I was dressed.

"Listen, I'm going to be at the gym the whole day. They should be releasing Brooklyn today at midday. Can you pick her up and bring her here to the house?"

"Really? So now you want me to taxi your bitch around? Damn, nigga. I say yes to one thing, and now you think I'm the motherfucking errand girl. Anything else you want me to do for your bitch?"

"Man, come on. I got to go."

I walked behind him with an attitude, watched as he got into his car, and pulled off. Then I got into my car and sat there for a minute. This nigga and his stinking-ass attitude were getting on my nerves. But that's all right. I got something for that ass. I lit a cigarette before pulling off.

It's been days since I've been to my apartment, and I dragged myself to walk up the stairs. This was a fucking dungeon compared to that big-ass house that I just left. I sighed as I walked to my door and opened it. I threw my purse on the couch and headed to my bedroom.

I was still tired, and I was nauseated as hell. I thought the stupid-ass doctor told me this would go away. His ass lied 'cause it ain't getting no better. I'm still vomiting and can barely keep anything down. At first, this shit was all fun and games, but right now, it was becoming a fucking burden to me. I crawled into my bed, pulled the pillow over my head, and allowed the tears to flow. I wasn't crying 'cause I was hurt. I was only shedding tears 'cause it wasn't fair how that bitch was living the good life, and here I was, cooped up in this dingy-ass apartment.

Later, I heard my phone ringing, but I ignored it. Instead, I buried my head back under the pillow, but the phone continued ringing.

"Hello," I yelled into the receiver without looking at the caller ID.

"Babes, where you at? Did you forget to pick up Brooklyn?"

Damn, I forgot this nigga asked me to pick up his bitch. I opened my eyes and glanced at the time. Shit, it was 12:30.

"I was sleeping."

"Sleeping? I really need you. I have some clients here, and I can't leave right now. Brooklyn has been blowing me up. I told her you were on the way to pick her up."

"A'ight, man, I'm 'bout to get up and go pick up your wifeee," I said sarcastically.

"Thanks, babes. I love you."

I didn't respond to him. Instead, I hung up and lay there for a few minutes before I got up. I don't give a fuck how long that ho was waiting. It's not going to kill her to wait some more.

After showering, I got dressed and left. My stomach was killing me, so I stopped by Wendy's to grab me a four-for-four junior cheeseburger deluxe meal. I knew I would bring it back up, but I was hungry and needed something on my stomach.

I pulled into the hospital parking lot and sat there for a few minutes, trying to get my thoughts together. Whenever I get around this bitch, I have to be someone else. The fucking cousin instead of the bitch that is fucking her husband.

Then I grabbed my purse and exited the car. I made my way to the entrance and walked into the waiting room, and there this bitch sat, waiting.

"Hey."

"Hello, Alyssa. You're kind of late," this ungrateful-ass bitch said with a slight attitude.

"I'm sorry, but I wasn't feeling too good. I tried to make it on time."

"That's fine. I'm just eager to get home. I hate hospitals," she said before walking off.

I followed closely behind that bitch, wondering who the fuck she thought I was. "I'm parked over there." I pointed to my car.

After we got in, I pulled off. "So, how are you feeling?" I inquired.

"I'm feeling way better than I felt a few days ago. Being in the hospital did me some good."

"Wow, that's great. Did the doctors find out what was wrong?"

"No, that's the crazy part. My tests all came back normal. I blame it on overworking and not getting enough rest."

"Well, boss lady, Jihad said that the doctor said you needed rest. That means I will be helping you out more at the office."

"Awee, you're such a sweet girl. You do more than enough already. I'm feeling much better, so I should be able to jump back into things soon."

Did this ho just say I was a sweet girl? I wanted to respond to her, but I held my composure. It wasn't easy, but seeing dollar signs was a big motivator. I was ready to drop her ass off, though.

I pulled up at the house, and she got out. "You're coming inside?" she asked.

"No, I'm not feeling good, so I'm about to head home and lie down. I spoke to your husband earlier, and he should be home soon."

"Okay, Alyssa, I appreciate you coming to get me. I'll let you know if we're working tomorrow."

"Okay, boss lady," I said with a bright-ass smile.

I didn't wait for her to go in before I pulled off. I was happy to get away from that old phony-ass bitch.

Then my phone started ringing. I glanced at the caller ID. It was Jihad.

"Hello."

"Hey, babes. I want you to know I do appreciate you. I know lately, all we seem to do is argue. But I love and need you in my life. I can't live without you, babes."

"Jihad, I don't know if I want to be with you anymore. When I met you, it was only supposed to be us—then boom, out of the blue, you have a fucking wife and child. I don't like to be around that bitch. It's not fair to me that

I have to hide that I'm pregnant by you. This is not what you promised me," I cried.

"Baby, c'mon, listen to me. I love you, and you don't have to hide the baby much longer. I need to keep it quiet until everything is finished with this bitch. I don't have much money now. I can say fuck everything and walk away now, but we won't have shit. We're having a baby, and we need money. Now is not the time to fold."

I sat there listening to this nigga, and part of me was telling me he was talking shit, but the other part said he was making sense. I only had a few thousand that I saved up since I started fucking with him. But with a baby, how long would that last? Leaving Jihad right now was definitely not a good move.

We talked for a while, with him professing his love for me, but I was getting sleepy listening to all this old, mushy shit this nigga was talking about.

"Aye, babes, I don't mean to cut you off, but I'm tired and need to lie down." I yawned a few times to show him I wasn't joking around.

"All right, babes, get you some rest. I'll slide through later."

"OK, boo. Love you."

I made sure I hung up the phone. I then dialed Jahmiel. I wasn't fucking tired. I was just tired of hearing Jihad whining. I lay on my back, waiting for him to answer the damn phone.

"Yo."

"Is that the way you answer the phone?"

"Hey, love, how are you doing?" His sexy voice echoed through the phone.

"Hey, you, I ain't heard from you in a minute. Damn, you just forgot about a bitch like that?"

"Nah, ma, but last time, shit got sticky with yo' punk-ass nigga, so I was giving you space. I figured I'd give you some time, and you'll reach out when you were ready for me to come give you this dick."

"Hmmm, is that so? What are you doing 'cause I'm wet, and my pussy throbbing." I got straight to the point.

"Damn, ma, *that's* what I'm talking about. Aye, give me 'bout an hour. I'll be over there to tear up that pussy for you."

"All right, babes." I smiled as I hung up.

Whew, the last time I invited him over here, Jihad showed up, but that didn't deter me from calling him again. Shit, Jihad better sit his old ass down. I mean, it's *my* pussy. I do what the fuck I want to do with it.

My body felt sore like someone was beating my ass with a bat. I made myself a cup of noodles, and then set my bathwater. I cut on the slow music, got into the tub, lay my head back, and closed my eyes. I needed this moment, even if it wasn't for long. I caught myself about to doze off, so I started washing myself. This water was so relaxing. I swear I didn't want to get out.

I looked at my stomach in the mirror as I oiled down my body. It was poking out, which wasn't too attractive to me anymore. I was ready for this to be over and done with. Shit, lately, I've thought maybe I should just have this baby and give it to the daddy. I didn't plan on being tied down with no child and not for no married man.

I slipped on some sexy lingerie without panties. I was horny and ready to get fucked. Then I heard the door banging. I hoped this was Jahmiel and *not* Jihad. I walked toward the door, and my nerves were a little bit on edge. Looking through the peephole, I sighed in relief when I realized it was not Jihad. I opened the door and dragged Jahmiel inside before shutting it.

"Damn, you a'ight? You act like you hiding from the damn police."

"Shit, that nigga that you met stalking my ass."

"Oh, word? You need me to get at the nigga?"

"Nah, babes, I got it under control."

"Hold up. What the fuck? You pregnant?"

"Oh yeah, I didn't want to bother you with it."

"Bother me? What you mean? It's my seed?" He looked at me with a stupid-ass look plastered across his face.

"Yes, it's your baby. You the only one I fucked without a condom."

"What the fuck you mean? You was fucking that pussy nigga too. How the fuck you just gon' throw it on me?"

"You need to calm the fuck down. First, I ain't call and bother you for shit. The only reason why we even having this conversation right now is because I called you over here. Let's get this fucking straight . . . I don't need shit from you for this baby. I only want the dick, and if that's too much to ask, you can get the fuck on, so I can get the next nigga over here to fuck me." This nigga done pissed me the fuck off. As a matter of fact, he was tripping. Shit, Jihad was already claiming my damn child. I didn't need him for shit.

"Yo, calm down. I'm just shocked. I ain't seen yo' ass in a while. Then you call me out of the blue, and I show up and see this. If it's my seed, I got no problem taking care of the kid. I just want to be sure. It ain't nothing for us to beef about, and you can get this dick anytime."

"Right, that's all I'm worried about."

I walked over to him, pushing him back on the couch. I then started unbuckling his belt. In seconds, I got his dick out of his boxers, knelt in front of him, and started licking his manhood like it was my favorite ice cream cone.

"Shit, oh shit," he said as he squirmed around in his seat. I didn't ease up any. I continued deep throating his dick until it hit the back of my throat, and I gagged. That didn't slow me down any. I started sucking his dick harder and faster. He grabbed my head and pulled it down in his lap. I wanted this nigga off my neck, so I sucked harder.

"Oh shit. Fuck, damn, maaaan," he yelled out.

I wish this nigga would shut the fuck up. I didn't want nobody to know he was up in here. After loud moans, he finally exploded. I set my mouth in a position to catch every drop. I used my tongue to lick up every one of them, then started massaging his balls. His dick got hard again. I spread my legs and slowly slid down on his dick. Then placing my legs on the couch and my arms on his shoulders, I started riding his dick.

"Take this dick, love." He slapped my ass.

I started bouncing this pregnant pussy on his dick while I tightened my pussy muscles. His dick was touching the bottom of my stomach as he slid in and out of this wet, pregnant pussy. It hugged his dick as I tightened my muscles, grabbed him, and exploded all over his dick. Then I sat there, holding him for a few seconds.

I remember the last time he was here and how Jihad popped up. It was getting late, and Jihad did say he was coming through. That was my cue to jump up. I headed to the bathroom, cum dripping down my legs as I walked. I grabbed a washcloth, wiped my pussy, and cleaned off my leg.

When I walked back to the living room, that nigga was still sitting there with his limp dick.

"Yo, you gon' get dressed?"

"Damn, shorty, it's like that? You throwin' me out?" He laughed.

"Nah, boo, it ain't like that, but you fucked me so good. I swear I'm tired as hell. You know, being pregnant drains me."

"Oh, OK. Lemme go piss, and then I'm out."

He got up and headed to the bathroom. I sat on the couch and grabbed my cell phone. Whew, I'm glad I didn't have no missed call from Jihad this time. Hopefully, his ass didn't leave the gym yet.

Finally, Jahmiel came out of the bathroom. "A'ight, shorty, I'm about to hit the streets. Yo, that pregnant pussy banging too. I'ma need some more real quick. Hit me up if you need anything."

"Okay, boo."

I nervously opened the door and was happy when he walked off. Then I quickly locked the door. Shit, Jihad had me all nervous and shit. OK, I guess I'm in the clear. I was tired as shit. That nigga had some good-ass dick. Jihad's dick was good, but not this damn good. This nigga got that "I can't leave that dick alone" shit.

I walked into my room and lay across the bed, but I decided to get on Facebook to see what was going on today. I swear I was sleepy as hell, so I decided to take a quick nap before Jihad popped up on me.

I must've been in a deep sleep 'cause it took awhle before I heard the door banging. I jumped up and took a few seconds to get myself together before grabbing my phone. I realized I had like ten missed calls from Jihad. I knew then it was his crazy ass at the door.

I opened the door, and he stormed in, looking all suspicious and shit. "Yo, what you been doing? I told yo' ass I was coming over," he said as he walked into the living room.

"Didn't I tell you I was tired? In case you're not aware, I'm pregnant, and my body is tired."

"Yeah, I know, but if I tell you I'm coming, I expect you to listen out for the door or the phone."

"I'm sorry, bae, but I was exhausted."

"Come here. I'm sorry. I just get real jealous when I can't reach you. I love you, babes. I know you a sexy bitch, and niggas be trying to get at you."

"Jihad, you know you the only nigga I want. Plus, what the fuck I look like fucking another nigga while I'm carrying your baby?" I said with an attitude. I feared he suspected some shit, so I had to be the first one to catch an attitude, just in case.

"Baby, calm down. I wasn't saying you fuckin' nobody. I just let my jealousy get in the way sometimes. Come here, babes." He pulled me onto the couch with him.

"Damn, babes, you sexy as fuck. I think the baby gave you bigger breasts and ass. Shit, just the way I love it." He started rubbing on me.

"Babes, damn, you ain't got no drawers on?"

Oh shit. I was supposed to put on some underwear after I fucked Jahmiel. Fuck. Before I could think, this nigga already had my legs parted, and his head buried deep in me. Oh, holy shit! I didn't take a shower after Jahmiel busted in me. All I did was wipe off.

"Babes, why your pussy smell like sex?" He lifted his head and asked me.

"Huh?" I tried to buy some time to gather my thoughts.

"Why yo' pussy smell like sex?"

"Baby, you trippin'. Earlier, I was feeling horny, and I fucked myself with my dildo. I was gon' take a shower, but I fell asleep."

"Oh, OK. You good. Just want to make sure it ain't no other nigga playing in my pussy."

"Bae, you really trippin' now."

He went back down and sucked the life out of my pussy with my legs wrapped around his neck. I lay on my back just thinking, is it sex he smelled, or was it the next nigga's cum? Either way, it was too late now 'cause he was making sweet love to my pussy.

After I exploded in his mouth, he turned me to the side on the sofa and entered me. I groaned as he slid up in me. My pussy was still sore from that dick beating I got earlier. The harder he fucked me, the louder I screamed. Jihad thought I was screaming from him beating up my pussy, but I was screaming 'cause my shit was sore from what the other nigga did earlier.

After he busted, we took a shower and ordered Chinese food. I was exhausted and sore, so I ate, and we ended up lying there for a little while. I was almost dozing off when I felt Jihad get off the bed.

"Where you going, bae?"

"It's getting late."

"So?" I looked at him.

"You know Brooklyn just got home from the hospital today, and she's going to wonder where the hell I am."

"You know what, Jihad? I'm sick of hearing about this bitch. Brooklyn this, Brooklyn that . . . Well, I wish Brooklyn would've died so I can live fucking freely with you," I yelled out with frustration in my voice.

"Calm down, baby. You don't want to upset my baby. I wish the bitch would've died too, but she's alive and kicking. I still have to play my role as her husband until I get my hands on all this money. Baby, please, be patient." He reached over and rubbed my hand.

"Jihad, I'm telling you, I am getting sick of this. Get your shit together—fast," I warned.

"C'mere, I got you, babes. I promise it won't be too long. Get some rest. We'll talk tomorrow."

"I need some money to pay some bills tomorrow."

"How much money you need?"

"Around $1,500."

"A'ight. I'll Cash App it to you by morning."

"Okay . . ."

"Sweet dreams, babes. I love y'all." He bent down and kissed my stomach.

I walked him to the door. He kissed me and hugged me tightly before leaving. I locked the door behind him, poured a glass of milk, turned off the lights, and headed to bed. I was mentally and physically exhausted. I cut on the TV in my bedroom. Lately, I've been binge watching *90 Day Fiancé*. Those foreigners be getting these stupid Americans to marry them and give them green cards. Soon as they get it, they be leaving their asses. That shit is actually hilarious because people are so damn stupid. I drank my milk and lay down. It's been a very long day.

Chapter Twenty

Brooklyn

This shit makes no damn sense. I've been home from the hospital for a good eight hours, and my so-called husband still hadn't made his way back here. What is *wrong* with this picture? I dialed his number, but it went straight to voicemail. I laid the phone down, trying to figure out what the fuck was going on. I wasn't feeling one hundred, but better than a few days ago. I still tried my best to remember what happened the day I fell out, but whenever I got to that time, I drew a blank.

I made a cup of tea and ate some crackers. I still didn't have any appetite. Hopefully, tomorrow, I'll feel much better. I was still debating if I was going to work. I needed to decide soon because I needed to call Alyssa so that she could come in. I looked at the time, and it was a little past eleven. I was about to call her when I heard the room door push open. I jumped around to see it was Jihad. I put down the phone as I got ready to confront this nigga.

"Hey, babes," he said as he walked over to me.

"Hey, babe, I've been home from the hospital, and you walk in here this time of night talking about 'hey, babes'? Where the fuck you been, Jihad?"

"Babes, I'm so sorry. I should've called you. I swear I ain't been myself since you got sick. I was scared God was gon' take you from me. When I found you on the floor, it shook me the hell up."

"What the fuck does that have to do with you coming home today?" I asked him.

"I went to the bar after I left the gym. I just needed to clear my mind. I'm sorry, babes."

I wasn't buying that story he was trying to sell me. I wasn't sure what was going on with Jihad, but I was a psych major and read people. Jihad was undeniably acting nervous as hell.

"Jihad, come here." I motioned for him to come to me.

"What's up, babes?" He looked confused.

"Come around here and pull down your pants."

He looked at me with a shocked look. "Pull down my pants?"

"Jihad, you heard me the first time. Pull down your pants so I can smell your dick."

"Brooklyn, you tripping. I thought you were over doing this dumb-ass shit. I ain't been doing a gotdamn thing. This is fucking childish. I thought you were sick." He appeared to be upset.

"Fuck what you're talking about. Come let me smell your dick."

"Brooklyn, here you go, and when you see I wasn't out doing shit, I want you to apologize."

He walked over to my side of the bed, pulled down his pants, and dropped his underpants.

"Here you go, Brooklyn. I been at the gym all damn day until I went for a few drinks."

I took his dick into my hand and smelled it . . . Irish Spring soap was reeking through his pores. I looked at him and shook my head. This nigga claimed he was at the gym all day, where I know damn well he was working, so he was sweating. So how the fuck would he be smelling like Irish Spring? Furthermore, that is one soap I never bought. I hate that pungent smell.

"See, you don't know what you talkin' 'bout. You need to apologize for this shit. We're married, for God's sake. You need to stop acting like you're one of these careless-ass bitches out here."

I looked at this nigga like he was fucking retarded. I can't prove it, but this nigga was up to no good. I don't know what it is, but I felt it in my guts.

He pulled up his pants and looked at me with an attitude. "You know, you will realize one day that I'm not like these other niggas out here. I fucking love you, and I ain't fucking around on you. I wish you would open your eyes and see for yourself. *You're* the problem, *not* me. You're insecure." He stormed out of the room, cussing under his breath.

I was tired and exhausted, so I pulled the cover on top of me, whispered a prayer to God, and closed my eyes.

It's been a week since I've been out of the hospital, and I feel better than I did before. I was back at work, and when I tell you my workload was overwhelming . . . I was happy that Alyssa was here with me because it wouldn't be possible for me to get all this work done otherwise. I was initially skeptical when Jihad told me he had a cousin looking for a job. But she positively is a blessing to me, especially now. I planned on keeping her around for a long time.

My phone started ringing. I looked at it and saw it was my Jas. I gladly answered the call.

"Hey, you."

"Bitch, please, don't,' hey, you,' me. I've been calling yo' ass for a few days now, and I haven't even got a callback or a text. Bitch, I was seconds away from putting a damn APB out on yo' ass," she said, sounding agitated.

"Girl, I ain't see no missed calls or texts from you, but before you go off on me, my ass was in the hospital—"

Before I could finish my sentence, she cut me off. "Hospital? What the fuck you talkin' about? You a'ight?"

"Yes, I wasn't feeling good for a few days. I thought it was the flu I was catching. Then I fell out."

"Fell out? You mean passed out? And I'm your got-damn best friend, so why I'm just now hearing about this? Did the doctor find out what's wrong with you?" She bombarded me with a bunch of questions.

"All my tests came back regular. The doctor thought I was just exhausted and dehydrated. Girl, I don't know what the fuck happened. Jihad said he heard a thump, and when he came upstairs, I was passed out."

"Really? Hmmm . . . This shit doesn't sound too right to me. I'm in court all day, but my ass will be over tonight. Bitch, I can't lose you," she said in a serious tone.

"Girl, that shit scared me for real, but I'm here at work, so let me know when you on the way. I'll probably order us some Chinese or something for dinner."

"Sounds like a plan, and please, call me if you need me. You know I'll drop everything and rush my ass over there."

"Okay, babes."

Lord, that damn Jasmine was not feeling this. I should've called her. Shit, I even forgot to call my mama and the rest of my family. It wasn't intentional, but it is strange to me. I strolled through my phone. I didn't see any missed calls or texts from Jas. But she just said she was calling and texting . . . Wait, Jihad had my phone while I was in the hospital. Did he delete my calls and texts, and if so, why would he do that? I will damn sure ask his ass later. He had no damn business to be all up in my shit. I shook my head in disgust.

Unexpectedly, I heard a knock on the door. "Come in," I yelled.

"Mrs. Lewis, I have three afternoon appointments set for you. Here are the files." Alyssa handed the folders to me.

"Thanks, Alyssa."

"You're welcome."

"Alyssa, I know this is not business, but I can't help but notice that you are pregnant."

"Oh yes, ma'am. I'm almost four months."

"I hope I'm not overstepping my boundaries. But Jihad did tell me that you were going through a difficult time. Is the father involved?"

She hung in her head, making me regret that I asked that. I could tell this was very painful for her.

"I'm sorry. I didn't mean to intrude."

"No, boss lady, you're not intruding at all. This is very painful for me. The minute I told him I was pregnant, he cussed me out and told me never to contact him again. I tried getting in touch with him a few times after that, but he ignored my calls, and now, he's blocked me from his phone," she cried.

I picked up some napkins on my desk and handed them to her. "Here you go. Wipe your tears."

"Thank you, boss. I'm so sorry. I didn't mean to burden you with my problem. I just been going through so much lately. I appreciate you so much for giving me this opportunity. I'm not going to let you down or my cousin."

"I'm glad I could help you, and seeing how hard you work, you have a permanent spot here if you decide to return after you have the baby. Listen, you're Jihad's cousin, which means you're family. I'll help you in whatever way I can. Now, girl, dry them damn tears and hold up your head. You're a beautiful girl, and you're not lazy. Trust me. It will all work out. Babies are a blessing . . ." My voice trailed off.

"Thank you so much. I told Jihad he was a lucky man because I could tell you're a great woman. I'm blessed that our paths crossed. Thank you so much, Mrs. Lewis."

"Listen, you can call me Brooklyn when we are not in a professional setting or around clients. You're also welcome, so go ahead and dry them tears. We got work to do."

"Yes, ma'am. I'm on it," she smiled.

"That's right. That's what I'm used to seeing, you smiling and happy. Don't give no nigga the power to dim your light. Now, go on so I can knock out some work."

She smiled and walked out. It's a shame how fucked-up these niggas are nowadays. It's all good when they're fucking you and not pulling out, but the minute you knocked up, they go MIA. I swear these niggas are fucking ridiculous.

"Mrs. Lewis, your first afternoon appointment is here."

"Okay, thank you, Alyssa."

I cleared my mind, straightened my desk, then got up and walked out to meet my client.

Shit, this was a long-ass day, I thought as I kicked off my Loui heels. I quickly slid out of the pencil skirt suit I wore. I was happy to be home. I jumped in the bathroom and took a quick, hot shower. Then I got dressed in a comfortable pair of pajama shorts and a top, walked into the kitchen, and stood there staring at this disgusting-ass shit. My expensive-ass kitchen was looking like a little hood kitchen. The sink was filled all the way up to the top, garbage was overflowing, and shit was all over my kitchen table. Dirty pots sat on top of my stove. I was pissed the fuck off. I've been sick, and *this* is how this nigga had my place looking? Where is that little grown-ass daughter of his? I stormed off, heading up the stairs.

I walked over to Briana's door and knocked a few times, but there was no response. I heard music blasting through the door, so I pushed it open. There she was, lying on the bed with her phone in her hand.

"Hang up the phone."

"No, I'm not, and what are you doing in my room?"

"Hang up the gotdamn phone." I lunged toward her.

"Back up, lady. You got issues. Where's my daddy?"

"Why is my kitchen looking like that? Scratch that. Why is your *room* looking like this? You have my shit looking like a fucking pigpen. You need to bring yo' ass downstairs and clean up my kitchen, then get up here and clean your damn room. I don't know what kind of filth you're used to living in, but this is *my* shit, and you damn sure ain't gon' live like that in *my* house."

"I need to call my daddy 'cause you trippin'. It's your kitchen, so *you* clean it up."

I turned around and looked at this little bitch. Who the fuck does she think she's talking to?

"Who the hell are you talking to? You little, ungrateful-ass girl. I took you in, gave you a great home, fed yo' ass on the daily, and all you do is run around here being disrespectful. I don't see yo' no-good mama or your daddy doing shit. How the fuck you think you living this good? *Me,* little girl. *I* make this happen. Now, get the fuck up and go clean up this shit."

I didn't wait for an answer. Instead, I walked over to the stereo and unplugged that shit. Then I made my way to the television and unplugged that shit as well, grabbed it, and made my way out of the room. Then I returned for the stereo. By then, her ass was on the phone with someone. I'm hoping it was her trifling-ass mama, so I can also address that bitch. I was sick of her little ass and wouldn't tolerate any more of this shit.

"You doing all this, and my daddy *still* don't want you. I hate you and can't wait until Daddy sees you for the wicked bitch you really are."

"I'm not going to sit here and argue with a little ill-mannered-ass child that still don't know how to wipe her pussy properly. You got an hour to clean up the kitchen and your room. If you don't do it, you need to contact one of your parents, or both, to come get yo' ass. Two grown bitches can't live under the same roof, and since this *my* shit, *you* need to find somewhere to go."

That was it. I had nothing else to say to her grown ass. I already see my life slipping away behind her ass. Yes, I know I'm grown, but these little bitches be coming out the mouth fly as hell. I wish I could punch her in her mouth, so she could know that I'm a grown-ass bitch, and this is *not* what she wants. I slammed the door behind me and called her father.

"Hey, love. I was just thinking about you."

"Hey, you need to come get yo' damn child out of my house before I catch a case on her ass."

"Huh? Calm down, baby. What's going on?"

"I'm calm, but you need to bring yo' ass home to get your child."

I didn't wait to hear shit he was saying. I hung up. I was angry as hell. It wasn't healthy for me to feel this much anger. I sat on the edge of my bed, trying to calm my nerves. Instantly, I got a tension headache. I got up, took my pill bottle off the dresser, and took two pills. I had a water bottle on my nightstand, so I swallowed them. I was so angry that I was shaking. Then I lay on the bed, trying my best to bring down my anxiety.

I was so caught up in this shit with this little girl that I forgot to call Jasmine, so I called her number and waited.

"Hey, girl, I forgot to call you."

"I figured you were busy, but I just got in. I'll be over there in an hour."

"Okay, boo."

I thought about making an excuse not to see her, but I needed to see my friend. She was the one closest to me and would always tell me the truth, regardless of whether I wanted to hear it.

Jasmine was at the door, so I walked downstairs. I opened the door to let her in.

"Hey, girl." She rushed in, hugging me like she ain't seen my ass in years.

"Hey, boo. Come on. Let's go in the sunroom."

"So, tell me how you really feeling?" she said as she took a seat across from me.

"Giiiirl, I still don't know, and you know what's crazy? I can't remember shit about me falling out."

"What you mean, you can't remember anything?" She looked at me strangely.

"I remember me being in bed. I wasn't feeling too good for a few days. But that day was worse. I could barely walk. Jihad had to bathe me."

"I ain't no doctor, but this shit don't sound right. So out of the blue, you just started feeling sick? Now, your memory gone? And nothing shows up in your tests?"

"Girl, I'm just as puzzled as you."

"What does Jihad think is wrong with you?"

"Girl, he's just as lost as us. He was at the hospital every day with me."

"Was he, and he didn't think he should pick up the phone and call me?"

"Girl, he was scared. He found me on the ground and went into panic mode."

"Hmm, I hear you. Listen, we need to get you to a specialist or something. This shit here don't sound right to me. Sounds like one of those ID channel stories."

"Bitch, here you go with yo' old investigating ass."

"You joking and shit, but I'm serious. I need you to get a second opinion. How do you feel now?"

"I'm feeling like a brand-new person. That's why I think it was just my body telling me I need to chill out."

"Let's hope so . . . Anyway, I know you said you didn't have him sign the prenup, but do you have a will?"

"A will? Damn, bitch, I said I was sick, not dying."

"I know what you said, but because your hardheaded ass didn't get that nigga to sign a prenup, I need to make sure you have a will. You not too young to have a will. Trust me, I see people our age die and don't have a living will. Don't you forget, you have an elderly mother that you're responsible for. Would you like something to happen and Jihad gets everything, leaving your mama out in the cold? Baby, I know you're still dick drunk, but I'ma need you to think with your head and not your pussy. This nigga lied about how much money he had. Then you found out he another broke nigga. What else are you waiting to find out? You're my best friend/sister, so I'ma make sure you handling your business."

"Brooklyn, what the hell happened between you and Briana?" Jihad busted through the door, yelling.

"You see Jas right here. Can you lower your damn voice?" I said to this nigga.

"Man, I don't give a fuck. I come home to find my daughter in tears and her mama calling my damn phone over twenty times 'cause you called her a bitch and tried to hit her. What the fuck is going on, Brooklyn?" That nigga got in my face.

I stood up. "Don't you dare come in here yelling at me in front of my company like I'm your child. Matter of fact, why the hell don't you get her ass out of my damn house?"

"What, bitch? Ha-ha, so you showing off in front of company?"

"*Bitch?* Nigga, *you* is the bitch. I don't give a fuck about y'all relationship, but one thing you won't do is disrespect her in front of me." Jasmine stood up and jumped in Jihad's face.

"Bitch, stay the fuck out of our business. Matter of fact, you need to get the fuck out of my house," he yelled at Jas.

"*Your* house? Nigga, where the fuck were you at when Brooklyn bought this? You know the truth, Jihad? I never liked yo' ass. Matter of fact, I told my friend she shouldn't marry your broke ass. My friend might be in love with your ass, but I see you for the piece of shit you are. You broke, you a fucking liar, and don't worry. I'm not going to stop until I find out what you're really up to. Shit, instead of talking crazy to her, you should be kissing her feet 'cause she picked up your ass and put you up in a mansion."

"Oh, *this* is what you and this bitch been talking about?" he turned to me and asked.

"Get the fuck out of my face, Jihad."

"Oh, so you sidin' with this bitch?"

"I don't mind being called a bitch 'cause I got a pussy, but what is *your* excuse for your bitchassness? Brooklyn should be the man, and you should be one spread-eagle and let her fuck you."

"Jas, oh my God. Stooooop."

"You right. You know what? I'm sorry, friend. I forgot you still love this bum-ass nigga. I'm gone. Call me when you finish with his ass."

"Really, Brooklyn? You gon' stand there and let this ho carry me like that?" This nigga looked shocked.

"Get the hell out of my face, nigga."

I didn't wait for a response. I walked off and opened the door, but Jas's car was gone. This shit was fucking ridiculous. I ran up the stairs to my room. This nigga lost his gotdamn mind and shit. I also wished Jas would've shut the fuck up. Now, both of them in their fucking feelings. *Fuck my life,* I thought.

Twenty minutes later, Jihad walked into the room. "Yo, when you got with me, you knew I had a daughter. We talked about this before, and you said it was cool for her to come live with us. Am I correct or not?"

"I said it was okay for your child to come live with us. The thing is, you didn't tell me her ass was grown. So first, she brought her man into my house to screw him, and now, her ass disrespecting me. I don't know how she talks to you and her mama, but I'm *not* her parent, and I'm not going to tolerate her little ass disrespecting me like that."

"She's a child, for God's sake, Brooklyn. You should know how to deal with children since that's your business."

"Don't fucking include my job. I get *paid* for that shit. This right here is fucking charity. So again, you need to call her fucking mother, so she can come get her disrespectful-ass child."

"This is *my* daughter we're talking about. She is *our* responsibility," he yelled.

"Incorrect, Jihad. That is *your* fucking child. She is *your* responsibility," I lashed out.

"Well, if my daughter has to go, I'll leave too. I thought we were going to work on this marriage, but I guess not." He looked at me and shook his head.

"Jihad, I don't care what you do. All this fucking talking is not going to change my mind. So, if you're leaving with her, please do so."

I was done talking to this nigga. I wasn't changing my mind. That little bitch had to go, and I wasn't changing my mind, even if it meant me losing my husband behind it. He stomped out of the room, calling me every name but the name of God. I was tired and didn't feel like going toe-to-toe with this nigga. I decide to call Jas. I know her ass was mad.

"Hello," she answered with an attitude.

"Damn, bitch, I'm only calling you to check on you."

"I'm good, but you need to go check on that fuck nigga that your loyalty is with—"

The phone went dead. "Hello, hello . . ."

The line was dead. I can't believe this was my best friend/sister carrying me like this. What the fuck did I do to her? Fuck this. I need some kind of explanation. I dialed her number about four times, and her voicemail came on each time. Either she blocked me or turned her phone off. Either way, her ass was out of pocket. Shit, to be real, Jihad was talking to me, and she jumped her ass into it. I didn't ask her to defend me. I'm a big girl. I can fight my own battles.

I needed a strong drink after all this shit, but I didn't want to go downstairs. I was done with Jihad for the night and couldn't risk bumping into him. So instead, I pulled the cover over my head and rocked myself to sleep.

Jihad

I don't know how niggas got multiple bitches and still maintain a clear head. But these two bitches were getting on my gotdamn nerves. Alyssa was the love of my life, and I was willing to do any and everything for her ass, but her little stank-ass attitude been getting on my fucking nerves. I beat her ass once, and lately, I feel like beating her ass again. The only thing saving her is the fact she's carrying my seed.

Now, this bitch Brooklyn was a whole different case of madness. This bitch really thought my ass, a fine, young brother with a good dick, could be in love with her ass.

Let's get this clear. This bitch's sex is boring as hell, and her pussy dry as hell. More than once, I had to spit on my hand and rub her clit. Shit, from the minute she walked into my place of business, signed up, and used her Visa card, I knew the bitch was paid. This was right around the same time I was going through money problems. I needed a way out, and this bitch looked like the perfect bitch to give this dick to. But now that I was married to the bitch, she thinks she owns me. Bullshit. I'm just buying time to get rid of her ass.

I sat in the car, hitting the blow while I waited for Briana to finish taking her stuff into the house. I know I should've waited, but I was angry and was feining. The minute the blow hit my brain, I felt like a new person. I glanced in the mirror and saw my daughter walking back to the car. Shit. I hurriedly checked my nose in the mirror and quickly wiped away the spot of cocaine sitting on its edge.

"Daddy, I'm going to miss you so much," Briana said as she leaned in my window.

"Baby, it's only for a few weeks. But trust me, Daddy has some things planned."

"Love you, Daddy."

I reached in my pocket, pulled out my wallet, took out $200, and handed it to her.

"Thank you, Daddy. You're the best."

"Nah, baby, you the best. Well, let me go before yo' mama comes out here with her drama."

"I know, right? I love you, Daddy. Talk to you tomorrow."

I watched as she skipped back into the apartment complex. This only increased the hate that I felt for Brooklyn. This bitch was cold and had no heart. She threw my daughter out like she was garbage, and for that alone, that bitch will pay.

***

I was about to pull off when my phone started ringing. I looked at the caller ID. It was an unfamiliar number, but it could be a new client.

"Hello, Jihad speaking."

"Hello, Jihad. This is Trina."

The name didn't ring a bell, but I didn't want to come off rude by letting the caller know I don't know her.

"Hello, love, how are you?"

"Do you remember me?"

"Uh, nah, but you can jog my memory real quick."

"We had a threesome together."

What the fuck? Is this a game? I figured it was one of the bitches I've fucked before playing game on me. I had to proceed with caution.

"Umm, I don't recall."

"Jihad, let's cut out the fucking bullshit. You, me, and Alyssa had a threesome at her house."

Damn, I wasn't expecting this. Still, I was curious to hear why she was calling me.

"Wait, is something wrong with Alyssa and the baby?"

"Noooo, relax, Jihad. Alyssa and the baby are just fine. I called you to talk about me and you."

"Me and you?" I was confused. I had no idea what this bitch was talking about.

"Jihad, listen, from that night that we fucked, I can't seem to get you off my mind. I mean, you can't tell me that I've not crossed your mind. I could tell you was loving the way I sucked your dick."

Was this some sick-ass game that this bitch and Alyssa had cooked up? These bitches had me fucked up. Yes, to be honest, that bitch's mouth was fire, and her pussy was wet and tight like she ain't been fucking. The memory of that bitch put a smile on my face.

"Listen, Trina, I don't know what kind of test this is, but you can go back to your girl and let her know I didn't fall for the fuckery. I only want her."

"Jihad, you really think I'm setting you up? I want to fuck you again. To show you how serious I am, I will send something to your phone."

"I hear you."

She hung up without saying another word. I shook my head at this craziness. This day just got way crazier than I could imagine. I cut the music up and pulled off. Alyssa's ass think she slick; hell, this was one of the oldest games. Bitches always use their homegirls to flirt with their nigga to see if the nigga will flirt back so that they can say the nigga cheating. Not I. I was too slick to fall for this bullshit.

I pulled up in the driveway and glanced at the time. It was almost midnight. I pray this bitch Brooklyn was already sleeping. I was sick of her and the mood I was in, if this bitch said the wrong thing, I might catch a case tonight.

Suddenly, a text message came in, and I quickly checked it. *Holy Jesus, son of God,* was the first thought that popped into my mind. About five pictures came in of this bitch showing her freshly shaved pussy. Shit . . . I squirted in my seat. My dick started throbbing, moving around in my boxers, screaming to be released. I used my hand and grabbed it, trying to calm it down. Why is this bitch playing with me like this? Like I won't fuck the shit out of her phat ass? I dialed back the number she had called me from earlier.

"What do you want?"

"I want you, Jihad. I'm going to text you my address. I'll be waiting for you, butt-ass naked." She hung up immediately.

My heart was telling me to go tear up this pussy, but my mind was telling me it was a setup. *Don't do it.* I sat in the driveway, weighing my options. I took a few more glances at the pics in front of me. Then I glanced at the crib, turned on my engine, put the address in the GPS, and pulled off. I ignored all the warnings that my mind was giving me. I was high on the blow, my dick was throbbing, and I wanted to fuck. It was a chance that I was willing to take.

I pulled up to the parking lot and looked around to see if Alyssa's car was parked anywhere. I didn't see it, and the parking lot was quiet. I grabbed the bill that had the rest of my blow in and also the small amount of what I had left. Then I quickly exited the vehicle and looked for the apartment number. This wasn't the best side of town, so I moved carefully. I should've taken my gun out of the truck. I saw the door slightly open, so I knocked.

"Come in, boo," a voice yelled out.

A little voice in my head kept saying, "*Nigga, leave now,*" but I ignored it and stepped inside.

In front of me stood this chick butt-ass naked with everything hanging.

"Pick up your lips, love, and close the door," she said, interrupting my thoughts.

"Huh? Shit, I'm tripping." I turned around and closed the door. "So, what is this all about? I thought you and Alyssa were best friends?" I quizzed, regretting I mentioned Alyssa's name.

"Jihad, yes, she is my best friend, but I enjoyed fucking you, and that is something worth risking our friendship over."

She moved toward me and pushed me down on the couch. She was a little stronger than I thought. Then she wasted no time pulling down my sweatpants and releasing my dick.

"Yo, I forgot to stop at the store and grab some Magnums."

"What you need those for? My pussy clean, and I'm on the depo. So, we good. I'm feeling horny as hell and don't want to waste another second."

"A'ight, shorty, I hear you."

Shorty dropped to her knees and instantly took my dick into her mouth.

"Aw, shit, this is what I'm talking about," I whispered as my dick touched the back of her throat.

I stretched my legs out and closed my eyes. This was some good shit here. Not sure how long this bitch has been sucking dick, but she was a beast at it. This is some shit a nigga would love to wake up to every day.

"Bitch, take this dick; take this dick. Who is your daddy?" I yelled out as I fucked her from the back. I had her at the edge of the bed with her body on the bed, and her ass scooted back up on my dick while I held her ass cheeks apart. She screamed as I thrust in and out of her.

"Aweee, daddy, give me that dick. Oh shit. Nigga, I want you bad. Jihad, yes, shit, yes," she screamed.

Her screams excited me more as I beat up the pussy without mercy.

"Oh shit, my pussy. Fuck, oh my God," she screamed out.

I was about to bust and wasn't easing up. Her pussy hugged my dick tight as I slid in and out. I gripped her ass tighter, pulling her down on the dick and preventing her from moving.

"Oh shiiiit," I yelled between clenched lips while I exploded up in her pussy. My legs buckled under me, and I almost lost my balance. Then finally, I pulled my limp dick out of her and fell on the bed.

I closed my eyes, trying to savor the moment. After a few minutes of lying there, I sat on the bed.

"You good, love? I hope this ain't it for us. You got some bomb-ass dick, and I want it on the regular. Shit, ain't nobody got to know we fucking."

I looked at her. I was about to say some off-the-wall shit, but shit, her head game was fire. Shorty snatched my soul. I know she and Alyssa were friends, but shit, it ain't my problem. It ain't like I'm trying to wife the bitch. I'm only trying to fuck.

"I definitely want to see you again. We just need to be careful when we're around Alyssa."

"I got you, daddy. Trust me. She won't know anything going on."

She got up and walked out of the room. I jumped up and got dressed, then looked at my phone. I had multiple missed calls from Alyssa, followed by some texts. Shit, I was tired as hell and needed sleep.

She walked back into the room dressed. "Aye, it's late, and I got work in the morning."

"Okay, I understand."

I walked out, and she followed me. "A'ight. Shorty, I'ma hit you up later."

"Okay, boo."

I looked around nervously as I stepped outside. Everything seemed normal, so I jogged to my car. I sat in the truck, opened up the bill, and snorted a few lines of the blow before I pulled off. Then I cut on the music as I cruised down the streets. It was late at night, so the road was empty. I was feeling great. I let the window down, allowing the cool breeze to sweep inside the truck. I haven't felt this good in a long time. I just hope it lasts.

I paid for a hotel for the night. I was too tired to fight with Alyssa or Brooklyn. I was in a good mood and didn't want any one of these bitches to fuck it up. After a shower,

I snorted some blow and lay there. I had to figure out my next move.

I knew Brooklyn was at work in the morning, so I went to the house and grabbed some clothes. I wanted to teach this bitch a lesson. She can't treat me any old fucking way and expect not to feel my wrath. I put the clothes in my truck and drove to Alyssa's crib.

I planned on spending a few days there so Brooklyn's ass can learn.

Chapter Twenty-one

Brooklyn

This was one of the days that I felt like I could do without working. The last few days were stressful. It's been three days now since I've seen Jihad. I've called him multiple times but got no response. I know that I told him I didn't give a fuck if he left with his daughter, but I miss my husband. I missed how we used to laugh and how he made me feel. Lately, all I've been feeling is anger.

I also didn't feel like being around people. I know I was coming off as selfish, but how can I sit around all day trying to fix other people's problems when my marriage is falling apart, and I can't fix that?

"Mrs. Lewis?" Alyssa entered my office.

I quickly wiped the tears that were flowing down my face. "Yes, is there a problem?"

"No, I was telling you I was going on my lunch break . . . Are you crying?"

"No, go ahead, hon."

"Brooklyn, I might be young, but I'm no fool. What is it? Is it my cousin? Don't tell me he's giving you trouble. I swear I will hurt that boy. Wait, is it another woman?"

"Why would you say that? Have you seen him with another woman?" I looked at her for confirmation. Shit, she was his family. She might know something more than I do.

"Oh no, never. I know my cousin loves and adores you. But he is also a man, and I know sometimes they don't know what they have until it's gone."

"I've never caught him with another woman, but I've always suspected there was someone. The late nights, him disappearing. The signs are there."

"Let me ask you a question . . ." She looked at me.

"Go ahead."

"You're an educated woman with money. If he was cheating, and you found out, what would make you stay with him?"

"Alyssa, you're young, so there might be some things in life you've yet to learn. When I married him, I married him for better or worse. I put a lot of time and effort into this relationship. There's no way I will sit back and let some little ghetto-speaking, hoodrat bitch come in and take away my husband. I'm willing to fight for mine."

"Wow. I hear that. Jihad doesn't know how strong your love for him is. I don't think he's cheating. He ain't that stupid to risk it all for some ghetto-speaking, hoodrat bitch."

"I have no proof, but if I find out, he will regret fooling with me. Anyway, you know what? This all personal, plus that is your family. Go feed the baby. Go on."

"Okay, I'll be back in a few."

After she left, I sank into my chair. It felt good letting that little bit of steam off just now. I swear I miss my husband and how we used to be close. Shit, I miss smelling his cologne. Why is he behaving like this? *Is* there another woman in his life? Tears welled up in my eyes. We haven't even been married a year, and we already have problems.

My intuition kept telling me to stop by the gym to see how things were going. So I did and noticed the parking lot was semiempty. This was weird 'cause this was usually the busiest time for the business. *Hmm, strange,* I thought as I walked into the building. A few people were inside, but it looked like a ghost town, unlike the packed gym we're used to.

I saw his brother, Jaseem, as soon as I walked in. He was talking to a woman, so I waited for them to finish their conversation.

A few minutes later, he walked over to me. "Hello, Brooklyn. How are you doing?"

"I'm good. I'm looking for your brother."

"Huh, why would you be looking for him here?" He shot me a strange look.

"What are you saying? This is his place of employment, right?"

"Brooklyn, you're married to the man. I thought I told you before you need to talk to him about his business."

"Wait. I have a right to fucking know. It was my fifty grand that helped save this business."

"Ha-ha. For you to be such an intelligent woman, you sure be acting green. If Jihad had put fifty grand into this business, the bank wouldn't have repo'd it. We have thirty days to vacate this building. He paid off what we couldn't pay on the current mortgage. See, barely anyone is in here. I put my life into this, and that no-good husband of yours ran it into the fucking ground. I lost every fucking thing in this shit. My wife's threatening to get a divorce and move up north with my children. I have nothing—not a gotdamn thing. Excuse me, but I got shit to do. I don't have a rich wife to write me a big check," he lashed out as he walked off.

I was stunned at his level of anger. I wanted to run behind him and comfort him, but I saw the pain in his eyes. I know he was angry, and it was best I leave him alone. I took one last look at the place before I dashed out.

***

As I drove down the street, all kinds of thoughts entered my mind. I cut Jihad a fifty-grand check. If he did not give it to the bank, what the fuck did he do with my money? This nigga . . . this nigga. Lies after lies. So, if he ain't been working, what the fuck has he been doing? The better question is, where the fuck has this married man been sleeping? I felt myself getting angrier by the second. I know I wasn't 100 percent well, so I tried my best to calm down.

"Lord God, I need a sign. Show me a sign that this man is not for me," I whispered as tears rolled down my face.

I was happy to be home from work. I was tired mentally and physically. I just needed a quick bath, something to eat, and to get some rest. I remember the doctor warning me not to overdo it too soon. I saw Jihad's truck in the driveway as I pulled in. I haven't seen his ass since the other night, so what the fuck was he here for? I wanted to confront him, but I needed to keep my mouth shut. I need to get to the bottom of what was going on first. Plus, I was too tired to deal with him and his bullshit right now.

I grabbed my briefcase and exited the car. Opening the door, I walked in. I was about to head to the stairs when Jihad appeared from the kitchen.

"Hey, baby," he said while smiling.

"What do you want, Jihad? A few days ago, I was all kinds of bitches, and now, I'm 'baby'? What the fuck you want?" I gave him a cold-ass look.

He took a few steps closer to me. "Listen, Brooklyn, I'm so sorry for everything I put you through. I swear I just need a few minutes of your time to hear me out. I promise if you're not satisfied after we talk, I'll pack my stuff and give you a divorce."

I looked at him. I wanted to tell him to fuck off, but I loved this man. *This* is the man I want to spend the rest of my life with. I was angry with him, but part of me was soft on him.

"Okay, but I'm telling you, I'm not making no promises. I can't keep living like this."

"I understand, babes. I'm making your favorite meal."

"All right. I need to freshen up real quick."

I let go of his hand and walked up the stairs. I don't know how to read this man. It's like he has two personalities. I shook my head and walked into our bedroom. Stepping out of my clothes, I walked to the shower. This warm water was giving me life right now. I closed my eyes, slowly soaped up my body, and washed from head to toe. I needed to relax my mind, and this was exactly what I needed to clear it.

By the time I finished freshening up and walking downstairs, he was finished cooking. I walked into the dining room, where he had the room in a romantic setting. Candles were lit, and "A House Is Not a Home" by Luther Vandross was playing.

His eyes lit up as I entered the room. He quickly walked around and pulled out my chair. Wow. This was the Jihad that I was used to. I took a seat as he placed my food in front of me. The smell quickly filled my nose. I was hungry and eager to take a bite.

Luther was certainly putting me in a mood, along with the glass of red wine he poured me. He finally took a seat across from me. We sat in silence, eating our meals. I must admit, the food tasted way better than it smelled. The steak was so tender it melted away in my mouth, just like I love it. This man definitely has some hidden talent, I thought.

"Here, I'll help you clean up." I got up out of the chair.

"Oh no, this your night to be off. I got this, so go sit in the living room and relax."

"Oh, okay."

Shit, I was too tired to fight with him. I lay on the couch with my eyes closed, listening to the sultry voice of Luther sweeping loudly through the speaker. Lord, is this the sign that I asked you for earlier? If it is, I welcome it with open arms.

I felt someone touch my leg. When I opened my eyes, it was Jihad kneeling in front of me.

"Hey, babes, sorry to startle you, but there's something that I need to say to you." He took my hands and placed his face in the middle.

This seemed serious, so I braced myself, just in case. If this nigga said some bullshit that I didn't want to hear, I was going to snap. So, I sat there staring him dead in his eyes.

"Brooklyn, ever since I laid eyes on you, I knew you were the woman I wanted to spend the rest of my life with. Truth is, I didn't have all the money that you thought I had. I was almost broke, with only a few thousand in my account. But I didn't let that stop me. I used it to take you out and eventually used the rest to buy your ring. I'm just a regular dude trying to make it with a woman I knew was out of my league. I love you, Brooklyn, and I know I fell short, but if you give me just one more chance, I can show you I can be everything you need me to be. I swear I can, Brooklyn. I will even move out so you don't feel pressured."

I looked at him, and he was crying. Not no fake tears; genuinely real tears. This man was broken. I rubbed his face as I pulled him closer to me. What did I do to this man that led him to believe it was all about the money? Tears welled up in my eyes. A queen's job is to lift up her king, not drag him down. I felt bad. I mean, I love niggas with money, but that wasn't everything. I wanted love. Here, I have a man that loved me, and because his account wasn't stacked, I've been treating him wrong.

"Oh God, no, I got to fix this."

"Come here, baby, come here," I tried to pull him up on the couch.

"Jihad, listen to me, boo. I'm so sorry if I made you feel like it was all about the money. I mean, yes, I wish my husband was doing great, but I know life isn't set up like that. You could've come to me and let me know. I would've still married you. Shit, I would've taken a less expensive ring. Baby, I love you, and I don't care if you rich or poor. I still want you." He lay his head on my chest, and I placed my face on his.

We cried together as we professed our love to each other.

"Jihad, you know, maybe we need to pray."

"Pray?"

"Yes, I'm not no religious person, but I feel like if we ask God to guide us, we will find our way to happiness."

"I agree, babes."

Without another word, I let go of him, and we dropped to our knees. I remember how my grandmother used to have us pray daily. I used some of her words. I prayed for God to lead my husband and me on the right path. It was no long prayer, but it was enough for God to know we needed help.

"Babes, I want you to know this is a new beginning for us. I got some things lined up that will bring some huge money in. Babes, trust me. Your man got a degree and the hustle to go out here and make it happen. All I need to know is my baby is behind me 100 percent. I can do any and everything with you beside me."

He was in an upbeat mood and was smiling. That prayer did us good. We need to start going to church on the regular now.

Before the night was over, Jihad sucked my toes, my pussy, and my asshole. That man had me climbing all sorts of walls in that living room . . . from the couch to the rug. My ass was carpet burned, but who is complaining? Not I. I enjoyed every bit of it, and I know he did too. I looked over at him, lying on his back, snoring with his hand on his dick.

I took my time and eased up off the bed. My damn alarm was going off for about a good twenty minutes now, and my ass kept snoozing it. I knew I needed to jump in this shower and get the hell to work. As good as the sex was, both of our asses can't be unemployed. The thought made my stomach turn. I quickly brushed that feeling away. I did make a vow for better or worse, and this right here was definitely the worst.

Jihad

When Papa told me this dick would take me places, I didn't believe him at first. Shit, now I see what that old nigga was saying was true. After lying up with Alyssa for a few days, I realized it was time to return to the crib. Alyssa was pregnant, the baby was coming in a few months, and I had already spent most of the money Brooklyn gave me. I knew I had to get back into Brooklyn's good graces, and I had the perfect plan to do it. It wasn't going to be easy, but I was that nigga, and my dick game and mouthpiece definitely could get the toughest bitch falling to her knees.

I got in before she returned home from work and got down to business. I know what Brooklyn loves, so I decided to make her favorite meal. That bitch had a weakness for a well-cooked steak. The minute she walked into the house and I started working my wonders, I knew the rest was easy. After feeding her and shedding a few tears, I listened to her pray. Yeah, you heard me right. This bitch dropped to her knees and started to pray.

The entire time I'm kneeling there, shaking my head, thinking, *This bitch is trippin' hard as fuck.*

After that little charade was over, I did what I do best . . . sucked and licked on every inch of that bitch's body. As bad as I hate fucking her, I laid the dick down and had that bitch screaming and running. I pinned her under me and fucked the shit out of her. We had to be going 'bout an hour before I busted all up in her.

It's been a week, and that bitch was acting like the perfect wife. She even gave me a debit card with my name on it. But she warned me it's only for emergencies. I agreed and let her know how much I appreciated her.

We were lying in bed one night after I fucked her good.

"Aye, babe, I was thinking 'bout that life insurance we'd discussed before."

"Yeah, what about it?"

"I want us to go down and get it done sometime this week."

I sat up and looked at her. "Are you sure? I mean, I'm not in a position to help pay for the premium. Plus, I don't want anyone to think I forced you into this."

"Jihad, stop. We're married. That means we are one. What's mine is also yours, so cut out the bullshit. This is for us, just in case something happens. In this day and age, you have to be on top of everything, and having life insurance is one of them."

"I understand, baby. I swear, what would I do without you?"

"Hopefully, you will never find out." She smiled at me.

We continued talking until the wee hours of the morning. After I was sure she was asleep, I sneaked off to the bathroom with my phone in hand. I heard it going off for a long-ass time but was scared to check it. I had over twenty missed calls from Alyssa, and tons of texts followed. I know she was mad as hell 'cause I haven't been around like I used to. It was difficult for me, but securing the Brooklyn bag was a must.

The next day, Brooklyn kept her promise. We both took out over a million-dollar life insurance policy on each other. I had to try my best not to show my excitement. So, if this bitch died, I would be a millionaire. That is what you call a *big* come-up. That night, I fucked her and sucked her real good to show her my appreciation.

I pulled up at the doctor's office. Finally, this was the day that Alyssa and I would find out the sex of our baby. I was kind of nervous but also happy. Briana is damn near grown, and I'm ready to have another mini-me. Hopefully, this will be the boy I've wanted so badly.

I parked and exited the vehicle. When I saw Alyssa's car parked a few cars down, I braced myself 'cause I knew she was still upset with me. I ain't been spending a lot of quality time with her. I tried explaining things to her, but she wasn't having it. Instead, she was letting her jealousy shadow our plans.

I walked in and looked around. There she was, sitting by the window. Our eyes locked, and she quickly turned her head. I walked over to her and took a seat beside her.

"Hey, love, how are you feeling?" I rubbed her leg.

"*Really,* Jihad? Why the hell you even bother to show yo' face in here?" she said in a high-pitched tone.

I saw a few nosy bitches turn around and look at us.

"Yo, what's your problem? I'm up here to make sure you and my baby are doing okay. But I see all you want to do is put on a show. Look around you. You're the only one up in here with a man by your side. Consider yourself lucky."

"Whatever, Jihad. The bitch you lay up with every night is the lucky one."

"Miss Jones, the doctor will see you now," the nurse said.

She got up, and I followed closely behind her. I don't give a damn about her attitude. She had to know that I was with her and ain't going nowhere.

Alyssa sashayed out of the doctor's office with an attitude. She wanted a girl, but it was confirmed we were having a boy. I was ecstatic. I wanted to jump around, but with the look on her face, I had to contain my excitement. She tried to get into her car without saying a word to me. I jumped in front of her and blocked her from opening the car door.

"Hold up. Why the attitude?"

"Why the attitude? I'm sick of you and your shit, Jihad. I'm going to have my baby, and I'm still living in that hellhole. Not only that but you were also supposed to be getting rid of this bitch. But instead, you playing house and shit. Do you know I have to listen to that bitch brag about how you been acting like a brand-new man? Do you know how much that shit hurt? No, you don't 'cause you don't give a fuck about me. All you care about is living your double life." She stepped away from me.

"Yo, is *that* what you think? *You're* my fucking life. I love you. I wish that bitch would've died that night she fell out. I want you, us, and our baby. You're giving me something that bitch isn't able to give me—a fucking son. You hear me? I love you, Alyssa, *not* that bitch."

"I hear your words, Jihad, but I'm tired of sleeping alone. I'm tired of calling you and your phone going straight to voicemail. I'm tired of it all." She busted out crying.

"Man, chill out. All this stress isn't good for the baby. You're my woman. Just have a little faith in me. That's all I ask. I'm almost there."

"I can't do this shit no more. Get out of my way, please." She shoved me.

She jumped into her car, and even though I was banging on the window, she looked at me, shook her head, and backed up. She then pulled off, leaving me standing there.

Fuck. I walked off to my truck. All this fucking stress was killing me. I needed a fucking break. I jumped into my truck and pulled off, heading to the gym. I needed to let off some steam before I fuck around and lose it.

This shit was fucking disgusting. The parking lot was empty. I sat in the truck for a few minutes, hitting the blow and taking in the scene. My life was spiraling downhill. Just a year ago, I was *that* nigga. I had bitches, and I had money. Now, look at this shit. I have nothing to show for it. The only thing keeping me going is the fact that a big payday is coming.

I got out of the truck and walked into the gym. No one was there, not even the receptionist. I know we're supposed to give the building up in a few days, but I convinced myself it wasn't really happening. Then as I stepped inside, reality hit me.

I knew my bitch-ass brother was here 'cause I saw his car parked outside. So I looked around and then walked to the office. He was sitting at his desk when I walked in. He looked surprised to see me.

"It's about time you showed your face 'round here. You need to get yo' shit up out of here before the sheriff and them show up Friday."

"Nigga, I know what I need to do. You ain't got to tell me shit," I lashed out and turned around to walk away.

"Hold on. Wait. Before you go . . . Where is all that money Brooklyn gave you to put into this place? How much was it, fifty grand, huh?"

"Bitch nigga, how the fuck is that *your* business? That's *my* bitch and *my* money." I turned around to face this bitch-ass nigga.

"Ha-ha, look at you . . . The high and mighty Jihad. Your bitch, huh? Does your bitch know you a fucking powder head? Does your bitch know you got a fucking baby on the way? Does she know you spend her hard-earned money on your side bitch? I bet you she doesn't know. Oh wait, maybe I should call her and let her know what a piece of shit she's married to."

"You bitch-ass nigga. You've always been jealous of me. I was always the one with the chick. The one Daddy favored. The one with more money. Admit it, nigga, you jealous. You wish you had my life. Instead, you stuck with that boring-ass bitch you married. Shit, maybe I need to give her some of this dick. Let her know what a *real* man feels like."

He leaped from around the desk, but I was too fast for him. I pulled out my gun and aimed it at him.

"Yeah, you better pull out that shit 'cause you knew I was gon' beat that ass," he laughed.

Pop!

I fired a single shot at his chest.

"Who's the pussy now, nigga?" I grinned.

"You shot me?" he yelled as he leaped toward me.

Pop, pop! I fired two more shots at him. I had to defend myself against this nigga. There was no way I was going out like a pussy. His body went down and hit the ground. I stood there looking at him, high as fuck off the blow. It took me a minute to grasp what the fuck I just did.

"Oh shit. Oh God, no." I rushed to him and got on my knees, leaning over him. He struggled to say something, but the words were not coming out.

"You-you-you," he tried to speak, but the blood started gushing out of his mouth, and his eyes started rolling over. Within seconds, he was gasping, and his breathing got heavier . . . until his chest stopped moving. I knew then he was gone.

"Noooo! Oh shit, what have I done?" I yelled and looked down at him.

Oh shit. I felt his pulse. There was nothing. I jumped up, tiptoed to the door, and slowly opened it. I peeped out to make sure no one was out there. I didn't see anyone. I closed the door and walked over to his body, making sure I didn't step into no blood. Then I went to the safe and opened it up. Damn, all the nigga had in there was a stack. I grabbed it and left it open. Next, I pulled out drawers and threw papers all over the floor, making sure whoever entered would think it was a robbery gone bad.

Then I deleted everything off the security camera and disabled it. I looked around to make sure I didn't overlook anything. I was sweating uncontrollably like the heat was turned up to 100 degrees. After taking one last look around before I walked out, I left the office door open. I didn't use the front door. Instead, I slowly opened the back door and peeped out before exiting the building. I calmed myself down as I walked around the building, carefully turning away from the security camera on the nail salon building next door. I had deleted our camera, so I wasn't worried that my face would show when I was on my way in.

I got into my truck and looked around before I calmly drove away. It was already starting to get dark outside, and barely anyone was out and about. I sped off as soon as I was sure I wasn't noticed. Jaseem's dead body kept flashing in front of me. I tried to get it out of my head. *Shit, what have I done?* I thought.

I headed home. I needed to be there before Brooklyn got in. I need to make sure I have some kind of alibi. I started thinking about what I would say or how I would react when the news reached me. I know I would have to be careful. The police would be involved, and I couldn't risk being linked to his death.

I got in the house, took a quick shower, and threw the clothes and sneakers that I was wearing in the trash. I watched too many episodes of *Forensic Files* not to know how to take precautions. After I got that out of the way, I poured myself a few shots of Grey Goose. I needed something strong to numb what I was feeling. I mean, I didn't fuck with my brother, but I didn't go in there to kill him. Oh God, my parents . . . Shit, his little girl . . . I needed something stronger than this, so I quickly got dressed. I needed to make a run. I used my last blow earlier and needed to find my connect.

Alyssa

After trying to avoid going back to the doctor for months, I finally decided to make a doctor's appointment. I hadn't heard from Jihad last night, so I had no idea if he would show. I thought about hitting Jahmiel up to see if he wanted to play daddy for the day. I called his phone and realized the number was disconnected. I don't know if I should laugh or cry. Here I thought I had two baby daddies, and they both were behaving like assholes. *Shit, I think it's time to find me a new nigga,* I thought as I made my way into the lobby of the doctor's office.

So, I spotted Jihad walking in with a smile on his face. I looked at him and shook my head in disgust. As soon as he opened his mouth, I made sure he knew I was pissed the fuck off. Shortly after, the nurse called me. I thought he would sit the fuck down, but instead, he followed me into the examining room. You could feel the tension, but I didn't give a fuck.

The ultrasound revealed I was having a boy, a little man to call my own. The look on Jihad's face was priceless when the ultrasound disclosed that he was having a junior. I was disappointed, to say the least. My whole time pregnant, I prayed for a little me, and this is what we got.

The relationship between Jihad and me continued to deteriorate. It was like he was purposely avoiding me. I didn't know why until his bitch started coming into work with a smile on her face. I knew something was up, so I inquired. She spared no feelings when she flaunted how happy her husband made her, and they'd been working out their relationship. If that bitch were any good at reading faces, she would have seen the smirk on my damn face. I was seconds away from letting that bitch know, woman to woman, that nigga ain't worth shit. But instead, I smiled at her. She was the dumbest bitch that I've ever met. Looking at her, I realized that I needed to figure out shit real soon.

I got off work a little late today. The bitch needed me to work late. By the time I reached the house, I was exhausted. Those long-ass hours sitting at that desk be killing my back, and no, that selfish-ass bitch didn't care about me and what the fuck I might be going through.

I hurriedly stepped out of my clothes and jumped into the shower. I needed this warm water beating down on my body. This was getting crazy. My stomach was getting so huge it prevented me from bending down too much. I was so ready to have this baby.

Shit, I took another look in the drawer. I realized I had no more weed in my little stash. I was too damn tired to go down the street to cop some. Instead, I reached for my bag and took out my cell phone. While the phone rang, I turned the television on. I had no idea what shows were coming on, but I hoped it was something good.

"Helurrrr," this bitch yelled into my ear.

"Damn, bitch, must you be that damn loud?"

"Oh, I'm sorry, Miss Sensitive Ass. Where the hell you been?"

"Girl, the usual. Work and playing house with this nigga."

"Uh-huh, I hear you. How is my godchild doing?"

"Bitch, you're not going to believe this shit . . ."

"What, ho? Blurt it out. You know my ass hate suspense."

"I'm having a boy . . ."

"Are you fucking serious? Hold up. What did Jihad say?"

"That nigga happy as hell, but I wanted a damn girl. So what the hell I'ma do with a boy? All their little clothes be ugly as hell."

"Bitch, you a lie. I bet you I find some dope-ass baby clothes for my godson. I can't wait to hit these stores."

"A'ight, bitch. Tell me you got some weed over there."

"You know I do, bitch. I guess yo' ass is out."

"Man, can you come smoke with me? I got money, but I'm too tired to fuckin' drive down the street."

"Bitch, you lucky you my dawg 'cause I was already in bed."

"Thank you, boo. I'll make it up to you."

She hung up without responding. I swear I love that bitch; blood couldn't make us no tighter. I swear I have no idea what I would do without her crazy ass.

Then my phone started to ring. I looked at the caller ID. It was Jihad. I rolled my eyes before I picked it up.

"Hello," I said dryly into the phone.

"Hey, babes, how are you feeling?"

"I'm doing good, Jihad." I was very short with him and made sure he knew I was.

"Damn, Alyssa, you still mad with a nigga? Come on, babes, we're having a baby together. Can you at least let the past go?"

"Jihad, in case you didn't know, this isn't the past. This is our future, and guess what? You're there, and I'm here. Listen, Trina coming over in a few, so I got to go."

"Why is she coming over?"

"Why not? You know that's my bitch."

"Yeah, a bitch that also eats pussy. I don't think you need to be hanging around her anymore."

"Jihad, what the fuck are you talking about? She's more than a sister to me. Plus, you ain't had no problem when she was fucking and sucking on you."

"Don't bring up that shit. Truthfully, that shit was wack and mushy. I only did it 'cause I didn't want to disappoint you. But, like I said, I have a bad feeling about her ass. Like she's jealous of you. I see how she looks at you when you're not paying attention. I'm not tryna come between you and your friend, but, baby, I'm from the streets, and I can smell fake from a mile away."

"I hear you, but as I said, that's my bitch, and she's never crossed me or given me any reason to believe she's shady or anything. So I don't know what you're seeing, but you're wrong about her."

"A'ight, shorty. Did you eat?"

"No, not yet, but I'll grab something."

"Cool. I got some things to handle, so I'll hit you up later."

"Uh-huh."

I was happy to be off the phone with him. This was his excuse lately, having to "handle" something. Then I wouldn't hear from him until the next day. I shook my head in disgust. I'm 'bout sick of him and his bullshit.

I heard the door banging, so I walked over and opened it.

"Damn, bitch, you big as a cow," Trina greeted me as she walked in.

"Hello to you. Thank you for making me feel bad about all this damn weight I done gained."

"Bitch, chill. You know I ain't mean nothing by it. Plus, your man owns a gym and is a personal trainer. So you'll lose all that. I hope you keep the ass, though 'cause it got fatter."

"Uh-huh. You can stop looking at my ass."

"Here, bitch. You sound like you were desperate."

She handed me a bag of weed and some paper. I wasted no time in rolling it. Then we started talking like we hadn't seen each other in years.

"Bitchhhh . . ." she said while her eyes lit up.

"What, ho?" I continued rolling the blunt.

"I saw Jahmiel the other day, and all he kept talking about was you and his baby."

I stopped what I was doing and looked at her. Shit. I had forgotten that I told him it was his baby the last time he was here."Oh my God, are you fucking serious? Did anybody hear him say that?"

"I mean, it was just me and him, but that boy couldn't shut up about it. So, you told Jihad he the daddy, and you told Jahmiel he the daddy. Bitch, both them niggas are crazy and will fuck you up. You better know what the fuck you doing. Shit, you said Jihad is married. If I were you, I would say fuck him. Jahmiel is young. He got money, and he ain't with nobody right now. Y'all could make a nice family."

"Bitch, who you work for, Dr. Phil or Iyanla? I love Jihad. I don't love Jahmiel. Plus, Jihad about to leave that bitch."

"Really, Alyssa? You *really* think that nigga's going to leave his wife that has money and come be with you?"

"Damn, bitch, who side is you on? It ain't about the money. Jihad loves me and our son. He knows if he doesn't leave her, he won't be in me and my baby's life."

"You're my friend, and I just don't want to see you hurt. I mean, you're too pretty to be anybody's sidepiece. You deserve better, you know?"

"I know, friend. Trust me. I won't be for too long. I already put some plans into motion. But in the meantime, Jahmiel's ass needs to shut the fuck up. I don't want him going around saying this shit. You don't know who knows Jihad. Man, this is crazy."

"Yeah, it is crazy, but that boy was happy as hell."

I took a pull off the blunt and sat there thinking. The last thing I need is for Jihad to believe our baby is not his. Truthfully, I didn't know which of them niggas got me pregnant. I pray it's Jihad's, but I just don't know.

"Bitch, enough about me. Who is it?"

"Who is what?" She looked at me crazily.

"Who is the bitch or nigga *you* fucking with? Bitch, your face is glowing, nails done, and hair done."

"You're tripping, friend. There's no one, trust me."

"Uh-huh, bitch. He must be married or broke 'cause you holding out on me. I'ma find out soon, though."

"Bitch, you're tripping. Trust me, if there was someone, you're the first one that would know this. You know I can't hold nothing from my bestie. Anyways, it's getting late, and you know how much I hate driving. We need to get together soon, so I can get a list of baby stuff you need."

"Okay, let's do that this weekend."

"A'ight, boo."

I locked the door and walked to my room. The weed mellowed me out, but it also made me sleepy. I got into bed, and before you knew it, my ass was dozing off.

Chapter Twenty-two

Brooklyn

I looked over at the clock on the nightstand, which was reading 12:45 a.m. I wasn't feeling too good. I was experiencing the same symptoms I had before. I eased up off the bed and rushed to the bathroom. I made it just in time before I started vomiting. I held my chest as I brought up all my food.

Oh God, what is happening to me? I thought as I brushed my teeth and washed my face.

I tiptoed back to bed, trying my best not to wake Jihad. Finally, I eased back into the bed, curling up in a fetal position. My body was warm, yet I was trembling with a cold sweat.

"Babes, you good?" I felt Jihad shaking me.

"I don't feel too good. I was throwing up. I feel weak."

"Damn, why didn't you wake me up, Brooklyn? Baby, you're hot as fuck. I'ma call the ambulance. We need to get you back to the hospital."

"No, I'm not going back there. Last time I was there, they couldn't find nothing wrong with me. Just get me some medicine."

"I'ma make you a cup of tea. But if this fever doesn't break, I'll take you to the hospital. I don't care if I need to be there with you the entire time."

Before I could respond, the doorbell rang. We both heard it 'cause we looked at each other.

"You expecting company, babes?" This was strange. Why would anyone visit someone's house this late?

"Nah, are you?"

"Hell nah. I'll be right back."

He left the room. He was gone for a good while, and I started to get suspicious.

"Noooo. Oh my God, noooo!" I heard a gut-wrenching scream from downstairs.

I placed my hands on the bed and eased up out of it. Then I heard voices, not just Jihad's, but a man's and a woman's. *What the fuck is going on?* I thought as I made my way to the stairs and down the steps.

The first thing I heard was Jihad yelling and two police officers holding him.

"What's going on here, Jihad? Why are you crying, and why are the police here?"

"Ma'am. You're?"

"I'm Brooklyn, and this is my husband, so can somebody tell me what the hell is going on?"

"Ma'am, Jaseem Lewis was found murdered in his place of business."

"What? Huh? Are you sure? What happened?" I started to feel worse than how I was feeling before. I turned to look at Jihad. He was on the floor now, crying uncontrollably.

I don't know where I found the strength, but I rushed over to him and dropped to my knees. I wrapped my arms around him as the tears flowed. I didn't know Jaseem well, but he was Jihad's older brother. I know they had their differences, but the fact remains they were brothers.

"I'm so sorry, babes," I kept whispering to him while I fought back the tears. This was fucking crazy. His wife and kids ran across my mind. Who would've done this? This was so wrong on so many levels.

"Mr. Lewis, do you mind if we ask you a few questions about your relationship with the victim?"

"My relationship? What the fuck you mean? He was my motherfucking brother, my big brother. Oh God, how am I going to tell my parents? My mama. Oh God." Jihad stood up, put his hands on his head, and started pacing.

"We know this must be difficult, but we're just trying to get some background on the victim. Y'all owned the business together, so you can probably shed some light on his life. We're trying to see if he had any enemies or if you know of any threats against your brother or the business."

"My brother didn't have no enemies. Everybody loved him. Did you check the cameras and the safe to see if there was a robbery? You know bums are always hanging outside. We had to call the police a few times to remove them."

"My detectives are combing all over the crime scene as we speak."

I wasn't feeling good, so I went to the downstairs bathroom. I'm glad I did 'cause I started vomiting again. I heaved until nothing came up but bitter fluid. Then I held my stomach as a sharp pain ripped through me. I wanted to curl up in a ball, but I needed to get back out there. My husband needed me.

"Okay, Mr. and Mrs. Lewis. Again, you have our deepest sympathy. I also promise y'all we will get the killer or killers."

"Thank you, Officer."

They left, and I locked the door. By the time I turned around, Jihad was in the living room. I heard glass breaking, so I rushed in there. I stopped dead in my tracks when I realized this nigga had knocked down one of my costly selenite table lamps. I had those shipped to me from overseas. I wanted to rip off his fucking head, but he was curled up in a corner, rocking from side to side. So I walked over and just sat in front of him, holding him.

"My brother gone, babes. He gone. They should've taken me instead. I'ma find whoever is responsible, and I'm going to kill them," he yelled, spit flying everywhere.

I didn't know what to say. I just held him while he cried, cussed, and cried some more. To see my husband hurting like this broke my heart. I wish there were something I could do to help him, but I knew there was nothing. Then I heard the doorbell ring again. I wondered if that was the police returning. I let go of Jihad and made my way to the door.

"Who is it?" I tried to yell, but I was feeling too weak.

"Alyssa."

I opened the door to see my assistant, Jihad's cousin, standing there.

"Hey, Alyssa, come in. I guess you heard what happened to all y'all's cousin?"

"Yes, I saw it on the 11:00 p.m. news. I tried calling you guys, but y'all wasn't answering so I got here as fast as I could. Where's Jihad? The news saying it seems like it was a robbery."

"Jihad's in here. Girl, he's going through it. I'm trying my best to calm him down, but as you can imagine, this is rough. I don't know who would do this to y'all's cousin."

She followed me into the living room where Jihad was sitting, his nose running and tears rolling down his face. He just sat there staring at nothing in particular. I tried to read him, but nothing was coming through. I knew from this day on his life would never be the same.

"Jihad, cousin, please, talk to me," Alyssa begged him.

He looked at her and grabbed her in a bear hug. My soul was hurting for them. Finally, I couldn't take it anymore. I looked at them and walked off upstairs. I needed to lie down for a little while.

"Brooklyn, Brooklyn!" I heard Jihad shaking me and yelling.

I opened my eyes and saw him standing over me with a cup.

"Here, you're still burning up. I made you some soup. You really need to let me take you to the doctor."

His eyes were bloodshot red, and it seemed like he'd been through hell and back.

"I know this sounds stupid, but how you feeling? Wait, is Alyssa still here? Is she doing okay?"

"Yes, she's downstairs lying down. I just got off the phone with my mama and daddy. Mama ain't taking it too well."

"What about Jaseem's wife?"

"Yeah, I spoke to her, but that bitch act like she got an attitude or something. I don't care about her ass. I just want to know if my nephew and niece are doing okay. I also talked to Briana, and she ain't taking it too good. I can't believe this shit, babes. I'm numb. I've been racking my brain, trying to figure out what the fuck happened. I feel like if I were there, this shit wouldn't have happened."

"Nonsense. If you were there, both of you might be dead. Well, you might want to go up there to get a full understanding of what happened. This is some fucked-up shit."

"Listen, babes, I'ma let Alyssa stay with you. I'ma put some clothes on and head up there and stop by the station, so I can better understand what's going on."

"Okay. Don't you worry about me."

"Well, drink the soup before it gets cold."

"Okay, Jihad. I love you, and we're gon' get through this."

He stopped and turned around to look at me. He didn't say anything. Instead, he smiled at me and continued walking out the door.

I tasted the soup. It was kind of sweetish. Hmm, must be from the sweet potato in it. I swear I love this man. He was dealing with something tragic, yet he found time to make me homemade soup with chicken, potatoes, and dumplings.

Knock, knock. "Come in," I whispered.

"Hey, boss lady, just checking in on you." Alyssa came in and walked over to me, putting her hand on my forehead.

"Hmm, you're still burning up. You sure you don't want to go to the doctor?"

"I'm sure, but can you get me a bottle of water out of the fridge?"

"Yes, sure."

I lay my head back on the pillow, hoping I would fall asleep soon.

"Here you go." She took off the top of the bottle and handed it to me.

I was so damn weak I struggled to hold the bottle.

"Here, I got it." She took the bottle and started feeding me.

"Well, lie down and get some rest. If you need me, call me on the phone. I'm going to be in the guest room."

My guest room? Why not the living room, I wanted to ask, but shit, she was here with me until Jihad came back home. I guess it wouldn't hurt if she lay in there.

***

Alyssa

After seeing that Jihad's brother was murdered, I decided to put aside my feelings and go be by my baby daddy's side. I tried my best not to pay his wife no mind. I was there for one reason only, and it was to comfort Jihad.

"Oh fuck, yes, Jihad, yessss," I yelled as I bounced up and down on his dick.

"Bae, calm down, please. You know Brooklyn is in the next room. Oh shit, babes, oh wee," he tried to whisper.

"That bitch is sleeping, boo." I continued bouncing up and down on his dick.

I really wasn't worried about this bitch hearing me. If you ask me, I was ready for her ass to know now. Jihad was the only thing sparing her feelings.

"Shit, shit, I'm about to bust," he yelled in a soft voice.

I squeezed my muscles together and moved my ass around in a circle. You couldn't tell me my ass was pregnant. Jihad grabbed my hips and pulled me down on him. The dick was hitting my stomach, but I braced myself and let it slide into my pussy. Three minutes later, he exploded in me.

I eased up off his dick, letting the cum slide down my legs. Finally, I got up and rushed to the bathroom in the guest room. I jumped in the shower and took a quick wash-off. Then I wrapped a towel around me and walked out of the room.

"Aye, babes—"

I stopped dead in my tracks. My baby daddy was sitting on the bed sniffing something out of a dollar bill.

"What the hell are you doing?" I ran over to him and knocked the money out of his hand.

"Why—oh shit, why you do that?" He hurriedly picked up the money, looking at the ground carefully.

"You a powder head? When did you start doing drugs, Jihad? Oh my God." Tears rolled down my face.

"Baby, come here. Oh God, you shouldn't have seen this." He tried hugging me.

"Get off me, Jihad. Fuck me seeing it. The real question is, how long *you* been doing this shit?"

I was disgusted. Is this the nigga that I was having a baby for? Oh my God, this shit can't be real.

"Baby, I'm sorry. I been so stressed out behind losing the business, and now they killed my only brother. I got a baby on the way. I need to provide for you and my baby. I'm under fucking pressure, babes."

"Hold up, what the fuck you mean you losing the business? What business you talking about? The gym?" My emotions went from hurt to anger in two point five seconds.

"Babes, don't worry. I got it under control now. Trust me. We're going to be good now. I love you, Alyssa. Just watch. I'm a give you the world."

I stood there looking at this nigga in disbelief. I didn't believe shit he was saying 'cause his ass was high as a fucking kite.

"This shit gets more ridiculous by the second. When I met you, you acted like you were paid out the ass—only to find out your bitch was the one with the money. Now, you lost the gym. So, I'm having a baby by a broke nigga?" I looked at him for answers.

"Baby, I'm not broke. Here, I got money. I got a card."

He looked for his pants, took out his wallet, pulled out a card, and handed it to me. I looked at it. It was a Wells Fargo bank card. His name was on it.

"Here, take it. Buy the baby stuff. All of it. I told you, I got you, baby." He shoved the card into my hand.

I pretended like I didn't want to take it, but since he insisted, I took it. I looked at it, then looked at him, acting as if I was still upset. But inside, I was jumping with joy. This nigga certainly came through. I wondered how much money was on here.

"Wait, is this a joke? Why you ain't give me the pin?"

"No, babes, I swear this ain't no joke. The pin is 7879."

"All right . . ."

I still didn't trust him. I needed to make it to the ATM to see what this card was hitting for.

I was still in disbelief that this nigga was sniffing powder. No wonder his mood swings were so off. I looked at him sitting there. I needed to get out of this room and get some air. So I walked out, leaving him there. I peeked in the bitch's room, and she was still sleeping. Then I made my way downstairs. I looked around. This could be all mine. Shit, this bitch needs to get out of the picture so I can get this money. Me and my baby deserve to be living in luxury.

"I thought you went home." Brooklyn's voice startled me.

I quickly put my feet down off the couch and sat up.

"No, Jihad came back late, and I didn't want to leave you here by yourself," I quickly lied.

"Oh, I was wondering where Jihad was. He didn't come to the room last night."

"I think he said he didn't want to disturb you, so he stayed in the guest room last night."

"Oh, OK. I thought that's where you stayed?"

"No, I came down here. I couldn't sleep. Jaseem was heavy on my mind."

"Did you talk to your family?"

"Yes, I spoke to them. This is a rough time for all of us. Really rough time." I started to cry.

"I can only imagine. I prayed for the entire family last night before I went to bed."

"Thank you, Brooklyn. We need it more than ever. Our family will never be the same."

"Good morning, ladies. Brooklyn, baby, what're you doing out of bed?"

"Good morning. I was looking for you. I realized you weren't in bed when I woke up."

"I told Brooklyn you were in the guest room because you didn't want to disturb her last night," I interrupted.

"Right, baby, I knew you wasn't feeling too good. Plus, you know I'm going through it. I didn't want to make it worse on you."

"Oh, OK. What did the police say happened?" she asked.

"It looks like it's a robbery. The crazy part is, it looks like the nigga took my gun out of the drawer and used it to kill Jaseem. So, I need to go make a statement today."

"A statement? What kind of statement?" Brooklyn asked.

"It's just procedure, babes. It hurts my soul that a nigga would take *my* gun and kill my brother. It looks like he surprised Jaseem. I'ma give them a list of our clientele. It could be one of them for all we know."

"Hmmm, do you need a lawyer? I can call my friend. He owns a law firm in downtown Richmond."

"Nah, babes. Trust me. I'm good."

I was doing fine until this nigga called her babes in front of me. Then I started feeling nauseated, and it was from my being pregnant. Jihad looked at me, and I shot him a dirty-ass look. I didn't give a fuck if that bitch saw me.

"Come on, baby, go lie down again. I'ma make you something to eat. We need you to feel better soon. I just lost my brother. I can't lose you too, babes."

He put his arm around her and led her out of the room and up the stairs. I let out a long sigh. I swear I was suffocating listening to how this nigga catered to this ho.

Shit, today was going to be a great day. I planned on hitting up the stores, spending a couple of stacks, getting my hair done, and a pedicure. I'ma hit up my bitch to see if she wants to join me. I grabbed the phone to dial her number. I know she wouldn't turn down no shopping.

"Boss lady, I'm about to step out for a few. Do you need me to do anything before I leave?" I said as I entered the bedroom.

"Oh no, Alyssa. Jihad already gave me something to eat, and I washed up. I'm going to answer a few emails and cancel the appointments that I had. Go ahead. Handle your business."

"OK, well, you know I'm only a phone call away."

"OK, love. Be careful out there."

I smiled and walked away. This bitch be acting like she's so fucking worried about me. Wait until she finds out *I'm* the bitch her nigga's going to replace her with. I wonder if she would still be sweet. I doubt it.

Chapter Twenty-three

Brooklyn

I felt so damn sick. I was unable to travel to Manassas for Jaseem's funeral. I felt really bad that I wasn't able to go support my man. This would also be the time for me to meet the rest of Jihad's family. Since we'd been together and married, I hadn't met anyone. This was crazy 'cause they live right here in Virginia. I've asked him about this numerous times, and the explanation he gave me was that he liked to keep his relationship private. I didn't believe him. I think Jihad grew up poor and was ashamed of his upbringing. This man has no idea that I love the ground he walks on and don't give a fuck if his family is poor or not.

My hands were shaking as I tried to make me a cup of ginger tea. I was even struggling to breathe. I'm not no doctor, but I could tell something was seriously wrong with me. Vomiting, headaches, nauseated for over a week . . . I was starting to get worried. I thought I would feel better, but I was only getting worse.

After I had made the tea, I slowly went upstairs. It took every ounce of strength in my body to climb those stairs. By the time I reached the top, I was struggling to breathe. I got in my room and flopped down on the bed after putting the cup of tea on the table. My eyes were burning out of control. I got up and walked to the mirror in the bathroom. I was shocked to see my eyes. They were bloodshot red and weak. I stared at the person in the mirror, and I didn't recognize me. Tears welled up in my eyes, and my head started to spin. I dragged my hand on the wall for support and finally made it to bed. Then I grabbed my phone and called Jas. I thought about calling my husband, but he was dealing with enough, so I called my best friend.

"Hello, I know you ain't calling me. I thought I made it clear that I don't have anything to say to you."

"Jas, do you still have the key I gave you to the house?"

"Yeah, why? So, now you want your key back?"

I was feeling weaker and weaker by the second. Everything around me was starting to darken.

"Brooklyn, why are you breathing like that? Hold up, are you OK?"

I couldn't answer. I was gasping for air. Finally, I fell to the ground, dropping the phone out of my hand.

"Brooklyn, oh my God. Say something. What's happening? I'm on my way. Hold on, baby, I'm on my way," she yelled.

God, please, don't let me die. Please, God, I thought. *My husband needs me, God. He needs me . . .*

"Brooklyn, baby, where are you?" I heard Jas yelling.

I wanted to answer her, but the sounds wouldn't come out. I was happy she was here 'cause I thought I would die before she got here.

"Oh my God, what the hell happened? The ambulance is on the way."

She lifted my head from the ground. "You're burning up. How long you been feeling like this? Where's Jihad's ass at?"

Tears rolled down my face. I just didn't have the strength to answer all her questions. Then within a minute, I heard the doorbell ringing.

"I'll be right back, baby. Hang on." She gently placed my head back down and rushed out of the room.

"She's right here. Please, help her."

By now, her voice was sounding like whispers. The room was turning upside and down. My body started to tremble. I thought I was cold until I began to convulse out of control.

"She's having a seizure. Get in here," I heard a man say.

"Do you know your name?" a doctor asked.

I was about to answer him, but it wasn't so clear. I had to think. My name . . .

Yes, Brooklyn."

"Do you know how you got here?"

I shook my head. The last thing I remembered was lying on the ground, and Jas was there.

I looked to the side and saw her standing there, looking like she was crying.

"Doctor, do you have any idea what would cause her to be this sick and cause seizures?"

"We're waiting on the lab to see what's going on with her blood. Her temperature dropped, and her heartbeat was irregular, so we're trying to find out what is causing that. I'm hoping we can have some answers for you soon. In the meantime, I have her on antibiotics and Acetazolamide. She needs to get some rest."

"Okay, Doctor. Thank you."

After the doctor left, Jas walked over to the bed and sat at the edge.

"How are you feeling, boo?"

"Tired and confused . . . memory kind of fucked up. Is Jihad here?" I quizzed.

"He's on the way. But listen, Brooklyn, I'm really worried about you. This is *not* normal. This is the second time you fell out, so it's got to be serious."

"I don't know what's going on, Jas. I was back at work and doing good until last week."

"Hmmm, I'm worried about you. I pray they come back with some answers today. If not, I'm getting some better doctors and specialists. Somebody's going to find out what the fuck is going on with you," she said on a serious note. See, Jas was a no-nonsense bitch. Maybe it was the lawyer in her, but when she makes up her mind about something, she means it.

We were still talking when Jihad walked in.

"Hey, babes, I got here as fast as I could. What the fuck happened?" he asked as he rushed over to me.

"Really? I called yo' ass hours ago, and you just now getting here? Why the fuck you ain't been bringing her to the hospital?"

Oh my God, these two were getting ready to start. I'm lying in this fucking hospital bed, fighting for my life, and they can't even put their differences aside for a second.

"Can y'all please don't start?" I finally mustered up the energy to say.

"No, you know what, Jihad? Brooklyn was healthy before she married your ass. Then all of a sudden, she's passing out and shit. I don't know what the fuck's going on, but something is fishy, and I'ma get to the bottom of this. I promise you."

"What the fuck is that supposed to mean? You think *I'm* the reason why my wife is sick? I knew you were a fucked-up individual, but this is low, even for you."

"I said what I said. I'm watching you, nigga."

Jas walked over to me and kissed me on the forehead. "Get some rest, boo. I'll be back to check on you tomorrow."

"Okay."

Without saying another word, she left. Jihad looked at me with an attitude plastered all across his face.

"What the fuck is *her* problem? I get she don't like me, but to accuse me of making you sick is pure disrespectful."

"Jihad, please. I'm too sick right now to deal with a bullshit-ass argument between you two. I love you, and I love her. However, both of you will have to learn how to be around each other without going at each other's throats. The shit is childish."

"I'm straight. I just don't want her ass around anymore."

"What's that supposed to mean?"

"I don't want her around anymore. I'm your husband, and if she can't respect me, you don't need her around— plain and simple."

This nigga must've lost his fucking mind. Either that or this medicine was making me delusional. I looked at him. I wanted to rip off his fucking head, but I didn't have the strength. So instead, I closed my eyes and hoped he'd drop the subject fast.

"Brooklyn, baby, I'm so sorry I left you home alone, but you know I've been dealing with my brother's death. But don't worry, babes, I won't leave you alone again." He rubbed my hand.

Even though I was pissed off at him, I still felt terrible for what he was going through.

"It's a rough time for us, but I promise you, we gon' get through it." I tried to sound strong for him. Truth is, I was feeling sick as hell. I was hoping the doctors would return with the results of my blood work. Last time, they didn't find anything strange in my blood, but I agree with Jas. This time, they *have* to give me some damn answers . . .

I opened my eyes and realized I was still in the hospital. I looked over and saw Jihad balled up on the sofa. Aw, that was sweet of him to spend the night with me. I know he would rather be at home in bed. My throat was dry. I reached over and poured some water. I was still feeling sleepy from the morphine they gave me for the pain, but I didn't mind 'cause I was in so much pain before.

"Hey, you. How are you feeling?" Jihad said as he opened his eyes.

"Feeling a lot better than when I got here. My memory still a little fuzzy, though. Hopefully, the doctor should have some answers for me today."

"Babes, I know how much you hates the hospital. If you want, I can take you home. I mean, I can take care of you."

"Jihad, aw, I appreciate it, but as much as I hate the hospital, I need to stay to get some answers and treatment for whatever is making me this ill. I'm scared the next time it will be my death."

"Sure, babes. Whatever you decide to do, I'm here with you."

I smiled at him. I wish Jas could see that he was different. He is not in this for the money. Why can't she see that he genuinely loves and cares about me? Jihad was right. He was my husband, and if she can't respect him, she definitely doesn't need to be in my life either.

"Good morning, Mrs. Lewis. How are you feeling this morning?"

"Doctor, I'm feeling much better, but did my blood work come back?"

"Absolutely. Have you been around or exposed to cyanide lately?"

"Cyanide? Why? Are you saying that's what is making me sick?" I looked at him, searching for answers.

"The lab results show lethal dosages of cyanide in your blood. How it got there is the question."

"Doctor, I'm a therapist. I go from my house to the office. I don't know how I would get exposed to cyanide. Are you sure that it might not be something else?"

"We are 100 percent sure. It's hydrogen cyanide poisoning. If you didn't get in here when you did, you could've died. But it's too early to tell if you will experience some long-term neurological problems."

"Doctor, my wife is right. She barely goes anywhere where she can digest that much cyanide. So there must be another explanation."

"I'm sorry, Mr. Lewis. I see this is hard for you, but our tests are correct. We can get a second opinion, but I'm confident the result will be the same. The nurse is going to give you a dosage of charcoal. I need you on 100 percent oxygen via an endotracheal tube, and because of the severity of the poisoning, I want to keep you for an extra couple of days so that we can monitor you."

"Thank you."

"Oh, and because of the level of cyanide in your blood, we've contacted the police department and the poison center. The police should be here shortly to speak with both of you."

"The police?" I looked at the doctor.

"It's just a precaution that we must take. It's unclear how the poison got into your system, and the police need to document this."

"Wait, Doctor, so you're saying someone did this to my wife?" Jihad yelled.

"I'm not suggesting that at all. However, we need to find out how it got into her body."

"OK, Doctor. Thanks."

I could see Jihad was ready to snap, and I was scared he might snap at the doctor, so I tried to smooth out the situation. After the doctor left, I looked at Jihad. I was speechless and confused. Cyanide poisoning . . . What the fuck was going on here . . . ?

That charcoal shit was nasty as hell, but I had no choice but to drink it. I felt sick but hoped this would make me feel much better. Then I tried to get some rest.

Jihad walked out soon after the doctor left. I thought he would stick around until the police officers came, but he said he had to handle some things. Then not long afterward, I heard the door push open.

"Good afternoon, Mrs. Lewis. I'm Detective Johnna, and this is Detective Saiid. How are you feeling?"

"I'm OK," I smiled.

"Well, we got a call from Dr. Lin. He informed us he suspected cyanide poisoning. Do you have any idea of who might've poisoned you?"

Are they fucking serious right now? I looked at their faces. Yes, these bitches were dead-ass serious.

"Listen, y'all, I have no idea how the cyanide got into my blood, but I'm sure no one was poisoning me. I don't know what story that doctor fed y'all, but he's wrong."

"We were hoping to speak with your husband, but I see he's not around."

"My husband? What do you need with him?"

"How long have you two been married?"

"Why? What are you insinuating? As a matter of fact, I'm done talking. Any further questions, you can contact my lawyer. Do y'all want her number?" I asked in an angry tone.

"I'm sorry, Mrs. Lewis. We didn't mean to upset you. We're only trying to get to the bottom of this."

"Well, y'all did. If you don't mind, please leave. I'm tired and don't feel good."

"Sure, we understand. Well, here is my card if you ever want to talk. Please don't hesitate to give me a call." She placed the card on the nightstand.

"We hope you feel better soon."

I didn't respond. Instead, I just stared at them. The fucking nerve of these people. I was sick of motherfuckers coming for my damn husband. I swear I'ma start checking everyone that comes at him.

***

It's been three days since I found out what was wrong with me, but I was no closer to finding out how the poison got into my system. I tried retracing my steps, returning to the first time I fell ill. Then the phone started ringing, so I grabbed it.

"Hello."

"Brooklyn, why the hell can't I see you?"

"What are you talking about now, girl?" I rolled my eyes to the back of my head.

"Bitch, I came up here twice and was informed that the patient requested that I not be allowed to visit. So what shit is this?"

"Jas, they're mistaken. I didn't request shit, and if you think I would do some foul shit like that to my best friend, then you really don't know me."

"If you didn't do it, then that nigga you married did it."

"Jas, there you go again, accusing him of some shit. Baby, you know these hospital people be mixing up shit sometimes. They could've easily made a mistake."

"I doubt they did. Are you still getting out today?"

"Yes, just waiting on the doctor to sign the release papers."

"All right. I guess I'll stop by later."

Shit, this wasn't a good idea, but before I could tell her that, she hung up. I was about to call her back, but Jihad walked into the room.

"Hey, beautiful, how are we doing today?"

"Hey, handsome, I'm feeling much better. I'm ready to get into my own clothes and my own bed."

"So, let's go then."

"Waiting on the doctor to release me."

"You don't need no damn doctor. I'm your husband. I got you." He walked over and kissed me on the forehead.

"You silly," I busted out laughing.

We talked a little, and then the nurse walked in. "Here are your release papers. Please sign here. And here are your prescriptions. The doctor wants you to follow up with your primary care physician."

"Thank you."

I was ready to go. Hopefully, I can keep my behind out of here for good this time. It felt great to get some fresh air finally, but it was humid, and that's when I realized I still had difficulty breathing.

"You OK, babes?" Jihad quizzed.

"Yeah, but it's still hard for me to breathe."

"Come on, let's get you out of this air."

After I got in the car, he got in and pulled off. I closed my eyes as he drove. All these clouds have been over our relationship since we got together. I wondered when our sunny days would come. When can we enjoy our marriage and love without all the destruction? Will it *ever* end . . . or was this just the beginning? God knows I can't take any more pain.

Jihad

Yes, I've been poisoning this bitch for a minute by putting cyanide in her homemade soups and juices that I was making her. This was the second fucking time, and this bitch survived this shit again. If it were up to me, I would've just shot her in the head, but that would cause suspicion. And nine times out of ten, I would be the number one suspect. Cyanide poisoning was supposed to cause a slow death, and a lot of times, when a person was sick for any length of time when they died, no one would look for cyanide in their blood. So, I was shocked when this fucking doctor confirmed she was poisoned. Then to make matters worse, this nigga said he informed the police. I was sweating profusely. I have no idea how Brooklyn didn't notice.

This wasn't good . . . the fucking police getting involved. I got the hell out of there before they arrived. I walked out of the room in a hurry and almost ran over one of the nurses on the way to the elevator. This had not been my week. First, it was my brother; now, it was Brooklyn. My name keeps coming up on the police radar. I know it's only a matter of time before they start digging . . .

"Hey, love," Alyssa greeted me when I entered the house.

"Hey. Fix me a drink, something strong," I demanded.

"Hmm, seems like you had a day from hell."

"You can call it that." I flopped down on the couch.

"Here you go. It's very strong. Now, do you want to tell me what's going on?"

"Nah, but you can give me some head. That will help ease the tension."

"Really? I've been nauseated all damn day. I can't give no head right now. Scared I might gag."

"Yo, you fucking another nigga?"

"What? Why the hell would you come at me like this?"

"I'm just saying, for the last few days, you been holding out on the head and pussy. You belong to me, so I should be able to fuck when I want to."

"Jihad, I'm not a piece of property. You don't *own* me."

I jumped up off the couch and grabbed that bitch by the throat. "Answer my question, bitch. Are you *fucking* someone else?"

"Oh, you're hurting me. Get off me, Jihad."

"Answer me, Alyssa," I yelled as I squeezed her neck.

"Stop, please. I'm pregnant. Please, Jihad."

Her cries got to me. I look down at her stomach, then let her go.

"Oh shit, I'm tripping," I mumbled.

She ran out of the room and up the stairs. I waited a few seconds, trying to calm myself. Then I made my way up the stairs.

I tried the door to the guest room, but it was locked. "Open the door, Alyssa. I swear I'm sorry, baby. I'm sorry, I'm just so jealous of you, baby."

"Go away, Jihad," she yelled.

I waited a few minutes and realized she wasn't budging. Fuck it. I walked away. I'm sorry I choked her ass, but she needs to watch her fucking mouth when talking to me. I do too much for this bitch for her to be so damn disrespectful.

I walked back downstairs and poured myself a glass of Goose. Then I called Trina.

"Hey, zaddy. I was wondering when I was gon' hear from you."

"Well, you just did, so can I come through and beat that pussy up real quick?"

"I'll be waiting, zaddy," she replied sexily.

"A'ight, I'm on the way."

I hung up and wasted no time putting on my sneakers and heading out the door. I hastily pulled away from the driveway. I was horny and looking forward to beating up that pussy.

I parked, got out, and walked to her door. She was standing there waiting for me. As soon as I entered, she hugged me and kissed me. "I missed you so much, baby. I been fienin' for the dick bad."

"Come show daddy how bad you miss him." I kicked off my shoes, along with my pants and drawers. Then I sat back on the couch, massaging my limp dick until it started to get hard. Shorty wasted no time. She dropped to her knees, gobbling up my whole dick. I closed my eyes as my toes curled and my insides shivered. This bitch was a beast with her tongue. This wasn't your average dick-sucking. She held the dick with one hand, then licked, sucked, and slurped on it while she massaged my balls with the other hand. I squirmed around in my seat.

"Shit, oh shit. Arrghh. Fuck, damn." I don't know what I was feeling, but it was bad in a good way.

She sucked harder until I busted in her mouth. Then she got on top, slid down on my dick, and rode it hard.

Slap, slap. I slapped her ass while she jiggled it on my rod. This feeling was good. I was hoping it would last, but it didn't. The pussy was so good I busted quickly. I didn't have time to pull out, so I just exploded in her. After sex, I lay back on the couch, trying to catch my breath. Shorty absolutely did a number on my body. I closed my eyes, trying to rest a little.

"Jihad, can I ask you a question?" She tapped me on the shoulder.

Shit, here we go. I bet this bitch about to ask for money. I know this shit was too good to be true.

I opened my eyes and looked at her as she sat beside me. "What's good?"

"Are you really in love with Alyssa?"

"Yeah, that's my girl. What's up? Oh man, don't tell me y'all set this up?" I looked at her suspiciously.

"Nah, I'm just saying. I don't get it . . ."

"Get what? What you talkin' 'bout, shorty?"

"I mean, here I am, single as hell, fucking you and sucking you good. But yet, a chick like Alyssa is the one that gets all the benefits."

"Shorty, you trippin'. I mean, you know that it couldn't be anything else between us. All we can do is fuck. So what do you want . . . money?"

"I don't want money. Jihad. I want *you*. My feelings for you have gotten so strong I can barely eat or sleep. Life ain't fair. I know I can be a better woman to you than her." She started crying.

"You trippin', shorty . . ."

"Am I? I mean, you wifing a bitch whose baby might be the next nigga's. A bitch that throws the pussy around. I mean, but hey, that's what you like, right?"

"Yo, hold the fuck up. What you mean the baby probably ain't mine. Did Alyssa tell you this?" I jumped up off the couch.

"Yeah, she told me. How else would I have known? You and that boy Jahmiel are the possible daddies. But shit, you the one with the money, so you are the father."

I looked at her to see if she was just blowing off steam. I know how vindictive chicks can get.

"You playing, right?"

"Whatever, Jihad. You have your head so buried up Alyssa's ass that you wouldn't see the truth if it smacked you dead in the face."

"This is some bullshit," I yelled out. "I'll kill Alyssa's ass. I swear I'ma kill that bitch *and* that nigga. I'm going home, and I'm going to kill this bitch."

"Really? So, you gon' tell her I told you right after we finished fucking?"

"Man, whatever. I don't give a fuck if she finds out we've been fucking. I'm going to rip that bitch's head off her body."

"I think you need to calm down. That baby could be yours, so you need to chill. You don't want to kill your child and go to prison."

I wasn't tryna hear shit she was saying. I was too fucking angry. So I just kept pacing and rubbing my head.

"Listen, baby, calm down. You can't go over there blowing up. It ain't like you been innocent. You've been fucking her best friend, remember? Don't you think she'll tell your wife, and all this will be one big mess?"

I didn't think about Brooklyn until she mentioned her name. Shit, I can't risk her finding out none of this. She and Alyssa had grown tight, and if anything happened, she would inquire. Shit, I need to think of another plan fast.

"I got to go."

"Baby, promise me you won't say a word to Alyssa. I don't want to lose our friendship."

"What friendship? Remember, we fuckin'."

I didn't wait to hear another word. I dressed, then dashed out of the house. I needed to get the fuck out of there.

I did a few lines of blow on my way to the house. The drugs helped calm me down, but my emotions were still running high. How could this bitch do this to me? I love her. I do everything for her—every fucking thing—and she's out there fucking this little chump.

Chapter Twenty-four

Brooklyn

I was so happy to be home once again. My memory was starting to return, and I wasn't feeling so weak. But I still was racking my brain, trying to figure out where the fuck that poison came from, and still couldn't come up with any valid answers.

I heard the doorbell. Jihad was downstairs, so I knew he would get it. I wondered who it was. It was a little past 5:00 p.m. I heard loud talking. Maybe it was Jihad and his cousin. I listened, but I heard Jas talking at the top of her lungs.

"You better get the hell out of my way. What the hell you mean I can't see my damn friend? Brooklyn, you better get this nigga," I heard her yell out.

I stumbled out of bed fast. This shit is crazy as hell. These fucking two are gonna be the death of me. I was almost out of the room when Jas flew up the stairs.

"What's going on?"

By then, Jihad's ass was making his way up the stairs, cussing. "Didn't I tell you I don't want this bitch around you no more?"

"Jihad, you need to chill the fuck out. I can't believe y'all doing this shit right now. I'm fucking sick, and this how y'all gon' act?"

"You know what, Brooklyn? You always choosing this bitch's side instead of standing up for your man. Fuck that . . . your *husband*," he yelled in my face.

"I'm not doing this right now."

I walked away from him after locking the door. Jas was already sitting on my bed. I turned around and looked at her. Why can't she just chill? She's supposed to be my bestie.

"Jas, why can't you just get along with him?" I shot her a dirty look.

"Brooklyn, are you fucking serious right now? I told you I was coming by. I didn't expect the nigga to be here. Furthermore, you're my fucking friend. So what gives him the right to fucking tell me I can't visit you? I'm telling you, this some crazy shit going on in this damn house."

I took a seat on the bed. Standing up makes me tired. I turned my head and looked at her, wondering what the fuck she was talking about.

"Strange? What the fuck you mean?"

"Just like I said, some strange shit's going on. First, you get sick, the doctors can't find out what's wrong, you feel better, and you come home. Then as soon as you come back home, you get sick again. This time, you're having seizures. Finally, the doctors said you have cyanide in your blood—and not a little, so it seems like someone was poisoning you."

"Hold the fuck up. You think it's Jihad?"

"Think? Bitch, I *know* his ass is behind this. Come on, you have never been sick before, and now you end up with *cyanide* poisoning? Bitch, you need to forget about how good that nigga fuck you and start thinking logically. Who has the most to gain if you drop dead? Remember, you did not make him sign the prenup. Look around you. All this shit you busted your ass to get will belong to his bum ass. Not your mother, but him. You know what? I love the fuck out of you, but you're acting real fucking stupid right now. Wake the fuck up."

"Can you lower your fucking voice? I understand you don't care for him, and he's not up to your standards, but you must understand I love him, he loves me, and we are married. I vowed to stick by my husband through the good, the bad, and the ugly. Why can't you just comprehend that?" The tears started rolling down my face.

This is my bitch, my right hand. Why can't she see this is who I choose to be with? Why can't she just be happy for me?

"Jas, let me ask you a question. Are you jealous of Jihad's and my relationship? I mean, I know you done had some fucked-up-ass men before, but Jihad is different."

"Bitch, are you *serious* right now? Is this the *best* you can come up with? I'm *jealous* of you? Bitch, he doesn't love you. He's a liar and a con man. Oh, and that bitch downstairs wearing your blouse—yes, that is *your* blouse. That is the *same* bitch I saw him with that night at the diner. You claim that's his cousin, but where the fuck she pop up from? Are you *sure* they are even related?"

"Bitch, you *really* tripping right now. Yes, that is his cousin. I swear you letting this lawyer shit get to your head. You actin' like it's a big old conspiracy set up to get me. There is *no* conspiracy. My husband is *not* after my money, and Alyssa *is* his cousin. I know you're used to it being just you and me, but it's *still* us. I'm just married now."

"Brooklyn, I see this conversation is not going anywhere. Bitch, wake the fuck up before you don't have a chance to wake back up for real. I love you with everything in me, but I can't sit back and watch you play stupid behind this nigga. If I were you, I would protect everything 'cause, baby, if this nigga don't finish you off, he's going to take you to the cleaners," she said as she stood up.

"You know this hurts so bad 'cause you're supposed to be there for me—*not* tear me down. Hmmm. I guess what Jihad said was true. You been jealous of me."

"Jealous? I'ma pray for you 'cause right now, you actin' like a stupid-ass bitch. These are the kind of bitches you and I laughed at for years, and now look at you. All for what? To say you have a bum lying up in your bed at night?"

"Get the fuck out of my house."

"You putting me out 'cause you can't face the truth?"

"You heard what the fuck I said. Get out of my shit," I yelled at the top of my lungs.

"You sorry just like that sorry-ass nigga. But you know my number. Hit me up when that bum takes everything you got—even your soul." She looked at me, shook her head, and walked out, slamming the door behind her.

I buried my head in the pillow and busted out crying. I've known Jas for over twenty years, and we have never had a fight this big. Never. This shit hurts. She handled me like I was a bitch on the street. How could she talk down to me like this after all we've been through?

Suddenly, I heard the door open. Jihad rushed over to me and wrapped his arms around me.

"Baby, are you okay? She didn't hurt you, did she?"

I didn't respond to him. Instead, I just cried. My heart was truly broken.

"Babes, for what it's worth, you're a great-ass friend."

"If I'm so great, why is my best friend acting like this? Why can't she just understand that I love you and I love her? There's no competition."

"Babes, I know you don't want to hear this. Sometimes you outgrow people. It seems like you outgrew Jas. But you got me and Alyssa now. We're a family."

I just continued crying, letting it all out. It's been too much for me to go through, mentally and physically.

Lately, I couldn't sleep at night. The conversation between Jas and me keeps echoing in my head. Finally, I turned and looked at Jihad. He was lying on his back, snoring. I took a long look at him. I wonder if what she said was true. Was he this wicked nigga that was only out to get my money? I was conflicted with my thoughts. I've seen both sides of him, but I wasn't sure which side to believe.

Today was the first day I could get out of bed and sit up. I sat in the sunroom with a cup of hot chocolate and a bagel. I had my laptop with me, so I decided to google cyanide poisoning, how it gets into your bloodstream, and how it causes dizziness, fast heart rate, and shortness of breath, followed by seizures. All of these are symptoms that I experienced. I also looked at what cyanide was used for. It was in pesticides, fumigants, and a bunch of other shit. It wasn't intended to be given to humans, and that's where the problem lies. I strolled down further. "Lethal exposures can result from accident, suicides, or homicide." My body shivered as I read that. I know damn well I don't smoke, nor was I around any kind of chemicals. But the word "homicide" stood out to me. Right then, Jas's voice popped back in my head, loud and clear . . .

"Hey, babes, you OK out there?" I heard Jihad holler as the door opened.

I quickly opened another page, pretending like I was looking up something else.

"There you are." He smiled at me while he walked over and kissed me on the forehead. My body tensed up. I tried not to let him notice it.

"You OK, babes? You seem unusually quiet today. Are you feeling all right?" He took a seat across from me.

"Yes, I'm fine. Just woke up with a slight headache, but I'm good."

"Anything good on there?" He pointed to the computer.

"Huh? No, I missed the news, so I was catching up on the latest. Same old shit, different day." I smiled at him. "Jihad, it's been a few weeks now, and Alyssa is still here. I mean, I know it's your cousin and all, but don't you think she should go home? You can't just visit a person's house, then stay there forever."

"Brooklyn, the only reason she was here was to help you when I'm not around. If you had told me it was a problem, it wouldn't have happened. I'll ask her to leave soon as she gets back."

"I appreciate her being here, but I know she has her own life. She has a baby on the way. So it's not fair for her to be here playing the help."

"I understand, babes. Trust me. I'll let her know. I'm going to make a quick run. Do you need anything?"

"No, I'm good. Gonna sit out here and relax for a while."

"OK, my love."

He started walking off and then turned back around.

"Brooklyn, you *do* know I love you, right?"

"Yes, love." I smiled at him.

I was happy that he was gone. My mind was speeding after what I had just read. Was I jumping the gun? I didn't have any proof that Jihad did this to me. I had to figure out a way to find out if he did or not. Was my life *really* in danger? Was I sleeping with the enemy? Too many thoughts invaded my head.

I tried my best to play it cool for the next couple of days. I would observe Alyssa and Jihad's interaction. It wasn't nothing more than family interactions. I think Jas was wrong about that. As far as Jihad, he was the loveable, doting husband.

"Babes, do you want me to fix you some soup?" The words that just came out of his mouth triggered something in me.

I didn't start getting sick until he made me soup. Could my husband be poisoning me through that damn soup? Wait, he also made me tea. That tea was extra sweet. Was that a cover-up so I wouldn't taste the cyanide? Oh shit, this has to be a mistake . . .

I jumped off the bed and walked down the stairs as fast as I could. I went straight to the kitchen and the cupboards. I searched for any bottle that seemed out of place, but there were only spices and seasonings. Nothing was out of place. I was kind of disappointed 'cause I was sure something was in the kitchen. Then I looked at the lower cupboards—still nothing.

I opened the garage door, turned on the lights, and carefully walked down the stairs. I walked to the cupboards there and searched them. Again, nothing. I was all up under the tables. I reached my hand up under one table, and my hand bumped into something hard. I looked under the table . . . and saw a gun. Why the fuck did Jihad have a gun taped under the table? I shook my head and got up. I looked around the room, but there was nowhere else to check. Hmmm . . . if I were Jihad, where would I hide some poison? Maybe it's not here because my husband was not poisoning me.

I took one last glance, then made my way up the stairs. Then I heard the door opening, so I rushed to the kitchen. It was Alyssa coming through the door with lots of bags in her hands.

"Hey, Alyssa, you went shopping again?" I swear, every day this week, she walked in with tons of bags. Even UPS delivered several bags. I guess the baby daddy came through with some money.

"Hey, boss lady. I've been buying my baby stuff with the money I made from working with you. I don't have that long to go, so I need to prepare for my son."

"So, you found out it's a boy?"

"Yes, you were not feeling well, so I didn't get a chance to share the good news with you."

"Oh, OK. Alyssa, did Jihad talk to you?"

"Talk to me? Why? What's wrong? Did I do something?"

"I was wondering when you're going home. Shouldn't you be getting your place ready to welcome the baby?"

"Oh my God, Jihad didn't tell you what happened?" She put her hand over her mouth.

"What are you talking about?" I asked. I could tell something was wrong by the way she was behaving.

"I'm so ashamed. I got put out of my place. I've been trying to find a shelter, but they have no space at the women's one in Hopewell." She busted out crying.

"Oh no, why you didn't tell me this?" I felt terrible that I even said anything to her.

"It happened while you were at the hospital. You were already going through enough, so I didn't want to burden you anymore." She started shaking uncontrollably.

"Oh no, you need to calm down. I didn't know about this. Where are your parents? They won't let you move back in?"

She continued sobbing. "I d-on-t kn-ow how-how much Jihad told you, but my-my parents were drug addicts. The-y both died wh-en I was young."

"Oh Lawd, I'm sorry. You know what? You can stay here. I'll talk to Jihad, and we can figure something out."

"No, I'll go find a room or something. I don't want to impose any more than what I've done," she said between cries.

This poor child was going through it. I pitied her and was angry at the no-good-ass nigga that got her pregnant.

"You're going to be fine. I'm sorry about this. I had no idea."

She hung on to me and hugged me tightly. "I love and appreciate you. I swear I'll find something."

"It's OK. Now, you need to calm down. All this crying can't be good for the baby."

She started wiping away her tears with the sleeve of her shirt. This chick was going through hell, I thought.

After she got her crying under control, I went to my room and flopped down on the bed. Whew, that was stressful as fuck. There I was, trying to put her out, and then she dropped this bombshell. I need a fucking drink. I've never seen one person cry so damn much. I know she's going through it.

Jihad

This bitch needs to be dead, I kept saying to myself as I paced back and forth. I was tired of being married to her boring ass. It's always, *Jihad, where you been? Jihad, what you doing?* Fuck, bitch, I'm grown. I felt like a fucking prisoner. Sometimes, it's hard to be around this ho, playing the loving husband role.

I noticed Brooklyn has been quieter than usual. I inquired about what was wrong, but she kept assuring me nothing was wrong. Bullshit. I can smell that lie a mile away. Brooklyn was definitely up to something, and I needed to find out what it was.

I tried my best to pacify the bitch 'cause whatever it was, I really didn't give a fuck. All I've been thinking about is plan B 'cause plan A fell through. Can't poison her anymore. That would be a disaster.

***

I've been trying my best to avoid Alyssa. After what I've learned, I can't look at her the same. She tried her best to talk to me, but each time, I quickly reminded her that Brooklyn was in the house and we had to be careful. Her ass was not buying that. So instead, I had to sneak to her room on different occasions and give her the dick, lie in there with her until she fell asleep, then I could leave the room, nervous that Brooklyn might be standing outside the door. Alyssa wasn't thinking straight, so I needed to do the thinking for both of us.

I was lying in the sunroom, just thinking of my next move. Then my phone started ringing. Shit, it was the fucking detectives. Ever since my brother's death, they've been hounding my ass. I pressed ignore on the phone. I already know what the hell they wanted. I plan to talk to a lawyer in the morning to be safe.

A few minutes later, I heard Brooklyn calling me. "Jihad, Jihad," she yelled.

"The detectives are here. They want to talk to you."

"What the fuck they want? Tell them I'm not here."

"You better come on. I think they got some news about your brother's death. This might be good."

Shit, this bitch was tripping. What could be good about some detectives visiting?

I got up and walked into the house with my game face on. I made eye contact with them as I approached them.

"Mr. Lewis, how are you holding up?"

"I'm maintainin'." I kept it simple.

"Well, we've been trying to catch up with you. Do you want to talk in private?"

"Nah, she my better half. I ain't got nothing to hide from her."

"Good, well, the ballistics are back from the gun used to murder your brother. Mr. Lewis, do you own a firearm?"

"Yes, I do. I already told the officer. It was at the office in the drawer by the desk."

"Yes, I read that. It was the gun that was used to murder your brother. This is the thing that puzzles me. If this was a robbery, wouldn't the killer go into the business already armed? Why dig around for a weapon?"

"Detective, you're asking the wrong person. You need to ask the killer these questions once you find them."

"I agree, Mr. Lewis. I don't recall if I've asked you this question before, but did you and your brother have any bad blood between you two?"

"Yes, you asked already, and I told you we good."

"That's another thing that has me puzzled. I spoke to your brother's wife, and she told us the two of you were constantly fighting over money. She said you had a couple of lawsuits against you and the company—"

"Detective, hold on. Is my husband a suspect in his brother's death?" Brooklyn stepped up and asked.

"No, ma'am, we are questioning everyone who knew the victim. He and your husband were business partners, so we're trying to clear up a few discrepancies."

"Detective, in case you didn't know, the business went under. The bank foreclosed on it. There is no money, so why would I kill my brother? I loved my brother, and yes, we had problems, but nothing that would make me kill my own flesh and blood. I had to look my mother in the eyes and comfort her. I loved my brother." The tears started welling up in my eyes.

"Detective, as you can see, my husband is still distraught about the murder of his brother. If there are any more questions, I suggest you contact our attorney. His name is Peter Vaughn, and here is his number."

"Thank you, ma'am. We will do just that. See you around, Mr. Lewis."

They turned around and walked to the door. Brooklyn opened the door, and they walked out. I let out a long sigh of relief. This was one of the times I was happy to be married to Brooklyn. She talked that lawyer shit that sent them flying out of here. Now, if only they would leave me the fuck alone, that would be nice.

"Listen, Jihad. I don't know if you picked up on that, but they're treating you like a suspect. I don't think you should talk to these motherfuckers without a lawyer present. I'll talk to Peter in the morning. But, trust me, they don't want to fuck with him. He's a beast in the courthouse."

"Brooklyn, what would I do without you? I swear, babes, I'll show you just how much you mean to me one day. Just watch."

In the corner of my eye, I saw Alyssa had walked down the stairs and stopped to look at me while I hugged Brooklyn. When our eyes locked, she shook her head and walked off. I wanted to run behind her, but right now, comforting Brooklyn was much more important.

Later that night, after I made sure Brooklyn was asleep, I tiptoed out of the room and into Alyssa's room. I know she was upset, so I needed to be with her. I opened the door, and she was lying in bed. I tried to get up behind her under the covers.

"Why are you here? Weren't you just in the bed with your woman?" she asked as she threw my hands off her. I knew she was mad, but I wasn't giving up.

"C'mon, babes, we about to have our baby. You know whatever I'm doing is for us."

"For *us,* Jihad? There can't be no *us* until that bitch in there is out of the way. You're legally married to her—not me. Me and your fucking child are a fucking secret!" she yelled.

"Man, chill out with all that yelling. You and my baby ain't no damn secret. I love y'all."

She sat up in bed and looked at me with tears rolling down her face. "*Really,* Jihad? If that's true, walk in there right now and tell her I'm your woman, and this is your baby."

"Are you fucking serious? I told you what I was trying to do."

"Exactly. All you keep feeding me is bullshit. You know what? Me and my child don't need you. Come tomorrow, I'm fucking leaving."

"Yo, you trippin'. You know what? Since you actin' like this, whose baby is this anyway?"

She looked at me like she'd seen a ghost. "What the fuck you mean by that?"

"You heard me. Is this my baby or that young punk that you was fucking?" I started to feel the anger creep up on me.

"I don't know what kind of sick joke you're trying to play, but I want no parts of it. It's kind of funny that soon as I tell you to go tell your bitch that we're together, now, you're acting like this ain't your baby."

"Bitch, shut up. Ain't nobody trying to do shit. I asked you a simple question. Is this *my* baby or not?" I shoved her face. I was using all my strength not to beat her ass.

"Keep your fucking hands off me, Jihad. I swear, I will go in the next room and wake that bitch up," she threatened.

Slap, slap, slap!

"Don't you *ever* threaten me, bitch. I swear, I will *kill* you." I jumped on top of that bitch and yelled in her face.

"I can't believe you keep putting your fucking hands on me. I'm fucking done. Get the fuck off me, Jihad."

"Bitch, you better pray to God this my motherfucking seed 'cause if not, they're going to find you at the bottom of the James River," I yelled, and I was serious as fuck.

She didn't say a word. She just lay there crying. I know there was some truth to this 'cause her ass wasn't defending it or telling me it's a lie. I was pissed the fuck off. I looked at that bitch, shook my head, and walked out of the room.

I went downstairs and got me a quick drink before sneaking into the room with Brooklyn. I thought she was asleep, but I was wrong.

"Hey, did you hear some kind of yelling?" Brooklyn turned around and asked me.

"Huh, yelling? Nah, I ain't hear nothing. I couldn't sleep, so I went downstairs for a drink."

"Hmm, I was probably dreaming. It seemed so real, though."

"Yeah, babes, you were shifting around. I think you were dreaming. Go back to sleep," I said.

That was close, I thought as I lay down. I was still angry at Alyssa, but I knew I had to be careful. This bitch done threatened to tell Brooklyn about us. I couldn't risk that happening.

Brooklyn and I talked to the lawyer earlier and explained to him what the police were saying. The lawyer asked me for the gun, and like I told the police, I told him I had left it in the drawer in the office. That was the last time I saw that gun. The lawyer was supposed to be one of the best in Virginia, so I felt confident as I walked out. I was ready for this shit to disappear. I been on pins and needles since they stopped by the house. I was careful, but this gun shit had them paying attention to me.

I pulled up at the gym. This was my second day coming up here since Jaseem died. I had a few things that I had to clean up out of here. I hired a moving company to move out the equipment. I planned to put all of it in storage until it was time to open another gym. I was going to let some time go by before I got back into the swing of things. By then, hopefully, I'll have enough money to start over.

I saw the truck pull up by the curb, so I got out of my SUV. I walked over and dapped them up, then opened the door. I stepped inside. I had an eerie feeling like Jaseem was standing there looking at me. I think it was just my conscience fucking with me.

"You a'ight?" one of the dudes asked me.

"Yeah, what's good?" I asked him.

"You were looking like you seen a ghost."

"Nah, I'm straight. Just make sure y'all get everything. Might need more than one trip."

"A'ight, boss, got you."

I walked off and then stopped at the door. I was hesitant, but then I opened the door to the office and entered. Blood was still on the floor where Jaseem bled out. I stepped to the side and went to the desk. I couldn't breathe in the room. I felt like I was suffocating. My stomach started to turn, and I rushed to the bathroom. I bent over the toilet. The BLT sandwich I had a few hours ago came right up. I didn't feel good. After I finished, I washed out my mouth and rinsed my face. I was feeling weak and nauseated. I needed to get out of this place ASAP.

I made my way to the truck and sat inside while the workers finished packing everything. I waited until they made two trips to the storage and came back. Shit, I must've dozed off 'cause I heard a banging on the window. I opened my eyes and saw one of the dudes who was moving the furniture.

"Yo, what's good?"

"Just letting you know we finished. The boss wanna know if you want to go in and make sure that's everything."

"Yo, tell him thanks. I got it."

"All right, boss."

I watched as he walked off. A few minutes later, they drove off. I got out of the truck, walked over to the door, and locked it. I was kind of hurt. This was my home for a long time. I hurriedly walked away. I needed to get the fuck away from here fast.

Alyssa

I couldn't sleep last night. Jihad and I had a big-ass fight, and that nigga put his hands on me again. See, I don't know who this nigga think I was, but this is the last fucking time he's going to put his hands on me like that. I eased up out of bed and walked to the mirror. My right eye was almost swollen shut. My face was bruised up. I used my hand and ran it across my black and blue face. I smiled, but it wasn't no good smile. I was beyond pissed. I was angry as fuck. I thought about calling the police on this nigga, but it would only make him angrier. Plus, I knew he was poisoning his wife, but I will keep that little secret until after I had my baby. Let's see how much he would pay for me to keep that.

I quickly got dressed and started throwing clothes in my bag. I heard when he left, and the bitch was probably in her room. I quietly took my stuff out and came back and grabbed the rest. I locked the door behind me, got in my car, and sped off. I needed to get the fuck away from here fast.

As I sped down the streets, tears rolled down my face. I was beyond hurt. This nigga keeps on putting his hands on me, and then later, he would apologize. I'm tired of this shit. There's no way I'll keep letting this nigga get away with this shit. I lit a cigarette and took a couple of pulls while I drove. Something needs to change fast.

I knew Jihad would look for me at my crib, so I went to my mama's house. As much as she got on my nerves, I missed my mama. I pulled into her driveway, parked behind her car, grabbed my purse, and walked to her door. I rang the doorbell and waited. Shit, I wish she would hurry the fuck up. It was cold outside, and I left in a little shirt and a pair of tights. I rang the doorbell several times and was about to dial her phone when I heard movements inside.

"Who is it?" she yelled.

"It's me, Ma," I yelled back.

She opened the door. I could tell she was shocked 'cause she just stood there staring instead of inviting me in.

"Ma, move out of the way. It's cold out here." I pushed past her.

"I bet you is. The whole of your stomach is hanging out. You know you're pregnant and should wear bigger clothes."

"All right, Mother. Don't start stressing me out."

I sat on the couch, rubbing my hands together, trying to get warm. Mama walked toward me, but then she stopped.

"Baby, oh my God. What the fuck is wrong with your face?" She ran to me and tried to touch it.

"Ma, please don't ask and don't touch it. It hurts."

"Did that bastard-ass nigga do this to you? I told you there was something about his ass."

"Ma, it's okay. I'm done with him."

"Did you call the police? You need to press charges against him. You're too young to have a man beating on you. Look how fucked up your face is." She lit a cigarette and kept pacing.

"Ma, please, just stop. I didn't call the police."

"Alyssa, you're too beautiful to be going through this. I don't care how good his dick is or how much money he has. You need to leave him the fuck alone. I wouldn't let him see the baby if I were you. Next time, he might kill you."

I was starting to think this was a mistake coming to Mama's house. I just wanted somewhere to crash. But here she was, being judgmental and shit. Trust me. I'm not no fool, and I don't need nobody to tell me Jihad was a piece of shit. It might've taken a minute to realize, but I could see clearly now.

She walked off toward the back, then came back a few minutes later. "Here, let me clean off your face. I swear I want to rip that fucker's head off with my hands." I could hear the anger in her voice.

"Ma, please, calm down. And trust me, I'm a big girl. I can handle myself."

"You need a gun; *that's* what you need," she said as she cleaned my face.

"Awee, Ma, that hurt." I shifted my face.

"Sorry, baby, but the peroxide will clean any germs. This bastard either needs to be dead or in jail."

Part of me felt the same way about Jihad, but the other part still loved him. I wish he didn't do this because my love for him was turning into hate.

After Mama finished, I lay back on the couch. I was tired and needed to lie down for a quick second.

"Baby, go lie on the bed. This couch ain't no good for you and the baby."

I got up, walked into her room, got in bed, and crawled under the cover. I was feeling all different kinds of emotions. I couldn't stop thinking about how nasty Jihad was to me. The main thing that puzzled me, though, was where the fuck did Jihad hear that my baby might not be his? Did that nigga Jahmiel tell that to someone? The truth is, only Jahmiel, Trina, and I knew about this. I know my bitch didn't tell anyone, so where the fuck did this nigga get this from? Figuring out this shit made my head hurt.

"Baby, you asleep?" Mama knocked on the door.

"Nah, Ma, just lying here."

She walked in, sat on the side of the bed, and started rubbing my leg.

"Listen, baby, I don't know what's going on between you and that man, but I do know if he loved you, he would never put his hands on you like this. You're the mother of his child. How dare he disrespect you like this. By the way . . . Did he ever leave that wife of his?"

Lord, I was hoping she had forgotten that he was married. This was a topic I didn't want to discuss with her.

"No, Ma, he's still married."

"I told you he was no better than your damn daddy . . ."

"Well, Mama, I'm not you."

"What's that supposed to mean?" She looked at me strangely.

"Ma, I didn't mean anything, okay?"

I knew her feelings were easily hurt, especially when discussing Daddy. After all these years, this was still a hurtful conversation for her.

"Listen, baby, I know you think I'm old and don't know what I'm talking about. But I do know you deserve better. You're my child, and I want you to have more than me. So, maybe it's time to stop thinking with your heart. Wake up. This man's not going to leave his wife. He's bullshitting. You need to start thinking about you and the baby 'cause that's all you'll end up with in the end."

"Like you did, huh?" I said sarcastically.

"You know what? One day, you'll come back and say, 'Mama, you were right.' Get some rest." She patted my leg, got up, and walked out.

Okay, I was being a bitch when I said that to Mama, but I lived my entire life listening to how my daddy dragged her. I didn't want to hear that shit. Plus, I'm not her. I'm not going to continue playing the fool.

Chapter Twenty-five

Brooklyn

I was getting sick and tired of being in this house. I stood in the window looking out. Finally, I was ready to get back to work. I felt terrible that I had to cancel all my appointments indefinitely, but I was starting to feel better now, so we'll see how the next week goes.

Speaking of work, it was kind of weird. I realized I hadn't seen Alyssa all day yesterday, so I went to the room to check for her. I knocked and waited, but no one answered. I turned the door and went in, but no one was there. Alyssa was gone, and so was her stuff. I closed the door and walked out. This was strange. When did she leave, and then she didn't say anything? Oh well, that was nice she found somewhere to go. Later, I'll check up on her. She certainly was on my mind a lot.

I spotted the mailman pulling up. I waited for him to put the mail in the mailbox, and then I walked out. It felt good to get some fresh air. It was a bit on the windy side, but I welcomed it. I'd been locked in this house too damn long and was starting to have cabin fever.

I saw the neighbor getting in her car. She waved as she pulled off. I opened the mailbox and took out the mail. Damn, Jihad must not have been checking the mail, I thought as I made my way to the door, sifting through tons of mail in my hands. Entering the house, I decided to take a seat in the living room to open the mail. Most of this shit was junk mail or credit card companies trying to get me to open a new line of credit. I was almost finished going through the mail when I spotted a Bank of America bill. I ripped it open.

What the fuck is this? I nervously combed through the pages. It was a bill for over ten grand. This was strange 'cause I never used this card. Oh my God! This was the card that I put Jihad on. What the fuck did this nigga charge that costs over ten fucking grand? I had told him this was only for emergencies. I started sweating, and I was getting angrier by the second. Did this nigga *really* do this shit? I held the bill, got up, and stormed up the stairs. I dialed his number. The phone rang without any response. I thought about leaving him a message but changed my mind.

I kept pacing back and forth. *You bastard. I trusted you.* Jasmine's voice echoed in my head, telling me he was only in it for the money. Now, it seems truer than ever. First fifty grand, and now this . . .

I sat on the edge of the bed, waiting and waiting for this nigga to get in this fucking house. It was a little past 9:00 p.m. when I finally heard the garage door opening. Then he walked up the stairs, entered the room, and cut on the light.

"Baby, why you sitting here in the dark like this?" He walked up to me.

I raised the bat and went straight for his kneecap.

Bap, bap, bap!

"What the fuck you do that for? Brooklyn, have you lost your fucking mind?"

"Nah, but you did, nigga. What the fuck did you use my fucking card to buy?" I kept trying to hit him, but the nigga kept running around the room.

"Yo, you need to chill the fuck out. I ain't used the fucking card to do shit. Bitch, you trippin' coming at me like that."

I looked at that nigga and lunged toward him. This time I missed. He grabbed the bat and wrestled it away from me.

"Now, if I beat yo' motherfucking ass, how would *you* feel? Go sit the fuck down."

"Nigga, fuck you. What did you do with my fucking card? Answer that, nigga," I yelled as I tried jumping in his face.

"Bitch, I swear you better back the fuck up." He raised the bat and pointed it at me.

"Or *what,* Jihad? You gon' beat me? You know I was such a fool for believing that you loved me. Jas was right. Your broke ass was only in it for the money."

"Look how you sound. Instead of finding out the truth or coming to talk to your husband like a real woman would do, you attack me. You know, I should've kept it moving when I first realized you're not the woman you portrayed to me. You a fraud, Brooklyn, and soon, everybody will see the *real* you. Money can hide the trash you are, but only for so long."

I stood there looking at this nigga. All that shit he was talking about didn't really matter. All I fucking cared about was my motherfucking money.

"I don't give a fuck what you say about me, Jihad. All I care about is what the fuck you spent my money on. You don't pay no fucking bills around here or buy food, so where did my money go?"

"Baby, I swear to God, it was a misunderstanding. When you call the bank and find out it was, then you owe me an apology. I love you, Brooklyn, and would never do anything like this to hurt you. I swear, baby, you have to believe me."

"Jihad, you need to get the fuck out of my house now," I screamed.

"Brooklyn, now, you know I can't do that. You're my wife. We're married."

"I don't give a fuck. I want you out of my shit," I yelled.

I ran up to him and started punching him in the face. The rage I felt gave me an extra boost 'cause I got a couple of licks in before he grabbed my hands and pushed me against the wall.

"Bitch, I done told you to keep your motherfucking hands off me. I don't want to beat yo' ass, Brooklyn," he yelled in my face.

"Boy, fuck you. I want you up out of my shit. I want a fucking divorce. I want you *out*," I yelled.

"Bitch, I'll kill you before I leave you. We in this together, you hear me?" He pressed his lips down on mine and bit me hard.

"You, stupid-ass nigga," I yelled as I bit his arm with everything in me.

"Damn, bitch, you bit me," he yelled.

He let go of me, then lunged toward me. I ran to my phone and thought about calling the police. I stopped short of calling them because I also bit him, even though he was the aggressor. Knowing the law in Virginia, if the cops came, both of us would go to jail. He walked out of the room, cussing under his breath. I ran to the door and locked it.

I quickly made my way to the mirror. The first thing I saw was blood. This beast bit into my skin like a savage animal. I reached for the peroxide and quickly cleaned my lip. It was starting to swell up on me. I needed to put some ice on it, but I was too scared to leave my room. So instead, I took a pain pill and got in my bed. I kept the phone close just in case this fool decided to bust up in here. I was so angry I barely slept. I kept twisting and turning all over the bed. I can't believe that nigga took my fucking money and then had the nerve to act like the bank don't know what the fuck they're talking about. This nigga got life fucked up.

I was up bright and early. I took my shower and dressed. When I looked in the mirror, my lip was still swollen, and dried-up blood was visible. I put a little Vaseline on it so it wouldn't look so bad. Then I put on my coat and grabbed my car keys. I stood at the door with my ear up against it. I didn't hear any movement, so I quietly opened it and tiptoed down the stairs.

"There you go." He appeared from the hallway.

"Jihad, go to hell."

I didn't even look at him. Instead, I kept walking, hoping and praying this fool wouldn't try nothing slick.

"Brooklyn, I love you, baby, and I'm not giving up on us."

I ignored him and walked out the front door. As I got into my car, I saw him standing in the doorway with a big old stupid grin plastered across his face. I shook my head as I drove off. This nigga was behaving like a psychopath. I wasn't taking any risks with him at all.

First things first, I stopped by the bank. I took his ass off my account and got a printout of everything my money bought. After the banker handed me the detailed report, I walked out. I got in my car and started looking at what this nigga was doing with my money. This has to be some kind of joke. Thousands and thousands on baby clothes, furniture, food, pedicure, hair salon . . . It took a few minutes to register in my head that these were all female shit. My husband used *my* card, *my* hard-earned money, and bought some bitch all this shit. But wait . . . baby clothes, baby furniture . . . This nigga has a baby on the way? I started feeling nauseated. My head started spinning. I opened my car door and threw up. I hung my head down for a few minutes, trying to catch some air. I didn't feel good. After a few minutes, I found the strength to close the door and rested my head on the steering wheel.

"God, what is this? Please, tell me this nigga don't have a baby on me," I said out loud as the tears slid down my face. I hit the steering wheel a few times. This can't be. I picked up the bank statement and looked at it again.

I grabbed my phone to call him, but all he would do was deny it, so I closed the door and headed home. It was dangerous for me to drive because I was dizzy and feeling weak. Then I quickly made a U-turn and headed in the opposite direction. I needed to make a stop before I headed home.

I knew I was probably the last person she wanted to see, but I had no one else. I was not in a good place mentally and physically. I parked my car in the visitor's space, got out, and walked into the law firm.

"Hello, good afternoon, Mrs. Lewis. How may I help you?" Anna, the receptionist, greeted me.

"Hey, Anna, Is Miss Wright in?"

"Yes, she is. Let me ring her up."

"Thanks."

I walked over and took a seat. I bent my head down, trying to control my emotions.

"Hey, you," I heard Jas say as she popped me on my arm.

I lifted my head and looked at her. Tears were rolling down my face.

"What's wrong? Come on, let's go to my office."

She put her hand on my shoulder and led me behind the two double doors. Jas's office was in the back, but don't get me wrong. It was the biggest and laid out. This bitch was definitely doing the damn thing.

After we walked in, she closed the door and pulled out a chair. "Here, take a seat. What the fuck's going on?" She sat on the edge of her table.

"Jas, I think you were right about Jihad."

"I know I was right, but what the fuck happened? Why are you crying?"

I took the paper out of my bag and handed it to her. She looked at me suspiciously. She then started reading. The room got quiet for a few minutes. I watched her facial expression while she went through the pages.

"Bitch, what the fuck is this? Whose account is this?"

"It's mine. I had given Jihad a card to use for emergencies, and this is what he did."

"This is all baby shit. Who the fuck got a baby on the way?"

"I'm trying to figure out the same fucking thing. The only person I know pregnant is his cousin, Alyssa."

"Bitch, I done told you that ho wasn't no cousin. Hmmm, this would be some crazy shit if this bitch-ass nigga had his side bitch living up in your house. Did you confront him?"

"I was going home but decided to stop here first."

"Hold on. What the fuck happened to your lip? Did he do this to you?"

I was ashamed. I couldn't respond, so I lowered my head and let the tears flow.

"Bitch, pick up your head. I know your heart's broken, but dry them fucking tears. You hear me? You're too strong of a woman to let this old bum-ass nigga play you."

I heard what she said, but my heart was hurting and probably broken into a million pieces. I tried to control the tears, but they just kept flowing.

"Here you go. As a matter of fact, let that shit out, and when you're finished, let's talk. Let's figure out how to get this broke-ass nigga up out of your life."Anna, please cancel and reschedule all my appointments for the rest of the day," she said into the phone.

She sat there quietly as I cried and cried. My head was pounding, and I was finally out of tears.

"Okay, now that you got that shit under control, bitch, you need to figure out what the fuck to do. First, we need a PI to investigate every fucking thing about this nigga. From his dirty drawers to his darkest secrets. Who he fucking, used to fuck—every gotdamn thing. Second, you need a divorce lawyer, and I know just the one for you. Brent White. He's excellent and a beast in the courtroom. And I need you to stop fucking him 'cause this what got you in this shit in the first place. Oh, wait, where's your gun at?"

"Huh?" I was sidetracked into my own thoughts.

"Bitch, where is your 9 mm Glock?" Jas seemed annoyed.

"Oh shit, I almost forgot about it. It's at home in my drawer."

"Well, bitch, you should've shot that nigga when he busted your lip like that. Brooklyn, we grew up together, so I know you ain't no soft bitch. So, I'ma need you to get it the fuck together."

"Jas, you don't know what the fuck I'm going through. I love this man . . ." My voice trailed off.

She got off the desk, walked over to me, and took my hand. "You're right. I may not understand it 'cause I ain't ever been married. What I *do* know is that nigga is a piece of shit, and you deserve so much more, Brooklyn. Someone that will love you for you, not your damn account. You brought this bum into your life. Now, you need to send him on his fucking way. Baby, I love you and hate seeing you hurting."

I saw tears roll down her face. I could tell she was hurting. I love this girl, and I wish I had the strength that she had. I couldn't do nothing but respect what the fuck she was saying. We hugged and cried together for a good five minutes.

"All right, bitch . . . Please, be careful with this nigga. You know the law. You got to give him a thirty-day notice to put him out. Also, you need proof—*lots* of proof. Remember, you ignored my warning to get the prenup and because of that, half of everything is his. So in order to discredit him, you need proof that he is dangerous. And let me take pics of your lip. I also believe that nigga was poisoning you with cyanide, so we need proof. That nigga ain't no fool. I think you should come stay with me until the divorce."

I quickly dried the tears from my eyes. "I bust my ass for years to get everything I got. There's no way I'm leaving my house. I'd rather die than leave my shit so this nigga can live," I spat.

I was angry now. I love this nigga, and *this* was how he played me? I think it was time that Jihad found out who the fuck this New York chick really was. I got off the chair and walked to the window, looking at the scenery outside.

Jas walked over to me and put her arms around me. "Listen, baby girl, don't blame yourself. You have a good heart. He's just too stupid to see that."

I reached over and rubbed her hand. This chick has no idea how much she means to me.

We sat and talked for a little longer, and then I decided to leave. I got into my car and pulled off. I stopped by the office for a bit to clear my head some before I headed home. Even though I was hurting, I was angry, and that anger had me plotting all kinds of shit.

I hate that I haven't been working, but I plan to return Monday. I know a lot is going on in my life, but I need to ensure I don't allow my business to go under. I busted my ass going to college and getting my degree. So I have to keep it under control.

I parked and got out. As I walked to the building, I saw someone walking away from the door. Probably a patient looking for me, I thought. As I got closer to the entrance, I recognized the face. What the fuck does this bitch want?

"What are you doing here? I thought I made clear that I don't want you anywhere near my business again," I yelled at Nicolette.

"Mrs. Lewis, please, just hear me out."

"I have nothing to say to you. I thought I made myself clear the first time."

I started walking off on her. I didn't forget what the fuck happened between that bitch and Jihad. Wait . . . *She* might be his side bitch. She ran behind me and jumped in front of me.

"Please, I only want to talk to you. All I need is a few minutes of your time."

I walked to the door and opened it. "You got five minutes before I throw out your ass."

I turned off the alarm, walked to the receptionist's desk, and sat.

"I think your husband set me up that day."

"Hmm, why would he do that? Do y'all know each other?" I looked at her with an attitude.

"No, I'd never met him until you two started dating. But you know me. I've been with you since you started this business. I've been nothing but loyal to you, so what sense did it make for me to come on sexually to your husband while he's here visiting you? I don't know what his motives were at the time, but it was a setup. I watched how he acted when you walked out of the office. Something isn't right about this man . . ."

I sat there listening while analyzing her. I could see in her eyes she was being genuine.

"My suspicion was right. I don't want to start anything between you and your husband, but I think the girl you hired is his mistress."

"Say what? Not only do you come in here accusing my husband of setting you up. Are you also accusing him of being unfaithful? You know, I gave you the benefit of the doubt. Thought you were going to apologize for what you did, but nah, you come in here with more accusations. Alyssa might not be as educated as you, but she's a damn good worker who's quick to learn."

"Brooklyn . . . I love you like a sister, and I'm telling you to be careful of those two. That man means you no good, and neither does that woman."

She looked at me with tears in her eyes and shook her head. Then she turned around and rushed out the door.

"Wait, Nicolette. Wait . . ."

She didn't stop, though. She ran out of the building. I sat there with my head on the desk. What the fuck is going on? Can my fucking day get any worse? It's like everything about Jihad was coming out. I don't know what to believe and what's a lie anymore.

I was mentally exhausted. I locked the door, then walked into my office. I left the lights off, crawled up on my couch, turned off my phone, and threw it back into my purse. I just needed to rest. I lay there crying in the dark, letting all my emotions pour out.

"God, please, take this pain away," I screamed as I grabbed my chest.

Then something strange happened. It was images of me walking, going toward the hallway. I was looking for my husband. I heard sounds. I was trying to make out the sounds. I pushed my guest bedroom door open, and I saw something. It was getting clearer. It was Jihad and a woman. Wait, it was his cousin, Alyssa. They were butt-ass naked having sex. I stood there looking. Then things started getting blurry. It was like I was watching myself in a movie. Suddenly, I jumped up. I looked around, and I was still in my office. What was that? It was everything that I forgot the night I fell out. It all came back to me.

Oh my God! This nigga had his bitch in my house the whole time, pretending they were cousins. This is crazy. I felt a sharp pain. I just sat there staring at the ceiling. Am I *that* fucking gullible? My mind replayed everything that had happened over the last couple of months. Oh. My. God. That bitch is also pregnant.

Something else popped into my mind as I went through my emotions. Jihad told the officers that he had left the gun at his workplace. But the day I searched the garage, his gun was taped under the table. This must be a second gun that he owns, but why? None of this was making sense. Why would Jihad lie? Oh my God. This can't be. I remembered my last conversation with his brother and how angry he was. Did Jihad kill his own blood? I couldn't take it. I buried my head in my hand, trying to convince myself I was tripping.

Jihad

Brooklyn's behavior wasn't getting any better. I was shocked as hell when I walked in, and she confronted me with the bill from the debit card. At first, I thought this ho was tripping . . . until I remembered that I gave Alyssa the card a few weeks ago. Oh fuck, what did this bitch do? Honestly, I only gave her the card that night she was going off on me. The plan was to take it back from her, but it slipped my mind.

Here I was, being attacked by this bitch. Brooklyn's ass don't know the *real* me, but she found out real fast when I bit the fuck out of her lip. I thought about killing that ho after she hit me, but I quickly remembered I had just killed my brother, and right now, it was too fucking hot.

***

I jumped out of the truck and headed to this bitch's apartment. I've been calling her for days, and her ass was not taking my calls. She even had the fucking audacity to cut off the fucking phone.

I banged on the door and waited, but there was no response. I continued banging until this old man popped his head out the door. He whispered some shit under his breath, then closed his door. He must've sensed that was the best thing for him 'cause I was all about some smoke. I got back into my truck and sent this bitch a few messages, waited a few minutes, and still nothing. That's when it hit me that her homegirl would know what was happening with this bitch. I dialed her number and waited for it to ring. My jaw tightened as anger swept through my veins.

"Hey, boo," she said gleefully.

"What's good, ma? Aye, have you seen Alyssa?"

"Is that what you called me for? I thought you were tryna come get some of this wet pussy."

"Chill, yo. You know I'll be there to beat up that pussy later. I just need to know if you heard from her."

"Jihad, you know that's my friend. I don't know what happened between y'all, but she is hiding over at her mama's house. But you can't let her know I told you."

I didn't even respond to her. I just hung up. Shit, where the fuck did that bitch say her mama live at? I tried racking my brain, but I kept coming up short. Finally, I slammed the steering wheel a few times. I was pissed the fuck off.

I was slowly losing it, that was . . . until I got a text on my phone. Someone invited me out to dinner. Even though I was pissed off, this dinner should brighten my night. I went home, took a quick shower, and left. I did notice before I pulled off that Brooklyn's car wasn't there. Where the fuck was this bitch at, I wondered. I had a date, and worrying about this bitch would have to wait until later. I looked at myself in the mirror. I had to admit I did clean up pretty well. I smiled. Even through all this bullshit, a nigga was looking GQ.

"Hey, you," I greeted my company.

"Hey there, Mr. Sexy."

"I was wondering why I haven't heard from you lately. I was starting to get worried." I planted a kiss on her lips as I pulled out the seat for her at the Longhorn Steakhouse Restaurant.

"No need to worry, handsome. You know I always come through." She smiled as she took a seat.

"Fo sho." I took a seat.

The waitress came, and we ordered drinks and our food. It was good to be in the company of a strong woman. One that doesn't come with all the drama and bullshit. I reached over to hold her hand while we talked and professed our feelings for each other.

An hour later, we finished eating. I pulled my wallet out to pay the tab.

"No, love. I got it." She winked at me.

She pulled out her AMEX credit card and handed it to the waitress.

"You never cease to amaze me." I kissed her hand.

"Be careful, darling. You know how turned on I get when you touch me."

"Well, that is *exactly* what I'm trying to do."

After the waitress returned her card and the receipt, we left. On our way out of the restaurant, I couldn't help myself. I grabbed her ass cheeks.

"Damn, babes, I really want you," she turned around and said.

"Yo, I would love to suck on that pussy right now."

She got in her car, looking at me all seductively. I also got in the car and stuck my finger between her legs. She was wet, just the way I love it. She started grinding on my finger. She was parked in the back, so I parted her legs, reached over, and buried my head between her legs. I took a few seconds to sniff her fresh scent. Then I started licking her pussy, inserting my tongue all the way up in her.

"Awee, yes, awe, loveeee," she screamed as she used her hand and pulled my head deeper inside.

I sucked on her pussy like it was the best thing I'd ever tasted. Her moaning only excited me more. Within minutes, she exploded in my mouth. I licked up every drop of her cum, cleaning her pussy with my tongue. She got up, unbuttoned my pants, pulled out my rock-hard dick, and wasted no time. She got on top of me and rode me in the parking lot. I was nervous about the thrill of getting laid by one of the baddest bitches in the world. I grabbed her ass as she grinded up and down my dick. I tried not to come, but the rush was too much. Finally, after about twenty minutes of thrusting in and out of her, I exploded in her tight pussy.

"Did we just do that?" She busted out laughing.

"Yes, we did, my love." I also started laughing.

"Now that our sexual appetite is satisfied let's get down to business. She is becoming a liability. What are your plans?" She changed from joking to serious.

"Well, poisoning the bitch didn't work, so I'm figuring out something else. I got it under control, my love," I assured her.

"You need to get it done ASAP. If you can't, you need to let me know so that I can find someone else. Jihad, you've really been doing too much. I'm tired of sharing you. All this needs to come to an end soon. Tie up all your loose ends." She looked at me.

I knew how serious she was. That was one of the things I admired about this lady, her no-nonsense attitude. I remember when she first approached me outside of my gym. I was drawn to her beauty, and then after we hooked up and fucked on the first night, I knew she was a savage. About two weeks later, she told me what her real intentions were. At first, I laughed at her, thinking it was a big joke. However, I soon discovered she was as serious as a heart attack. Initially, I was reluctant, but when she started talking numbers, it piqued my interest. It didn't take much to convince me to get on board. We had to be careful, though 'cause we couldn't risk being seen together. The rest is history.

This bitch gon' stop playing around with me. I wish I knew where the fuck her mother stayed. I went over to her friend's house, thinking if I gave her the dick, she would give me the info, only to find out she didn't know. I felt that bitch was lying 'cause they had been best friends since they were young. That selfish bitch just don't want me to get in touch with Alyssa. I looked at her and shook my head as I walked out of her apartment. I hope she enjoyed that fuck because it was the last fuck she got out of me. I don't have time to keep playing games with these silly bitches. I jumped in my truck and sped off.

There was no way Alyssa would stay at her mom's house for long. I know how much she said her mother got on her nerves. So I decided to park on the side of the apartment. That way, if she pulled up, I would see her. It was now three days later, and still no Alyssa. To keep my mind straight, I was high off coke. I ran through almost $500 worth lately. My nose was hurting, and I was tired and agitated. I'm not sure how much longer I could sit here. To be honest, my balls were sweaty, and I needed a shower badly. I was thinking about pulling off . . . until I spotted a car pulling in. I ducked but could still see the color and make. As if there's a god, here go this snake bitch pulling in. She parked, got out, and walked into her apartment building. I waited a few seconds, then ran up the stairs behind her.

I waited for her to open the door, then put my foot in. Her eyes widened when she saw my face.

"Surprise, honey." I pushed her ass in and locked the door.

"Jihad, what are you doing here?" She acted shocked while digging in her purse.

"What the fuck are you doing, bitch?" I snatched the purse away from her and threw it on the couch.

"Jihad, you're scaring me. You need to leave."

"Or what, Alyssa? I thought you loved me. Or was that a lie? You con me out of money, lied about having my baby, and ran up a fucking bank card. You fucked me over, shorty. What do you think I have to lose now?"

She tried dashing toward the bedroom, but I grabbed her by her braids and yanked her back toward me.

"Bitch, where the fuck you going? You don't have no fucking words now, huh? I gave you everything, bitch. Carried my wife behind you, and *this* is how you repay me?"

I started choking that bitch until she fell on the ground. Then I got on top of her and started punching her ass. My rage was uncontrollable, and being on coke gave me superman powers.

"Please, stop, Jihad. Please, I'm going to lose the baby," she screamed.

"Bitch, fuck you and this baby. That shit ain't mine." Now, I punched her in the stomach.

That bitch raised her hand and grabbed my balls, squeezing them so fucking hard. It threw me off. I jumped up and tried to grab the bitch again, but she got up and ran. I wanted to get her, but her little ass was already through the door. I rushed to the hallway, but I didn't see her.

"Come back here, Alyssa. I swear to God I'ma kill you," I yelled in the hallway.

That old-ass neighbor popped his head out again. I felt his ass was calling the police 'cause I saw him on the phone whispering. I looked at him, and he quickly slammed the door. My balls were aching, so I hopped down the stairs, looking around to see if I saw the bitch. She was nowhere to be found, but her car was still parked outside. I got happy, but that soon changed when I heard police sirens coming into the parking lot.

I tried to run, but police cars surrounded me. "Stop and put your hands up," an officer yelled.

I started to run again, thinking I could still get away. "I said stop before I shoot your ass." He pointed the gun at my face.

I stopped and put up my hands. They rushed over to me. "What's your name?"

"Jihad Lewis."

"Turn around and put your hands behind your back."

"What I do, Officer? I was just walking to my vehicle. I didn't do anything," I kept saying.

"Suspect is secured," he said into his radio.

"Officer, can you tell me what I did?"

"We were called because you beat up a pregnant woman. You have the same name as the suspect and fit the description."

"Officer, I swear to God, I ain't beat up nobody. I just broke up with my girlfriend, and she said she would hurt herself and tell y'all I did it. I swear, I ain't touch that girl."

"Jihad Lewis, you're under arrest for battery. You have the right to remain silent. Anything you say can and will be used against you in a court of law. You have the right to an attorney. If you can't afford an attorney, one will be appointed to you by the courts," the pig said.

"Nigga, fuck you."

Ain't this a bitch? This ho called the police on me. A few minutes later, I spotted them rushing Alyssa out on a stretcher. They wheeled her in an ambulance, and it pulled off in a rush. Fuck. Reality was starting to set in, and the coke was beginning to wear off. I hope I didn't kill the baby. God knows I don't want to be charged with murder . . .This was my first time in jail. Most of my life, I was able to stay clear of catching a case, even though I've done some shit. It was now evening, so I was brought in front of the magistrate. The old bitch denied my bond because of the nature of the assault, and they weren't sure if the victim and the baby survived.

Man, fuck all that. I wanted to go the fuck home. That bitch deserved everything that was coming to her. She knew I wasn't to be fucked with. Yet, she had me out here looking like a whole fool. Fuck that. I was Jihad, that nigga. I ain't gon' let no bitch take me for no bitch-ass clown.

Alyssa

I knew Jihad was searching around town for me, but I was at my mom's ducking him. I still loved him, but after what he did, there was no way I was going back to him. I took a lot of shit from him because he was spending money on me. He was also the first man that I truly loved. However, the longer I stayed with him, the more I realized he was a liar. Truth is, Jihad had no intention to leave that bitch. If he wanted, he could've killed her. His ass kept giving her a little bit of the cyanide instead of giving that bitch a deadly dose. I watched enough of the

ID channel to know that bitch would've been dead in no time, and no one would've been suspicious of the cause of death. So, that made me think that nigga does love that bitch.

Now, I was tired of being at Mama's house. I had to go outside to smoke my weed, and every day she got up, she preached the same shit over and over. "These niggas ain't shit."

"You sure you want to go back to that apartment? Baby, I told you, you could stay here with me. I don't mind the company," my mother said as I packed my bags to leave.

"Mama, I'm okay. I figure Jihad's ass is probably off chasing behind his wife. Plus, I'm not gon' live my life being scared of him."

"Baby, niggas like him don't like to lose. It's a power thing with them. He will do whatever it takes to control you. I say you need to press charges on his ass."

"Ma, I got this, okay?"

Ugh, this was one of the reasons why I was ready to go. Mama was so damn annoying. I know she means well, but she was becoming overbearing. Finally, I finished getting my stuff together. She helped me to the car, hugged me, and I left.

As I pulled up at my apartment complex, I thought everything was fine. I scanned the parking lot and didn't see anything strange. Thank God, I thought as I got out of the car. I was tired, so I only grabbed my purse, thinking I would return and grab the rest of my stuff later.

Something didn't feel right, but I brushed it off as my anxiety—until I tried closing the door behind me. There was Jihad forcing himself into my apartment. I tried to close the door, but I wasn't strong enough. He barged in, slamming and locking the door behind us. I tried reaching for my phone, but he grabbed my purse. I was scared for my life. His eyes were glossy, and he looked like he was on that coke again. I searched his eyes for emotions, but there were none.

I thought of running to my room and jumping out the window, but he grabbed me and started beating me like I was a ho on the street. The whole time he was doing this, I was praying to God. I didn't want my baby to die inside of me. I tried blocking his blows, but they kept coming. I couldn't give up. I had to fight. Not sure where I got the energy, but I grabbed his balls and squeezed them with everything in me.

In that split second, he made the mistake of letting go of me. I used that opportunity to run out the door. I ran down to the second floor, where this lady from the courts lived. I wasn't sure she was home, but I banged on her door. She opened it, and I collapsed at her front door. I was crying. I tried telling her what was wrong, but it took a few minutes for me to talk clearly. Finally, she called the police for me. As we waited for the cops, I was shivering. I knew Jihad was still lurking around.

Suddenly, I started to feel sharp pains in my stomach. Oh no, I prayed I wasn't losing my baby. The lady told me to lie back and put up my legs. By the time the police and ambulance came, I was bleeding. After speaking with the police, they rushed me out into the ambulance. I was so distraught. I couldn't believe Jihad did this to me. The man that's supposed to love and protect me.

"Push, push, hon. Come on, you're doing good," the nurse that held my hand said.

I was hurting, but I knew I needed to push out my baby. So I used everything in me and made a big push.

"There you go, honey."

I looked up and saw the doctor holding my baby. I was so weak I couldn't lift my head up much longer.

"Is he alive?" I whispered.

"Yes, he is. Congrats, honey. You did great." The nurse walked over to me and rubbed my arm.

I didn't feel good. Suddenly, the room started getting dark.

"We need oxygen. Code blue. I repeat, code blue!" I heard the nurse yell before I completely passed out.

"Welcome back, baby," Mama said as she stood over me, smiling.

"What you mean, and where's my baby?" I frantically asked.

"We almost lost you. The doctors worked hard on you to bring you back. Little man is in the nursery."

Now I remember how I got here. Jihad beat the shit out of me, which forced me to go into early labor. I had my baby three months early. Tears welled up in my eyes as I recalled how he punched me.

"Baby, I'm glad you're still here with us. Your son is in the incubator. His oxygen level was a little low, and he wasn't sucking the bottle, so they're feeding him through a tube. The police also came up here. They got that bastard in custody."

"Damn, when did all this happen? How long was I out?"

"You had the baby yesterday, but after you passed out, the doctor put you in a medically induced coma. How do you feel, baby?"

"I'm tired and hungry. How did you know I was here?"

"The police called and told me."

"There you are. How are you feeling?" a nurse walked in and asked.

"I want to see my baby."

"Okay, let me get a wheelchair to take you to the NICU."

"Baby, I'm so proud of you," Mama said.

I smiled at her. I wasn't so proud of myself right now. I let my love for this nigga almost cost me my life. I was angry, and revenge was on my mind. My entire soul was in the incubator in human form. He was tiny but gorgeous. Tears poured down my face as love filled my heart. I made him. I made someone this beautiful.

"Hey, little man." I smiled at him.

I read the tag on his leg, and it said, *"Baby Jones."* He was supposed to be a junior but fuck that nigga. I'll figure out a new name for my baby.

It was hard going back to the room without him. I just wanted to hold him, to tell him everything was going to be okay. Later, the doctor explained that I might be going home without him if he didn't suck on the bottle. I was hoping he did because, honestly, I don't want to leave him up in here.

So, I was racking my brain trying to come up with a new name for my baby. That's it . . . Malik. I used to fuck this nigga named Malik. Nigga was fine as fuck, but crazy as hell. Oh well, that was going to be my son's name. Malik Jones. I love how it rolled off my tongue. It sounds way better than that fuck nigga's name.

I bawled my eyes out as my mom drove me away from the hospital. I was heartbroken having to leave my baby up there with those people.

"Baby, calm down. It's only temporary. Baby boy will be home soon."

"I know, Mama, but it still don't stop me from hurting."

"Do you want to come to my house for a few days until you feel better?"

"Ma, no. I just need to go home. I need to have some time by myself."

"I understand, baby. Well, I'm going to stop by the store and grab you a few things first."

I hate that sometimes I'm a bitch toward my mother 'cause no matter how bad I treat her, she always comes through for me. Honestly, I need to let some of this anger go for real.

While Mama was in the grocery store, I sat in the car just thinking. So many things puzzled me. My biggest thought was how Jihad knew I didn't know who my baby daddy was. No matter how I tried to dismiss it, it came back nagging at me like a bad toothache. I hated to go there, but there was only one way to find out.

I pulled back when I first entered my apartment. Emotion flooded my heart as I looked at the spot where that nigga had me while he beat me.

"You okay?" Ma sensed something was wrong.

"Yeah, I'm good."

I walked to my room, changed my clothes, and got in bed. Ma warmed me up some Progresso soup. I drank it, took some pain medicine, and lay down.

"OK, baby. I see you're tired. I'm about to run. I'm going to bingo, but I'll call you to check on you later."

"OK, Ma."

"All right, baby." She started walking out.

"Ma," I called out to her.

"Yes, baby, something wrong?" She turned back around.

"I love you."

"Aw, I love you too, baby. Come lock this door and don't open it unless you know for sure who's there. That boy might make bond and come after you again."

I got up out of bed and followed her to the door. We hugged, and she left. Then I locked the door and put the chain on it, just to make sure. Then after pouring a little bit of juice, I got into bed.

I called Trina's phone. It went straight to voicemail. I called right back. Her ass was probably calling someone. I waited a few seconds, then called again.

"Hello," she answered in a low tone.

"Damn, bitch, I almost died, and you ain't nowhere around?"

"Girl, what are you talking about?"

"I had your godson."

"Really? Congrats, girl," she said in a dry tone.

"Yo, Trina, bitch, what's going on with you?"

"Damn, Alyssa. Why something has to always be going on with me? I said, congrats. What the fuck you want me to do—jump up and down? Oh, I forgot, you're Alyssa, the queen. Everybody needs to jump up and down for you."

I had to pull the phone from my ear and check the number, so I could be sure who the fuck I was talking to. This bitch was talking recklessly, but why? My mind started to work. I was feeling suspicious. Could *this* be the reason why she was coming at me like this? I felt confused. Before I could gather my thoughts, the phone line went dead.

"Yo, did this bitch just hang up on me?" I asked a question that I already knew the answer to.

I called her number back a few times, with no answer. I swear if I weren't feeling weak, I would drive over by that bitch's house. I sat up in bed, huffing and puffing. I know this ho didn't do shit like fucking around with Jihad. Then I remembered that threesome I gave him. After a while, I called her back.

"Alyssa, what the fuck you want?" she answered with an attitude.

"Bitch, just answer one question for me. Have you been fucking my baby daddy?"

"First of all, he's *not* your baby daddy. You don't *know* who the fuck got you pregnant. Second of all, yeah, bitch, we fucking, and what's that got to do with you?"

"Bitch, are you fucking *serious?* We best friends, and you fucking my nigga? Bitch, you a nasty ho," I spat.

"Girl, I know your little feelings hurt 'cause you never thought your precious Jihad would fuck with me. Well, I got news for you. This nigga stays eating this pussy. Anyway, not going back and forth with you, Jihad doesn't belong to you. So, we all sharing him."

"Bitch, when I see you, I'ma beat your ass, I swear to God."

"Alyssa, please, you better learn to fight first, bitch. Don't threaten me while that nigga over there beating your ass. Now, let me go take a shower. I heard bae just got bonded out."

That ho hung up before I could respond. Then angrily, I threw the phone on the ground, grabbed my pillow, buried my head in it, and started bawling. I didn't care if my neighbors could hear me. My heart was broken, and it hurt badly. *Me and this bitch grew up together. How the fuck could she do this shit to me? How?* I thought as I cried.

Now, it made perfect sense. She was the one that told Jihad about me not knowing who my baby daddy was. I trusted this bitch. Never in a million years would I have thought my right-hand bitch would do this to me. A nigga gon' always be a nigga, but a bitch I call my sister that I told my darkest secrets to hurt me to the core. I just wanted to die. I was tired of living.

"God, please, take me. Please, just take me."

Chapter Twenty-six

Brooklyn

The first thing on my to-do list was to change my locks. So, bright and early Monday morning, I contacted a locksmith in the area, and the young man came out. He changed all the locks for me and gave me new keys. I also called the alarm company but was told the earliest they could come out was Friday. So maybe I should've told them motherfuckers that my life was in danger. Then they would come out immediately.

I was late meeting up with the private investigator. Jas had recommended a friend of hers. We were meeting at his office on Franklin Street.

"Hello, good afternoon. My name is Brooklyn Lewis. I have a 1:00 p.m. appointment with Mr. Rex."

"Yes, Mrs. Lewis, he's expecting you. Follow me, please."

I followed her into his office. "Mr. Rex, Mrs. Lewis is here."

This tall, dark-skinned brother with a bald head stood up, walked around the desk, and shook my hand.

"Nice to meet you, Mrs. Lewis. Please take a seat. Thank you, Miriam."

He pulled out the seat for me, and the receptionist left. Then he walked back to the other side and took a seat.

"So, let's get down to business. In our phone conversation, you said you think your husband is cheating on you."

"Mr. Rex, listen to me. I'm not some desperate house-wife that wants to know if the nigga is cheating so we can go for counseling. I *know* the nigga cheating. But I need you to get me solid proof, so when I walk into my lawyer's office, I'll have all the proof I need to demolish his ass in court. I don't mean to come off cocky, but I got plenty of money, and I don't want to give this bum not one cent. So, please, dig up any and everything you can on him. I want to know what the nigga eats, what drawers he wears—I mean *everything*."

"Well, I'm just the man to get you everything you need. Give me forty-eight hours, and I will have everything you need. My fee is four grand to cover everything."

I reached into my purse, pulled out five stacks, and handed it to him. He looked at me like I was crazy.

"Mr. Rex, I just need you to know the importance of what I need done."

"I got you, Mrs. Lewis."

"Okay, let me know when you find something."

I got up and walked out. It feels so good to be getting my mental strength back. For so long, I've been down for this nigga so much that I was blind to see that he was a fucking snake. I'm not going to lie. My heart hurts badly, but I know I have to be strong. I need to fight to stay alive.

I called Jas's phone when I got in the car, but her phone went straight to voicemail. Knowing her, she's probably in court. I promise that when all this shit is over, me and her going on a seven-day cruise. Just us girls. I love this bitch. I have no idea how I would make it without her. A bitch or nigga can catch it if they fuck with her. I left her a message, threw the phone into my bag, and pulled off.

I was eager to hear from the PI. I know it was probably some shit that will hurt me, but I'd rather know than still be in the dark about who this nigga really is. Jihad had me fooled for so long. Now that I sit back and look at everything this nigga told me, I don't know what was a lie or the truth. Just thinking about him made me angry.

I stopped by the bank and ensured his name was up off all my shit. I also canceled that life insurance policy that he had me take out. All this made sense now. This nigga stayed convincing me to do some shit that benefited him. Why was I so blind behind this nigga? Over some fucking dick? I hung my head in shame. My grandmother raised me way better than this. How could I be so fucking stupid?

I got to the house and sat outside in the car for a little while. I just needed to get my head together before I entered the house. I can't wait to be able to put this bum out of my house for good. I know I must follow the law, but I don't want to see or be around this nigga again.

I walked into the house, threw my purse onto the bed, and quickly undressed. I walked through the house, and it seemed like his ass still wasn't here. I let out a long sigh of relief. I decided to bathe. My back felt a little stiff. Maybe if I soak in some Epsom salt, it might help me.

I walked downstairs in my panties and bra and poured me a glass of wine. My nose caught something. I tried to figure out what it was. It was a familiar smell, but I couldn't recognize it off the top of my head.

Hmm . . . I looked around, walked over to the sunroom door, and looked out, but nothing was out of place. "Ha-ha," I laughed. So here I was in my house, acting all suspicious and shit.

I cut off the hallway light and made my way up the stairs. I took a few sips of the wine, then got into the tub. I leaned my head back and closed my eyes. This water felt so good. I could lie here all night. I was relaxed . . . until I heard my phone ringing. Shit, it could wait, I thought.

After sitting in the tub for a while, I decided to shower. I cut on the water and let the hot water cascade down on my body. After I washed off, I cut off the water and grabbed my towel. That's when it hit me. The scent that I smelled downstairs was Chanel Grand Extrait. That was strange. It was an expensive perfume; the only person I knew who used it was Jas. Yo, stress got me tripping, I smiled as I walked into my bedroom.

I picked up the phone to check who was calling. It was the private investigator. I felt nervous as I dialed his number. I felt bubbles in my stomach like I wanted to throw up.

"Hello, Mrs. Lewis. How are you doing?" he asked.

"I'm good. Do you have some good news for me?"

The phone went quiet for a second or two. "Are you there? I mean, go ahead, spit it out. Trust me. I can handle it."

"Mrs. Lewis, this is crazy. It's the first time I followed a person and couldn't get anything."

"What do you mean you couldn't find anything? I thought you were good at what you do?" I was getting annoyed.

"That's the thing. This man is clean. I followed him around. He stayed at a hotel. He went out by himself and came in by himself. I even followed him to Chili's where he sat alone and ate. I even have one of my detective friends look him up, and he's as clean as a whistle. I can't tell you what to do, but I can tell you, your husband has been faithful."

"This is bullshit. I know that bastard hasn't been faithful to me. I don't know how he got around you, but he did."

"I'm sorry this is not what you want to hear. But many women would jump for joy hearing that their husband wasn't cheating. Instead, you *want* him to cheat. I don't mean to pry into your business, but why are you so determined to make this man out to be a cheater?"

"What did you just say to me? I didn't hire you for your fucking opinion. Matter of fact, you're fired, and I will let Jas know just how horrible of a job you did. Now, good fucking bye." I hung up immediately. The fucking nerve of this fuck nigga.

I was so fucking angry. I called Jas's number again, but still no response. I hoped she was okay. If her ass don't pick up by tomorrow, I'm stopping by her house. Hopefully, everything is good.

I was going to bed, but then something popped into my head. I jumped on my computer and went through my files. "Found it," I said as I put the address in my phone.

I threw on a jogging suit, put a cap on my head, and put on my sneakers. Then I went into the bottom of my drawer under my nightgowns and pulled out my gun. I checked to make sure it was loaded. I put it in my purse and ran down the stairs.

Before I pulled off, I put the address into Waze. I know this might not be a good decision, but at this point, I was desperate. No one else would help me, so I needed to take control.

It took me about twenty minutes to get to my location. This wasn't the best part of town, but that didn't deter me from going. I pulled into a run-down apartment complex. I saw people coming in and out of the building. I put my phone on record, placed it in my purse, and walked out.

I walked up to the third floor, looked for 3E, and knocked on the door. At first, no one answered, so I knocked again, this time louder.

"Who is it?" Alyssa asked.

"It's Brooklyn."

"I'm kind of busy, Mrs. Lewis."

"I'm worried about you. Plus, I brought your check."

Within seconds, the door slowly opened. My eyes widened. The bitch wasn't pregnant anymore.

"Hey, you. I was worried when you left so suddenly. Can I come in?"

"I didn't clean up today. Haven't been feeling good."

"Child, trust me, I'm not here for that," I smiled.

She walked away from the door. I guess that was her way of saying come in.

I stepped inside the small apartment. It smelled like ass and stale pussy mixed together. I wanted to run outside to get some fresh air, but I stood there looking at this bitch. Without the makeup and the fake proper English, she was just a regular hood bitch. So, *this* was the piece of shit my husband was sleeping with? Anger swept over me, but I had to try to remain calm.

"Here, you can take a seat," she offered.

I didn't feel like sitting, though. I saw baby boxes all over the place.

"Alyssa, you can cut the fake act now. I know who you are."

"W-wh-at do you mean?" She looked at me like she was confused.

"I'm not sure if Alyssa is your fucking name, but I know for a fact you're not Jihad's cousin. You're the bitch he was fucking. Matter of fact, that fucking monkey you were carrying is *his* baby."

"I don't know where the fuck you're getting your story from, but don't come up in my house calling my fucking child no monkey. If you really want to fucking know, I didn't know that nigga was married. I found out later. By then, I was in too deep. As far as working for you, that was all his idea."

"Bitch, quit lying. I know your kind, the lazy kind, the kind that sits around and waits for a nigga to take care of them. I feel pity 'cause you actually thought you were in competition with me. We could never be on the same level. Look at you. You're a low-level piece of trash."

"I wasn't tryna go there with you 'cause, believe it or not, I started liking you. But since you're up in my shit being disrespectful, here it goes . . . If your pussy was so good and your money was so plentiful, why did your husband choose to leave you for a hood bitch? I'm not going to sit up here arguing with you. I don't want that nigga no more. All you and him can do is write that motherfucking check for my baby."

I was tired of hearing this bitch's mouth. I pulled the gun out of my purse. "Shut the fuck up, bitch, and get over in that corner. Move, bitch, before I shoot you," I yelled and pointed the gun directly at that ho's head.

I spotted some toys and shit she had in the front room. I grabbed them, throwing them on the ground, smashing them.

"Stop! What are you doing? That's my baby's stuff," she screamed.

"Where's the bleach, bitch?"

She just started crying and holding her head down. "Bitch, where's the bleach? *Get* it," I ordered.

She got up and ran to the bathroom. I was close behind her. I quickly grabbed it from her. Entering the room where the baby crib was set up, I took the bleach and sprinkled it all over everything. Next, I ordered her to open all the drawers and sprinkled the little left in the gallon bottle over it.

"I'm calling the police. You fucked up my son's clothes. Bitch, you're going to pay."

I took a couple of steps closer to this ho's face. "Listen to me, little bitch. I could care less if that illegitimate bastard eats or dies. I find it hard to accept that I believed your fucking lies and fake tears. I listened to your pathetic stories and took you into my house. You are the lowest level of a slimy-ass bitch. I hope you die a slow death, you and that little monkey. Now, don't you *ever* come near me again, or I will blow off your fucking head," I said through clenched teeth.

"Ha-ha, bish, I'm not the first and certainly not the last. I can't help if your pussy is dry and can't keep your man happy at home. You mad 'cause he loved me and not you," she screamed.

"I should blow out your fucking brains, but I figure your poor ass will suffer enough. Next time you get pregnant by somebody's husband, make sure that nigga is the one that is paid and *not* his wife. You silly ho. Good pussy can only take you so far. I pity you, bitch, 'cause as much as you crept around with my husband, all you're left with is a wet pussy and a fucking baby. How you feel *now*, ho?" I spit dead in that ho's face before I walked off.

I wanted to rip this bitch's head off, but instead, I laughed and kept walking. There's a thin line between sanity and insanity. God knows I was borderline crazy right now.

Jihad

A nigga was finally freed after being in a fucking jail cell for three days. I was happy that bail was granted. It took a few hours, and then I was out.

"Hey, love," I kissed her.

"Hey, you. Welcome home, babes."

We hugged briefly, then got in the car, and she pulled off.

"I couldn't say shit over the phone because it's recorded. But tell me, Jihad, what the fuck were you thinking when you beat up on that bitch? I thought you told me the baby wasn't yours, and you didn't fuck with that bitch anymore. I'm starting to feel like you've been taking me for a fucking joke. See, Jihad, I'm not that weak bitch that you married. You can't play these kinds of games with me."

"Listen, baby, that's the God's honest truth. There are no secrets between us anymore. I told you everything."

"I hope so 'cause I'm getting sick of you and all these bitches. I mean, when it was one bitch, it was easier. Now, it's three bitches."

"Three bitches?" I turned to look at her.

"Relax, darling. I know everything that goes on. I know you was fucking that fat, little bitch."

I couldn't even say anything 'cause I thought I was careful. This woman was dangerous. I'ma have to keep an eye on this one.

Soon as I got to her house, I took a quick shower. I came out of the room with my dick hanging. She pushed me back on the bed and dropped to her knees. Then she slowly stroked my dick until it got hard. Next, she started licking the tip while massaging my balls. I was feeling horny. It's been days since I fucked. Sucking my dick was cool and everything, but I wanted to fuck. I needed to be up in some pussy.

"Come here, babes." I pulled her up to me.

I got up, turned her around, and spread her ass. I entered the pussy from the back as I grabbed her breasts and started pounding her. Shit, this was good. The pussy was gripping my dick tightly like a suction cup.

"Oh shit. Daddy, fuck me," she screamed as she threw her ass back on me.

This was the kind of shit that turned me on. An educated bitch acting like a hoodrat. If she could see behind her, she would notice the grin on my face as I fucked the shit out of her.

"Who pussy is this?" I asked as I smacked her ass.

"Yours, daddy."

"That's right. Now, take this dick," I demanded.

She threw her ass back some more. I went in deeper. That was short-lived, though. I felt my veins getting bigger, and my dick head was throbbing.

"Oh shit, babes. I'm about to cum. Oh shiiiit." I tried to hold it in a little, but the urge was too strong. Finally, I exploded in her pussy.

A few seconds later, I pulled out my soft dick and sat down. I was tired, and my legs felt weak.

"Are you okay?"

"Yeah, I couldn't be better. Shorty, that pussy is some good."

"What did you expect, darling? I'm a boss bitch." She winked at me as she walked off to the bathroom.

I lay back on the bed, thinking I needed to go. I needed to cop some blow. It's been days, and I was fiening like a crackhead. I needed to figure out something to tell her so that I could bounce.

"Okay, now that you fucked, I guess it's time to eat some good food, huh? I know the slop they were feeding you wasn't good at all."

"I'm not really hungry right now, babes. I'ma run to the crib and grab something real quick."

"To the crib? I thought you said you were staying away from there for a while?"

"I am, babes. I'm coming right back," I assured her.

She shot me one of those "I don't believe shit you saying, nigga" looks.

"I'm serious, babes. I know how important it is for me to stay away. You know I ain't gon' fuck up our plan this time."

"Jihad, I keep telling you, this is it. If you don't stay on task, we will never get our hands on that paper. Nigga, I love fucking you, but I love the money more."

"I hear you, love."

I knew she was serious. This bitch was as cold as they come. Sometimes, I wonder how I even crossed paths with her. I love her, but I must be careful with her. I got in the shower and washed off real quick.

"Aye, babes, do you have a few dollars that I can borrow, and where did you put the keys to the truck?"

"Sure, hold on."

She went into her purse, pulled out some bills, and handed me three of them.

"Thanks, babes. I promise I appreciate everything you do for me. I can't wait to repay you."

"No thanks needed. As long as you suck this pussy and fuck me good, then we straight. I got my own money. I just can't fuck myself that good like you can."

"You sure know how to stroke a nigga's ego. I love you, babes."

She didn't respond; instead, she smiled. I got dressed in a sweatsuit she bought me and then left.

Instead of going straight to the crib, I texted my connect to let him know I was coming through. Being without coke is like going without food to me.

Epilogue

Brooklyn

As soon as I got into the house, I rushed downstairs, reached up under the table, and pulled down the gun. I held it in my hand and looked at it. This nigga wants to fuck with me, so I will finish him off for good. I placed the gun in my purse and zipped it up.

I was tired. Shit, fuck that. I was mentally exhausted from everything that was going on. I downed two glasses of wine and was on my third. I lay my head back on my pillow and pulled my covers up beside me. Taking my phone out of my purse that was also in the bed with me, I checked it to see if I had any missed calls from my mother or Jas. I could tell my mother was worried about me after we spoke earlier. I assured her I would come to NY to visit her after all this was over. I made an appointment with an attorney for Monday. That would give me the weekend to get all my stuff together.

I was disappointed that I didn't have any missed calls. What was going on with Jas? I hadn't heard from her in a few days. Plus, she has not returned any of my calls. I plan on going over there. I wish I hadn't drunk this much wine, or I would surely have left the house already. I want to tell her she was right about the fake-ass cousin.

However, a little voice in my head told me, "Bitch, lie down; you're tipsy." So I rested my head on the pillow and closed my eyes. The locks had been changed, so I knew I didn't have to worry about that nigga coming up in here. Jas said I couldn't just put him out, but this was *my* shit, and until a judge told me otherwise, that fuck nigga would *not* be in here.

I was falling asleep, and I felt it. It was only 7:00 p.m., but shit, it ain't like I had anything else to do. So I put down the phone and decided to call it a night.

"Bitch, you thought it was so easy to get rid of me."

I thought I was dreaming, but it sounded so clear. I'd just fallen asleep. There's no way I started dreaming this quickly. I was scared to open my eyes.

"Get the fuck up, bitch."

That nigga yanked me off the bed and threw me onto the floor. I hit my head on the floor. Then he started to hit and stomp me. Each time I tried getting up, he kicked me down again.

"Bitch, I told you it wasn't over until I *told* you it's over." So now, he started stomping me hard.

I curled up in a ball, trying to use my hands to block my face. I thought I was going to die, but something in me woke up. I was determined to live. I grabbed his legs and pulled them from underneath him. He slipped backward and fell to the ground. I jumped up off the ground and dove onto my bed. I grabbed my Glock under my pillow. I turned around, and he reached over, trying to catch me, but I dove over to the other side of the bed.

Pop!

I aimed the gun at his shoulder and fired a shot. I got scared when blood saturated the grey sweatshirt he was wearing.

"Oh my God. Jihad, I'm so sorry." I only wanted to scare him. I'd never shot anyone before, and I was trembling all over.

"Bitch, you shot me! I'm going to kill you. You hear me, Brooklyn? I'm going to kill youuuu," he screamed.

He tried to get to me by coming around the bed. His eyes were cold, and the look on his face was gruesome. My survival skills kicked in. I knew he would kill me if he got ahold of me, so I jumped up on the bed and ran to the other side. I dashed to the door with the gun by my side. I was halfway down the stairs—when I stopped dead in my tracks.

Jas was coming up the stairs. She stopped when she saw me.

Wait, what is Jas doing here?

"Hey, girl, I heard a sound. Is everything okay? I was coming to check on you," she smiled.

No, something didn't feel right. Her smile wasn't warm. It was forced. I was confused.

"How did you get in here?" I asked in a serious tone.

"Brooklyn, are you okay? You're behaving strangely. You know I got a set of keys. Remember?"

"No, Jas, you don't have keys. I changed the locks earlier." I knew then something was very wrong. Why was my best friend standing in my house lying to me?

"Oh, babes, you got her. I thought I would have to go find her." Jihad stopped on the second stairs. "By the way, Brooklyn, I knew you had changed the locks, so I used some old lock-picking tools to enter."

I put my back against the wall and aimed the gun. Some sick shit was going on. This is my husband and my sister/best friend. I tried to make sense of all this, but I couldn't . . .

"Babes? W-h-a-t is this? Jas, what's going on?" I felt my chest tightening.

"Bitch, don't act like you don't understand what's happening here. Jihad, your husband, is my lover."

"You playing, right? What are you saying, Jas? Please, explain to me," I pleaded through tears.

I searched her face for some kind of understanding, but there was none. Instead, she wore a cold, psychotic look. I felt sick. I leaned on the wall for support.

"Jas, tell me this is a fucking joke. You hate him. *You* were the one that kept telling me he was using me. Then you told me he was trying to kill me."

"Brooklyn, my bestie. You're book smart but not a lick of street smart. Let me tell you something. Ever since we were growing up, I couldn't stand your rich, spoiled ass. Our grandmother treated you like a fucking princess while I got treated like Cinderella. It was always about Brooklyn. Bitch, as we got older, I started hating your ass more. You act like because you have money, everybody should bow down to you. Bullshit. I sat back and watched you until I came up with the perfect plan. See, you had everything together except a man. I knew yo' ass was thirsty and hungry for some dick. So I found the handsome, sexy Jihad to get at you. Yes, I had to play like I don't like him so that you wouldn't catch on, and it worked. You had no idea that behind your back, we were fucking. How stupid can you be?"

"Jas, you're my sister, my only friend. How could you do this to me? We slept in the same bed and ate out of the same pot. I love you, Jas," I cried.

"Bitch, I don't fuck with you. I've been hanging around for years trying to figure out how to kill yo' ass and get this fucking money. See, we had the perfect plan. The hospital wasn't supposed to find the cyanide in your blood. The plan was to keep you sick until you passed in a few months. Then no one would question what happened. I would come to your funeral, breaking down, just like everyone expected me to. I would console your grieving husband. He would wait a few months, then file the insurance claim. Half of everything he got would be mine."

"What are you saying? *This* was *your* plan? You want me dead over some *money?* All you had to do was ask. I would've given you anything," I cried.

"Little old Brooklyn. Bitch, you shocked? If this makes you feel any better, *I* was the one who told him to make it easy on you. Like, make you go to sleep and not wake up, but that didn't work, so we had to devise another plan. Bitch, I didn't want your handout. I wanted your fucking *life* and *all* your money."

Tears rolled down my face as I stood there listening to my sister, my ride-or-die bitch spit venom into my face. My feelings were mixed. I was feeling angry and hurt.

That bitch took a few steps toward me. I looked at her through tears, raised the gun, and pointed at her.

"Brooklyn, put down the fucking gun. We know your soft ass ain't going to do shit. I had to beat bitches up for you since we were young. You're a weak-ass bitch. That's why you can't get a good man. They fuck you and use you for your money." She lunged at me.

Pop, pop, pop!

I didn't see my loving best friend, who always had my back. All I saw was a cold, evil bitch standing there. I couldn't be fooled anymore. I fired three shots at her and watched as she fell backward down the stairs.

"Noooo! You bitch, you killed her. Jassss!" Jihad screamed.

With his eyes burning in rage, he tried to come at me. I raised the gun again and fired, hitting him in the chest. Shocked, he grabbed his chest while looking at me.

"Brooklyn, pl-plea-please, help me," he pleaded while blood gushed out of his mouth.

I looked at him as he reached out his hand. I thought about grabbing it. I love this man. I don't want him to die . . .

I started to reach out my hand, but then I pulled it back. "Nigga, fuck you and this bitch. Say hi to my daddy when you get there."

I stepped past him while he struggled to breathe. Next, I heard a big grunt . . . then silence. I continued walking up the stairs. Finally, I rushed to the bathroom and started throwing up. I couldn't stop crying, and I was shaking uncontrollably.

I wiped the tears from my face, sat on the bed, and tried to control the crying. I needed to calm down before I got on this phone. It was hard, and my soul was crushed. The two closest people to me were dead on my floor, and I was responsible for their deaths. God, give me the strength . . .

"911, what's your emergency?"

"I need the police . . ."

The End